Violence in the Contemporary American Novel

Violence in the Contemporary American Novel

An End to Innocence

James R. Giles

UNIVERSITY OF SOUTH CAROLINA PRESS

© 2000 University of South Carolina

Published in Columbia, South Carolina, by the
University of South Carolina Press

Manufactured in the United States of America

04 03 02 01 00   5 4 3 2 1

Library of Congress Cataloging-in-Pulication Data

Giles, James Richard, 1937–
   Violence in the contemporary American novel : an end to innocence /
James R. Giles.
   p. cm.
   Includes bibliographical references (p.) and index.

   ISBN 1-57003-328-5 (alk. paper)
   1. American fiction—20th century—History and criticism.
2. Violence in literature. 3. Literature and society—United
States—History—20th century. 4. City and town life in literature.
5. Inner cities in literature. 6. Minorities in literature. I. Title.
PS374.V58 G55 2000
813'.5409355—dc21   99-6277

To the graduate students in my American literature classes at Northern Illinois University for all that they have taught me

Contents

Preface ix

Acknowledgments xv

Introduction "Innocence Dying Younger" 1

Chapter 1 Dedalus in the *Dood Kamer*
William Kennedy's *Quinn's Book* 8

Chapter 2 The "Context" of American Innocence
Caleb Carr's *The Alienist* 26

Chapter 3 The Ducky Boys and the
"Urban Punk Killing Machine"
Richard Price's *The Wanderers* 44

Chapter 4 A Postmodern Children's Crusade
John Edgar Wideman's *Philadelphia Fire* 56

Chapter 5 Nature Despoiled and Artificial
Sandra Cisneros's *The House on Mango Street* 70

Chapter 6 Violence and the Immanence
of the "Thing Unknown"
Cormac McCarthy's *Suttree* 84

Chapter 7 Redemptive Landscape, Malevolent City
Scott Momaday's *House Made of Dawn* 100

Chapter 8 Discovering a Substitute for Salvation
John Rechy's *The Miraculous Day of Amalia Gómez* 113

Conclusion Girl X and the Country of Last Things 129

Notes 137
Bibliography 149
Index 155

Preface

As I imagine has happened to others, my study did not turn out exactly as I first envisioned it. It had several inspirations, the first coming from a perceptive reader of the manuscript that eventually became my book *The Naturalistic Inner-City Novel in America,* published in 1995. The reader pointed out that the most recent text that I had discussed in any detail was Joyce Carol Oates's *them,* which appeared in 1970, and suggested that something new must have happened in the naturalistic urban novel in twenty-five years. She or he was right of course; so I set out to see precisely what had happened. My focus on naturalistic urban fiction led inevitably to an awareness of the crucial role that violence plays in it. I discovered quickly that, while the writers I was reading depicted violence in all its detail and horror, they did not limit themselves to traditional literary naturalism, or even realism, in doing so. Thus, my book evolved into a discussion of eight urban novels that were sometimes naturalistic, sometimes realistic, and sometimes surrealistic, but all underscored by a trope of violence. I was struck, in addition, by the innovative variations on traditional fictional genres that I discovered. My book, while different from what it was when it began, is also, I hope, richer.

It is also by necessity limited. There is simply not room to discuss all the American writers who have, during the past three decades, written about the city and specifically about various manifestations of violence in it: for instance, James Baldwin in *If Beale Street Could Talk* (1974), Rudolfo Anaya in *Heart of Aztlán* (1976), Gloria Naylor in *The Women of Brewster Place* (1983), Tom Wolfe in *The Bonfire of the Vanities* (1987). E. L. Doctorow's *Billy Bathgate* (1989) and Sherman Alexie's *Indian Killer* (1996) among others might have been chosen for discussion here, and in fact almost were. So might have been other texts by the writers who are included here: for example, any of William Kennedy's other Albany novels, any of John Edgar Wideman's Pittsburgh novels, John Rechy's *Bodies and Souls* (1983), or Richard Price's *Clockers* (1992).

Yet the selections here are not arbitrary. They are intended to be representative of the dominant concerns and modes one discovers in the contemporary American urban novel of violence. All but one emphasize variations on what Arthur Redding in a recent study has discussed in terms of "structural" or "systemic" theories of violence: "violence—occasionally subsumed under bureaucracy or ideology, under economic, gender, and class configurations, or under the micropolitics of power—forms an integral, vitiating ground of any dynamic system whose purported equilibrium is merely a pretense."[1] As illustrative of theorists of this kind of violence, Redding lists "Darwin, Nietzsche, Marx, and, perhaps, Foucault" and comments that "here violence is understood as the ballast of ideologies; as in the semi-secret cargo of a slave trader's ship, there is blood in the hold of every way of seeing" (p. 5).

My study is hardly a theoretical one, but Redding's comments shed useful light on the eight texts on which it focuses. Violence in them is never an organized moment of rebellion by members of an oppressed group against their oppressors—it is never liberating. Rather it is violence by isolated members of the oppressed either against others in their own social and racial group or against isolated individuals in a parallel socioeconomic group. To an alarming degree, violence in these eight texts is perpetuated by adults against children or, even more alarmingly perhaps, by children against children. Women are also often targets of physical and psychological assaults by males.

Despite the emphasis on an oppressive class structure that underlies these novels, they exhibit, in style and subject matter, a rich diversity. Cumulatively, one finds in them variations on a wide range of fictional genres: the naturalistic protest novel, the historical novel, the detective novel, the postmodern novel, the novel of spiritual quest, the initiation novel, the feminist novel, and the novel of magic realism. They also represent a variety of racial, ethnic, and gender perspectives; but they were not chosen in an attempt to be "politically correct," whatever that means. Rather the multicultural nature of my study is the inevitable consequence of its subject matter.

In an impressive recent book, *October Cities: The Redevelopment of Urban Literature*, Carlo Rotella emphasized the 1960s as a key transitional period in the history of urban American, the moment when a national obsession with the inner city as an allegedly violent and foreign space to be isolated and avoided by the middle class began to dominate the national consciousness.[2] Rotella is correct to emphasize the significance of the Sixties fear of, and flight from, the city as a historic shift.

As Richard Lehan discusses in his exhaustive study *The City in Literature: An Intellectual and Cultural History*, the city has historically been associated with "the Other," an inevitable result of the essential diversity of urban settings. Lehan first asserts that "the city came into being when a surplus of food allowed a diversity of tasks. Diversity is a key to urban beginnings and continuities, and diversity is also the snake in the urban garden, challenging systems of order and encouraging disorder and chaos." He then convincingly argues that "such diversity led inevitably to the 'Other'—an urban element, usually a minority, deemed 'outside' the community. But in mythic-symbolic terms, an embodiment of the Other is the mysterious stranger, the Dionysis figure in the early city, the mysterious man from nowhere, who disrupts the city from within."[3] Lehan further discusses the shift in such postmodern novels as Thomas Pynchon's *The Crying of Lot 49* away from a focus on a "mysterious stranger" to an obsession with conspiracies. One of course has no trouble thinking of the exotic and often, if not always, menacing mysterious stranger figure in British and American novels, e.g., Fu Manchu, Dracula, Gatsby. Sometimes such figures assume cumulative personas (San Francisco's Chinese Americans for Frank Norris and Jack London) and sometimes become spaces, rather than characters, located inside the city (Stephen Crane's Bowery, Frank Norris's Polk Street).

Another excellent recent study, Kevin R. McNamara's *Urban Verbs: Arts and Discourses of American Cities* (199), focuses on a number of cultural "texts" (Henry James's *The American Scene,* Theodore Dreiser's *Sister Carrie,* the architecture of Hugh Ferriss and the team of Robert Venturi and Denise Scott Brown, William Carlos Williams's *Paterson,* and the 1948 film *The Naked City*) as illustrating a historic tension in American culture to celebrate and contain urban diversity, again usually associated with the various ethnic groups.[4] In the Sixties, the urge to contain so thoroughly dominated the urge to celebrate that, for many middle-class Americans, the city ceased to be exotic and fascinating, but became ominous and deadly.

The threat of and obsession with violence was the determining factor in this dramatic shift in the American view of the city, and, as Rotella points out, the fear of violence was rooted in two sixties obsessions: crime and race. It offered moreover a dramatic and vastly oversimplified way of "understanding" the complexity of the shift from an industrial to a post-industrial urban America. Desiring to get past such dangerous and inherently racist oversimplification, I wanted to make central to my study the benefits of the unique insights into urban violence afforded by those people who are usually its victims—African Americans, Native Americans, Chicanas, Irish Americans, gays—as well as economically oppressed heterosexual males.

A further reason for the multicultural bias in this study is the critical redefinition of American literature and the brilliant fiction that has inspired that redefinition over the past three decades necessitate that the reexamination and expansion of the traditionally established canon of American fiction. The appearance of novels by writers from marginalized groups has resulted, in fact, in an ongoing reappraisal of what constitutes the "United States," the results of which are concisely stated by Edward W. Said in his afterword to the 1994 Vintage paperback edition of *Orientalism:* "the United States . . . today cannot seriously be described except as an enormous palimpsest of different races and cultures sharing a problematic history of conquests, exterminations, and of course major cultural and political achievements."[5]

Said, in fact, exercises a considerable influence on this study, having furnished me with something of a critical coda, a scholarly goal, if not precisely a method:

> Modern thought and experience have taught us to be sensitive to what is involved in representation, in studying the Other, in racial thinking, in unthinking and uncritical acceptance of authority and authoritative ideas, in the socio-political role of intellectuals, in the great value of a skeptical critical consciousness. Perhaps if we remember that the study of human experience usually has an ethical, to say nothing of a political, consequence in either the best or worse sense, we will not be indifferent to what we do as scholars. (p. 327)

I am especially indebted to his concept of "contrapuntal reading."

In the context of discussing such British novelists of imperialism as Kipling and Conrad, Said writes, "In practical terms, 'contrapuntal reading' . . . means reading a text with an understanding of what is involved when an author shows, for instance, that a colonial sugar plantation is seen as important to the process of maintaining a particular style of life. . . . The point is that contrapuntal reading must take an account of both processes, that of imperialism and that of resistance to it."[6] Critics have discussed the ways in which "foreign" inner cities have been historically perceived as exotic internal colonies by white American writers.[7] In the texts treated in this study, voices from such marginalized spaces as the inner city and the Native American reservation answer back, and Said's recommended mode of reading provides a valuable context in which to hear them.

The extremes of strictly formalist approaches and of much of the deconstruction of the 1980s that denied the possibility of finding transcendent meaning in literary texts do not work for me, which is not to say that these approaches are lacking in validity. They simply cannot serve the purpose of a critical approach that assumes an ethical function for literature as well as a recognition of the political realities of the cultures in which individual works of literature are written. The Said model demands such a recognition, and I have gained valuable insights for my study from journalistic accounts of specific assaults against Chicago children. Reports in the *Chicago Tribune*, as well on as the major Chicago television news programs, of the especially horrible cases of an eleven-year-old boy named Robert "Yummy" Sandifer and a nine-year-old girl identified only as Girl X seem a virtual gloss on the novels examined here.

It should also be said that, during the past thirty years, the American urban novel has been, to a considerable degree, the creation of writers working out of distinct racial, ethnic, gender, and sexual perspectives—one thinks for instance of Baldwin, Naylor, Anaya, Ralph Ellison, Paule Marshall, Bernard Malamud, Saul Bellow, Edward Lewis Wallant, Cynthia Ozick, Amy Tan, Edmund White, and Armistead Maupin. And again, I believe that only an approach such as the one outlined by Said is adequate to describe the full complexity of American literature. That literature is indeed an ever-changing portrait of "different races and cultures sharing a problematic history."

Though essential as they all are, the anonymous reader of my earlier manuscript, Said, and journalistic accounts of violence in Chicago were hardly the only inspirations of this study, which simply would not have been possible without a number of earlier investigations of the American urban novel and of violence in American fiction. Since graduate school, my knowledge of these two subjects has been informed by Blanche H. Gelfant's *The American City Novel* and W. H. Frohock's *The Novel of Violence in America,* while John Fraser's *Violence in the Arts* was an exciting discovery of the 1970s. In more recent works, Amy Kaplan, Arnold L. Goldsmith, Sidney H. Bremer, and Michael Kowalewski have contributed their own definitive insights. The even more recent studies by Rotella, Lehan, and McNamara were invaluable in helping me focus my study.

Acknowledgments

As with all I write, this book would not have been possible without the help and encouragement of Wanda Giles, Karen Blazer, and the staffs of the interlibrary loan and the research departments in Founders Memorial Library at Northern Illinois University. I want also to acknowledge the support and encouragement of Heather Hardy, the chair of the Department of English at NIU, as well as the scholarly advice and encouragement of my department colleagues in American literature, especially James Mellard, Rose Marie Burwell, Craig Abbott, Gustaaf Van Cromphout, and Ibis Gómez Vega. Virtually from the beginning, Barry Blose of the University of South Carolina Press guided the book to its publication, and Bill Adams's sensitive editing greatly enhanced my text. Wanda Giles provided several essential readings of the manuscript.

Violence in the Contemporary American Novel

Introduction

"Innocence Dying Younger"

For almost two weeks during the late summer of 1994, readers of the *Chicago Tribune* were told the story of the life and death of Robert "Yummy" Sandifer. The essential details were as follows: on the streets of Chicago's South Side, Robert Sandifer who, at the age of eleven already had an extensive criminal record (twenty-three felony convictions and five misdemeanors since January of 1992), shot and killed a fourteen-year-old girl after previously wounding two sixteen-year-old boys. Returning home on a Sunday evening, the girl, Shavon Dean, was hit when only fifty feet from her door by Sandifer, who was actually firing at six young men playing football on a nearby corner. Quickly identified as the shooter, the eleven-year-old immediately went into hiding, as the Chicago police began an extensive but unsuccessful search for him. Early the following Thursday, they found his body: "Robert was lying on dirt and bits of broken glass in the mouth of a pedestrian underpass emblazoned with gang graffiti. He had been shot twice in the back of the head, execution style."[1]

The next day, two brothers, Cragg and Derrick Hardaway, aged sixteen and fourteen respectively, were arrested and charged with Sandifer's murder. Like their victim, the Hardaway brothers were identified as members of the Black Disciples street gang. Derrick informed the police that he and Cragg had found the terrified Sandifer boy and walked him to a waiting car, then told him to get inside because "the gang was going to take care of him, [and] that 'he had to go out of town.'" They then drove him to the underpass, where Cragg ordered Derrick to stay in the car while he walked away with Yummy. The two brothers gave different accounts of what happened next. According to Derrick, he later "saw Cragg running from the tunnel with his right hand covering his pocket, although he reportedly did not see a weapon." Cragg insisted that he merely "escorted Robert into the tunnel, where another gang member named 'Kenny' waited." Police authorities said that the brothers were being held in part for their own protection because of the suspicion that because gang members were "perhaps already plotting against" them: "[t]he Hardaway boys, too, are apparently fearful the gang will strike out."[2]

In addition to recording the grim details of the two murders, the *Tribune* coverage examined the short life of Yummy Sandifer and the backgrounds of the Hardaway brothers. Sandifer, whose nickname originated in his love of cookies, had suffered, in his eleven years, extensive and horrific physical abuse. In 1986, a caseworker for the Illinois Department of Children and Family Services had examined the then three-year-old boy and recorded his findings:

> ". . . observed to have old scars on face; numerous old linear (cord like) marks on abdomen . . . 1/4" healing (scabbed) cigarette like burns on back of neck & on lower R shoulder blade; 4 healing cigarette like burns on buttocks; old linear cord like marks on L leg."

> Similar descriptions were entered for his siblings.

> Looking at that report almost nine years later, Cook County Public Guardian Patrick Murphy translated some of the passages. The cord-like marks, he said, meant the boy was probably whipped with an electrical cord.[3]

It was generally agreed that most, if not all, of this torture had been inflicted by Sandifer's then twenty-one-year-old mother, who was fifteen when her first child was born and who regularly left her younger children in the care of their six-year-old brother. For the next eight years, the state sought a permanent and safe place for Yummy but failed, sending him in 1994 for thirty days to a notoriously insecure environment, the Audy Home: "'Eleven years old in the Audy Home is not very good,' said Martha Allen, a DCFS spokeswoman. 'You have—for lack of a better word—mature juveniles there, and he was a bit young.'"[4] Eventually, the boy was removed from the Audy Home and placed in the custody of his grandmother.

In some significant ways, life had been different and better for the Hardaway brothers. Their mother was an active member of the local school council and was "a concerned parent who came to the school whenever she was called," and both parents were described as "'nice people,' who could not control the boys outside their home." Moreover, Cragg was, when he attended school, academically brilliant, winning honors in math and science. Yet both Cragg and Derrick, like Yummy Sandifer, had extensive criminal records, Cragg having been charged on May 25 with "attempted murder, two counts of aggravated battery and weapons violations." One neighbor commented: "'They just can't control CR,' . . . 'He's the bad one. I don't think he really had a heart.'" Moreover, however well-meaning the Hardaway parents, the boys' lives, even when at home, were filled with danger: "Neighbors said the windows in the rear of the family home had often been shot out over time by rival gangs."[5]

On the day following the arrest of the Hardaway brothers, the *Tribune* ran two front-page stories under the umbrella heading "Innocence Dying Younger." One investigates the origins of the Black Disciples gang and describes the appeal of gangs to young people in the city, and the other describes the murder of an eighty-four-year-old woman by another eleven-year-old boy with no apparent connection to Yummy Sandifer.

There were several especially shocking aspects of Yummy's story beginning of course with his age—at least chronologically, he was still a child when he killed and was in turn killed. From infancy, his world was characterized by pain and alienation. Having suffered almost inconceivable physical abuse before he was three, he was then abandoned into an inner-city landscape marked by relentless poverty, racial and class oppression, and turf warfare. The only space Yummy ever knew was always brutally contested, and it is hardly surprising that he was transformed into a victimizer before he succumbed irrevocably to his own victimization.

Details from the *Tribune* coverage not directly related to the senseless tragedy of Yummy's life had equally frightening implications for the nation's future. Windows in the Hardaway home had "*often* been shot out . . . by rival gangs," and another eleven-year-old had committed another shocking murder. It seemed that violence against and by children had assumed the proportions of an epidemic in Chicago with the *Tribune* not infrequently running stories describing a condition of warfare against "our children."

Moreover, as any observer of mass media in America can testify, it is not only in Chicago that innocence seems to be dying younger. Stories of warfare against and between children, especially adolescent members of gangs, have become commonplace throughout the inner cities of America. Judging from newspapers and television, one can only feel that urban violence has become a norm that threatens to first silence and then destroy not only children, but eighty-four-year-old women, and indeed people of all ages. For a privileged middle-class audience, it is only the especially shocking case of a Yummy Sandifer that attracts attention. As always happens in such times of national crisis, our writers have assumed a responsibility not only to record the plague of violence that so threatens the survival of children and indeed a redemptive national innocence, but to seek explanations for its origins.

Don DeLillo has, for instance, been concerned throughout his career with the idea of a uniquely American violence. David Bell, the protagonist of his first novel, *Americana* (1971), abruptly gives up a successful career at a television network in order to undertake a search for some unifying and redemptive meaning in America and, along the way, experiences isolated and generally disturbing moments of insight concerning the absence of any such meaning. One such epiphany is especially relevant here: "there was a vein of murder snaking across the continent beneath highways, smokestacks, oilrigs and gasworks, a casual savagery fed by the mute cities, and I wondered what impossible distance must be traveled to get from there to here, what language crossed, how many levels of being."[6] This passage can, in fact, be read as a kind of quick summary of the thematic and narrative concerns that dominate all of DeLillo's fiction. His characters are constantly and inexplicably threatened by "casual savagery," by violence and death at the hands of esoteric and invisible, but nevertheless quite real, enemies; forces once specifically human and identifiable in origin assume mindless, supernatural form and threaten to engulf and destroy everyone who wanders into their path. Like Thomas Pynchon and Norman Mailer, DeLillo is a witness to and recorder of national paranoia.

His narrators usually, but not always, encounter this inexplicable "vein of murder" in urban America. DeLillo is responding to a postindustrial society devoted to the consumption, rather than to the production of goods; and few American writers have described the hollowness residing at the very core of American consumerism as powerfully as has DeLillo. For instance, the characters trapped in the New York City of *Great Jones Street* (1973) are desperately attempting to acquire, and then vanish inside, a powerful new drug; they increasingly find the brutal and brutalizing landscape of the city quite literally unbearable. The magical new drug functions as a trope for commodification, the reducing, in a circular manner, of everything and everyone to a commodity, something that is either worthy or unworthy of purchase. Those individuals without the power to purchase are deemed unworthy of being purchased, as lacking in human value, and form a rejected and seemingly mad subculture in *Great Jones Street*. One enters such a subculture at no little risk.

Bucky Wunderlick, the former rock-star protagonist and narrator of the text, is sickened and bewildered by what he sees everywhere around him in the city:

> Pigeons and meningitis. Chocolate and mouse droppings. Licorice and roach hairs. Vermin on the bus we took uptown. I wondered how long

> I'd choose to dwell in these middle ages of plague and usury, living among traceless men and women, those whose only peace was in shouting ever more loudly. Nothing tempted them more than voicelessness. But they shouted. Transient population of thunderers and hags. They dragged through wet streets speaking in languages older than the stones of cities buried in sand.[7]

Older and every bit as impenetrable, as incomprehensible, these lost beings have no purchase price and have therefore dropped through the bottom of society. While silence tempts them, they reject it and choose to shout their existence, their inherent value as human beings, to whoever might be listening. Virtually no one is. And those like Bucky Wunderlick who are listening do not share a common language with "the hags and thunderers."

One thing is nevertheless unmistakable. The shouting of the these "traceless men and women" is clearly threatening, even if the precise nature of the threat remains vague. While the expression of their rage may be incoherent, it is certainly possible to speculate about its origins. Having been defined by a consumer society as valueless because they have lost the power to purchase, they rage at those who have not been so brutally objectified. They perhaps even sense that one way to force a recognition of their existence on those who have learned not to see them would be through violence. Thus, in DeLillo's world, there is a reason for those who remain secure in urban society to fear those who do not. *Mao II* depicts a New York City as a world capital of greed and superficiality that seems every bit as foreign, as dangerous as Beirut; meaningful communication is impossible in the "civilization of locks" that is New York.[8]

While DeLillo's novels are essential to anyone seeking to understand the nature of contemporary American urban culture, he is, in the final analysis, not primarily concerned with urban crisis as such. Urban America rather serves DeLillo as a space in which to explore more abstract concerns such as the limitations of words, the bewildering complexity of names that have become disassociated from any comprehensible signification, the limited possibilities of language to pick the locks of the postindustrial world. As *Underworld*, his brilliant 1997 fiction devoted to exploration of the many ways in which technology, violence, and the commodification of waste dominate our age, eloquently demonstrates, his is truly a national and an international focus. Thus, New York and indeed the American city are, in De-Lillo's fiction, not as important for their own sakes as they are for settings out of which to explore other concerns. David Bell's doomed quest for a redemptive national meaning culminates in a remote and desolate west

Texas. One critic provides an especially succinct summary of DeLillo's central thematic concerns: "the nature of speech—its fringes in noise and silence, its association with violence, and its balances of performance and communication."[9]

In their own powerful fictions, eight contemporary American novelists—William Kennedy, Caleb Carr, Richard Price, John Edgar Wideman, Sandra Cisneros, Cormac McCarthy, N. Scott Momaday, and John Rechy—focus more specifically on violence in urban America. In contrasting and distinctive ways, they explore the "vein of murder," "the casual savagery" that permeates our cities. They also explore the "systemic violence" originating in an oppressive and exploitive economic system that leaves blood in "every way of seeing" and, in so doing, give voice to the marginalized and seemingly voiceless "others" of America's inner cities. Hoping to pick the locks of urban violence, they work within a variety of genres and traditions, including the mock historic romance, the detective novel, the jeremiad, the naturalistic protest novel; and they focus upon a wide variety of American urban centers. The earliest of these fictions, Momaday's *House Made of Dawn*, was published in 1968; while the most recent, Carr's *The Alienist*, appeared in 1994. Two were published in the 1970s (Price's *The Wanderers* and McCarthy's *Suttree*), two in the 1980s (William Kennedy's *Quinn's Book* and Sandra Cisneros's *The House on Mango Street*), and three in the 1990s (in addition to *The Alienist*, Wideman's *Philadelphia Fire* and Rechy's *The Miraculous Day of Amalia Gómez*). Except for Momaday's text, they were written after the 1960s "sea change"[10] in the perception of the American city and reflect a sense of violence as the dominant single aspect of urban reality.

In fact, these eight texts cumulatively depict an urban world in which violence has ceased to seem extraordinary, a world in which exploitation and death are ever present. Violence in them is never a positive form of action; rather it is always reactive and directed either against members of one's own social and ethnic group or against others in parallel groups. Out of five of them, a landscape emerges that would probably seem especially familiar to Yummy Sandifer, one in which children and adolescents are the victims and sometimes the perpetrators of violence. But the "vein of murder" "fed by [our] mute cities" threatens adults as well as children. Eleven-year-olds *and* eighty-four-year-olds are threatened by the "casual savagery" of urban, and especially inner-city, America. Windows in the Hardaway home were "often" shot out, and anyone of any age standing inside them might have become a victim. It would be understandable if the Hardaways retreated from these windows and from all windows and attempted to survive in what little safe space they could find; but, even if they did, escape from the racial and class oppression in which they are trapped hardly seems a possibility. Three of the texts focus on adult protagonists who continue looking outside the windows of their selves and find, in quite different ways, spiritual salvation in violent urban wastelands.

Ethnic antagonisms, racial and gender divisions, and class oppressions are norms in this cumulative fictional world; and it is largely, though not entirely, out of these factors that violence emerges, a violence that threatens to silence the voices of the inhabitants of this oppressive landscape. Violence in these texts is never intended to produce political change; it is never revolutionary in a political sense. Rather it is depicted, except by Cormac McCarthy, as "structural," "systemic," as a kind of random totalitarian force with roots in the very origins of the nation. William Kennedy and Caleb Carr explore these origins while attempting to "pick the locks" of a peculiarly American violence.

Chapter 1

Dedalus in the *Dood Kamer*

William Kennedy's *Quinn's Book*

In his 1988 masterpiece of black humor, *Quinn's Book,* William Kennedy creates a countermyth that simultaneously echoes and parodies the traditionally accepted history of the nation with its valorization of capitalism, individualism, and the Puritan work ethic. Like DeLillo, Kennedy is concerned in *Quinn's Book* with the relationship between words and the nation, rather than with the city alone. Yet by bringing a mythical focus supported by a pervasive black comedy to his recurrent fictional setting, Albany, New York, he constructs an urban and national history that explores systemic violence rooted in ethnic and racial oppression. The roots of the 1960s "sea change" in perception of the American city go back a very long way, Kennedy implies. Blood "is in the hold of every way of seeing" in *Quinn's Book*. Few novels better illustrate Michael Kowalewski's admonition that "American fiction is not for hemophobics.... In studying fictional violence one must explore the power of words to sicken and befoul as well as freshen and redeem."[1] In its evocation of violence and death, often linked to sexuality, the text is deliberately outrageous, constantly undercutting the implied reader's assumptions about the American success ethic and the norm in human behavior. The shocking nature of many of the novel's violent moments is, in fact, intensified by the parodic mode in which they are narrated. Moreover, *Quinn's Book* richly illustrates Lehan's ideas about the complex role of "the Other" in traditional views of the city, as well as McNamara's thesis about a historic urge to control and repress the rich diversity of the American city.

Still, it must be said that the inadequacy of language, of writing, to capture the reality of violence is a central concern in Kennedy's text. As foreshadowed by the title itself, a central thematic and structuring motif in *Quinn's Book* is the education of its orphaned and uneducated Irish protagonist Daniel Quinn as a writer. Thus, the novel often reads as a parodic and naturalistic American version of Joyce's *Portrait of the Artist as a Young Man*. Daniel Quinn, even with considerably more reason to be so (he is after all *literally* fatherless as well as motherless), is less conflicted about his Irish American roots than is Stephen Dedalus about his Irish origins. It is in part because of his devotion to his ethnic origin that Quinn succeeds as a writer even while losing faith in the purpose of writing itself. The realities of Albany and the nation are simply too violent and chaotic for Daniel Quinn to bear credible witness to them.

But William Kennedy bears witness to them, often by seeming not to do so. The plot of his novel is provocatively episodic, leaving several central strands of the narrative unresolved. This plotlessness works as a mode of challenging the validity of the modernist novel as practiced by Joyce and the "lost generation" American writers. In a metafictional manner, Kennedy doesn't just let the seams of his narrative show—he calls attention to them. His text ironically and repeatedly emphasizes that violence, senseless death, and ethnic conflict have historically made affirming and healing communication difficult and, sometimes, impossible in America. In his *Understanding William Kennedy*, J. K. Van Dover points out that *Quinn's Book* echoes Kennedy's first novel, *The Ink Truck*, in implying "the failure of advocacy journalism."[2] Van Dover asserts, in fact, that more than "advocacy journalism" fails in *Quinn's Book;* the text is "an anthology of modes of oral and written communication" (p. 117), which cumulatively demonstrates "the inadequacy of language" (p. 120).

Quinn's book fails, but that failure becomes an integral part of the aesthetic success of *Quinn's Book*. Kennedy's text undercuts the most idealistic aspects of American mythology. Meaningful witnessing and communication pose severe challenges for Daniel Quinn and the novel's secondary characters; the text contains several instances of attempted silencing of witnesses to exploitation and injustice, including one character literally having his tongue cut out. But, by constructing his powerful countermyth of American history, Kennedy ultimately affirms not merely the adequacy, but even the magic, of language, of writing.

Central to the text's countermyth and to its affirmation of the power of language are two memorable genealogies, which together provide an ironic and blackly humorous summary of central tropes in American history and especially of how such dominant cultural idealisms as "the American dream," the Puritan success ethic, and the heroic conquest of the frontier were compromised from the beginning. Kennedy's simultaneously evocative and ironic prose fuels the densely layered implications of the two genealogies. The first primarily recounts the superficially improbable adventures, covering more than two centuries, of the entrepreneurial Staats family. It satirically echoes Nick Carraway's, and F. Scott Fitzgerald's, lyrical evocation on the concluding page of *The Great Gatsby* of "the fresh, green breast of the new world" "that flowered once for Dutch sailors' eyes."[3] Kennedy's Irish American emphasis in *Quinn's Book* recalls Fitzgerald's ethnic background and is central to a considerably more bleak historicizing of America than one finds in *Gatsby*—rather than viewing "the American dream" as something lost and compromised in a recent past, Kennedy presents it as something that was illusory and corrupted from the beginning.

Ostensibly narrated by Daniel Quinn, the Staats family history opens with the admission that it is impossible to trace it farther back than "the sixteenth century, about the time Holland was . . . preparing to shape the New World in the image of the Dutch coin."[4] From the beginning a largely unchecked capitalism characterizes the Staats dynasty in the New World. A trader of "counterfeit wampum" (p. 220), Wouter Staats, the first of the family to come to America, appeared at Fort Orange, New York (the future Albany), and inaugurated the family's exploitation of the Native American. In his history of the Staats family, Kennedy so overtly highlights links between European imperialism, white American capitalistic power, and ethnic oppression that the kind of "contrapuntal reading" recommended by Edward W. Said in *Culture and Imperialism* becomes unavoidable.[5]

Wouter's son Johannes, the first Staats to be born in North America, is described as "a noble-headed youth who grew up to serve in the militia as an Indian fighter, gaining knowledge of the wilderness and its inhabitants to such a degree that upon leaving the military he entered the fur trade (beaver pelts) and earned the wealth that began the family fortune" (p. 22). While his father specialized in nonviolent exploitation, Johannes participated in the organized and sanctioned white aggression against the Indians that would culminate in their near extinction. "The Indian Wars" also made him expert in exploiting the physical landscape of "the New World." His "noble-headed" embrace of violence against Native Americans and nature itself truly makes Johannes the first American Staatsman.

Later, he became an ardent defender of religious freedom, even for Jews, apparently never noticing any contradiction between this idealistic behavior and his experience as an Indian fighter and exploiter of nature. Moreover, the two members of the Staats dynasty who appear in the present tense of the text, the wonderfully eccentric Hillegond and her son Dirck, are respectively active in the Underground Railroad and devoted to speaking out against the racial and ethnic hatreds that plague nineteenth-century America. The text seems to be implicitly pointing to the schizophrenic legacy of famous American aristocratic dynasties, to the improbable mixture of brutal oppression and idealistic devotion that has marked the histories of such families as the Vanderbilts, the Rockefellers, and the Astors.

Kennedy uses the ancestral figure of Johannes's eldest son, Dolph, for some wonderfully absurdist satire of the fondness of the American capitalist oligarchy for self-glorifying iconography. Dolph, a key figure in the transition of power from the Dutch to the English, commissions for the Dutch church a stained glass window of "the glazed image of a supine infant whose physiognomy combined the blond ringlets and eyebrows of a Dutchified Jesus, with the crossed eyes of Dolph's only son, Jacobus" (p. 23). Upon reaching maturity, Jacobus marries Catrina Wessels, "the wall-eyed niece of the Patroon," an "absentee landlord" who owns "an estate of seven hundred thousand acres . . . on which some one hundred thousand tenant farmers and lesser vassals paid rent and servitude *in perpetuum*" (p. 23). The narrator, presumably but improbably Daniel Quinn, comments further about the vast estate of the Patroon: "while this colonizing was doubtless the great expansionist stroke that created our present world, it was also the cruelest injustice American white men of the New World had ever known, and would precipitate warfare that itself would continue for decades" (p. 23).

By introducing the exploitative system of tenant farming into the Staats family chronicle, Kennedy accomplishes several things. He establishes the dependence of the nation from its inception and even beyond (the Patroon's holdings are, by the mid-nineteenth century, two hundred years old) upon the subjugation and exploitation of marginalized human beings; he raises a consideration that will extend the implications of his narrative well beyond Albany and the northeastern section of the nation; and he suggests historic and thematic considerations that will eventually dominate the novel, especially what, along with the genocide of the Native American, must be "the cruelest injustice" that *any* men and women in "the New World" have ever known—American slavery. The optical disabilities of Jacobus and his bride function as black comic symbols of the failure of the family, and by extension the historic American capitalist oligarchy, to see clearly the brutal oppression supporting its dynasty. It is this same failure to see, which is in actuality a refusal to confront the unpleasant aspects of reality, that allows Dolph to transform his only son into a religious icon. On the surface, such failure of perception may be quaintly comic, but its effects on others are brutal and tragic.

As an adult, Jacobus establishes a sawmill on a section of the Patroon's property, near which "a handful of Irish immigrants in the employ of the Manor, were throwing up one humble dwelling after another in what would eventually be called The Colonie" (p. 24). Along with the horrors of slavery, a central focus of *Quinn's Book* is the exploitation of Irish immigrants in America. In fact, the fifteen-year-old Daniel Quinn is the orphaned son of an Irish immigrant, who along with his wife and daughter die in a cholera epidemic that ravages the Irish community of Albany in 1849. It is this childhood tragedy that introduces Daniel to sudden and horrific death, which will become the single most recurring experience of his adult life. The kind of "humble dwelling[s]," in actuality mere shacks, that abruptly appear on the Patroon's estate during Jacobus's life will be the breeding ground for cholera and other diseases that regularly and inevitably assault the immigrant families that are crowded into them. By describing the origins of "The Colonie," Kennedy makes the implicit point that the violence historically inflicted by the capitalist oligarchy upon the powerless (tenant farmers, immigrants, and slaves) has at times been indirect, the result of a truly criminal neglect. Daniel, whose assumed obligation to voice the silenced conscience and consciousness of his oppressed Irish race continues even after he loses faith in the potentiality of writing to eradicate such oppression, understands that the Irish story is inextricably bound up with the Staats family history. As always, exploiters and exploited are united in a symbiotic relationship.

Jacobus's grandson, "called Amos after the rustic Hebrew prophet," dies at the age of sixteen a hero of the American Revolutionary War. Amos is a local Paul Revere who makes a miraculous thirty-mile horseback ride to notify the city of Albany of the surrender of the English general Burgoyne; the ride quickly assumes legendary status with the switch that Amos used on his horse being planted and growing into "an enormous tree that for several generations was known as Amos's Oak" (p. 26). The implications of this incident are obvious—the newly emerged nation quickly creates its own pantheon of heroes, all of whom represent the dominant white culture. These figures are canonized to help the nation forget and deny its brutal exploitation of African slaves, Irish immigrants, Native Americans, and women.

Kennedy makes this point overt in the present tense of the narrative when a perfectly preserved "Amos in his soldier's cap and uniform, arms crossed on his chest, a warrior's medal on his chest" is disinterred and put on display in the *"Dood Kamer"* or "Dead Room" of the Staats family mansion. Daniel Quinn and Maud Fallon, the beautiful young woman whom he pursues throughout the novel, stand marveling at the glorious intactness of Amos when the body simply explodes. Not at all unnerved by this unexpected combustion, Quinn and Maud proceed to kiss with "the dust" of Amos "falling over our heads and shoulders" (p. 42). This deliberately outrageous scene functions as a synecdoche of the novel—just as it does to Amos, the text is devoted to exploding the supposedly heroic mythology of the dominant American culture.

Amos's father, Jacobus, finally dies during "an apoplectic fit in 1780 while chasing a family of brazen Irish squatters off his land." Thus, he emotionally explodes in a way that anticipates the fate of his son's body seventy years later. Jacobus's grandson Petrus marries "the bounteous and bawdy Hillegond," builds in conjunction with the Yankee Lyman Fitzgibbon an iron works and factory that are central to the economic well-being of Albany of the present tense of the novel, fathers Dirck, and becomes "Albany's richest man" as the nineteenth century begins. With Hillegond and Dirck, we enter the present tense of the text.

Two of the most striking things about this extensive family history are the seemingly arbitrary manner in which it is introduced into the text and its apparent digressiveness. As fascinating as Hillegond and Dirck are as characters, they are secondary to Quinn and Maud and, at least in terms of plot, to both "La Ultima," the (to put it mildly) irrepressible Magdalena Colon, and the prototype of Irish American upward mobility, John the Brawn McGee. Moreover, the Quinn of the first half of the novel, an uneducated Irish orphan, can only know about the Staats family from local Albany legend; and one wonders why, in his rather desperate circumstances, he would even be interested in it. One assumes, of course, that the mature Quinn, who has become a nationally famous journalist, has researched and/or created the story of the Staatses. Still, its abrupt appearance early in the novel positioned within an account of Quinn's immediate experiences, along with its rich detail, initially seems arbitrary.

The Staats history is a kind of narrative riff, a bit of sustained and often fanciful improvisation appearing suddenly in an account of events that have only a tangential relationship to it. Upon finishing the novel, however, the reader realizes that these few pages constitute a virtual abstract of everything that surrounds it, an absurd, often improbable and always directly or indirectly violent, summary of the countermyth that sustains Kennedy's novel. Edward C. Reilly perceptively points out that "the key to understanding

Quinn's Book is Kennedy's emphasis on patterns anticipating the twentieth century and 'preconsciousness'";[6] and, in fact, Kennedy is re-creating in an absurdist manner, the violence, racism, and capitalist oppression, that defined the nation from its start and even before. The story of the Staatses reads like an outrageously exaggerated *Knickerbocker's History of New York* narrated from an Irish American point of view.

Balancing it is the considerably briefer history of the Plum family in America. In the present tense of the novel, the members of the Plum family are frightening representatives, devoted to criminality, of Albany's lumpen proletariat. Two brothers, nicknamed Peaches and Outa, especially recall characters in a Nelson Algren novel; the Plum brothers are grotesquely and self-destructively irredeemable. Moreover, the story of their ancestry is dominated by sadism, murder, and incest. "The first Plum in the New World" was Ezra, who at eighteen arrived in Albany in 1759 and was hired as "the city's official whipper." Later he was moved up to the post of "city hangman" (pp. 82–83). It is a safe assumption that few, if any, of the old Dutch or Yankee aristocracies were flogged or hanged by Ezra; rather he almost certainly tortured and executed individuals from socioeconomic classes as exploited as his own. Ezra, in fact, personifies the participation of the poor and outcast in their own oppression. As might have been anticipated, he died a violent death, though probably not, as one would expect, at the hands of a victim of his torture or a relative of someone he had executed; instead, the "unknown assailant [was] widely believed to be his grandson, Jeremiah" (p. 83).

Ezra's son Bliss is, if possible, even more rapacious, establishing that "murder ran in the family," killing two of his cousins who had just arrived in America from England, "thus removing them as competition for an inheritance Bliss coveted" (p. 83). Bliss, though, does not get to enjoy the inheritance because, once his crime is discovered, he is appropriately enough, hanged. The black humor inherent in Bliss's name becomes even more overt in the story of his son Jeremiah, "conceived during Bliss's three-week marriage to a woman named Blessed Benson" (p. 83). Jeremiah, the probable killer of his grandfather, inherits the Plum property upon the execution of his father and becomes the patriarch of the family in the novel's present text. His wife, Priscilla Swett, "almost eviscerat[es] a woman neighbor with a carving knife in an argument over the neighbor's fur hat, which Priscilla, called Pris, had stolen" (p. 83). Priscilla's first name is undoubtedly intended as an ironic echo of Priscilla Alden, the famous New England Puritan woman; moreover, the entire Plum family, like William Faulkner's Anse

Bundren in *As I Lay Dying*, is determined not to sweat any more than they have to.

There are other Plums: one is a murderous bounty hunter, and one is a notorious horse thief. Climaxing the family saga is Peaches, the lower-class bully and petty criminal of the novel's contemporary period, "whom Priscilla claimed as her own in order to cap a scandal, for Peaches was actually the offspring of his own sister, Hanna, when Hanna was fifteen. And the sire was Hanna's father, Jeremiah" (p. 83). At least superficially, the Plum genealogy, especially in the context of the Staats', might be troublesome for a Marxist. Never remotely part of the aristocracy of the emerging nation, their sordid history is also devoid of any of the idealistic devotion to social reform that occasionally distinguishes their Dutch counterparts; they might be seen then as a kind of elitist parody of the American lower classes. A more perceptive reading, though, would approach the Plums as representing, in part, the enforced ignorance, and the brutish existence suffered by the American lumpen proletariat especially during the middle of the nineteenth century.

Most important, the Plum family story functions as a means of underscoring, through exaggerated and sordid details, the more unpleasant and exploitative moments of the Staats family history, which is itself marked by murder, savage cruelty, and outrageous sexual transgression (the Plums plumb the social, economic, and moral depths). It constitutes the dark underside of the Staats story, functioning as a symbolic depiction of the historic outrages committed by the oligarchy. An apparent digression, the Plum history completes the countermyth that informs Kennedy's text. Moreover, these two family narratives merit extensive discussion here not only because together they symbolically sum up everything else in *Quinn's Book*, but also because they outline a revisionist view of American history reminiscent of those we will discover in Carr's *The Alienist* and Wideman's *Philadelphia Fire*.

After these two genealogies, appearing as early in the text as they do, Kennedy's reader is hardly surprised that the initiation of Quinn will be marked by unrelenting violence and death, that he will discover Albany and the nation to be one large *Dood Kamer*. Moreover, they are recounted by the adult and now famous Daniel Quinn, who has come to understand the historic role of the Irish as victims and scapegoats of the upper class and the nativist lower classes, respectively. The crusading newspaper editor, Will Canaday, who acts as a mentor for the young Quinn, teaches his protégé that in the past as in the present, "violence [has been] the norm of this bellicose world" (p. 49). The cholera epidemic, which occurs in 1849 seven months before the novel opens, constitutes Quinn's initiation into violence and death.

Like Wideman in *Philadelphia Fire*, Kennedy follows the lead of Camus, using widespread disease or plague as a trope of human blindness, superstition, and carelessness. In a letter to Maud, Quinn describes the outbreak of cholera and the events that anticipated it. Initially, "a stranger in old clothes" (p. 61) abruptly appears in front of a neighborhood woman's home and informs her, "[D]eath is moving in me" (p. 62). His limbs then proceed to die one at a time. It is only after others have died that the stranger is seen "as both carrier and emissary of the plague" (p. 62). The symbolic role of the old man is obvious—he is an absurdist grim reaper, an embodiment of death whose body is dying a part at a time. Of course, no one understands the warning he brings until it is too late; characters in novels and stories from Poe's "The Masque of the Red Death" to Camus's *The Plague* never do.

Subsequent warnings cannot be so easily ignored, though the response to them is hopelessly misguided. Local ministers start to preach that the plague is the result of the sinfulness of the community, and when "one brave soul" dares to call one of the ministers a "madman" and suggests that the pigs who roam the city streets are a more likely cause of cholera than any "sins," he is struck down with a plank.[7] One remembers that, in *The Plague*, city authorities are reluctant to state officially that the rats which overwhelm the city are the cause of the epidemic that devastates Oran. Moreover, this episode from *Quinn's Book* must recall, for contemporary readers, the sudden and tragic outbreak of the AIDS epidemic during the 1980s, especially the refusals by national, state, and big-city administrators to take it seriously and its cynical exploitation by certain fundamentalist religious leaders. In a general sense, the cholera epidemic in Kennedy's novel highlights the prevalent human tendency to deny and to seek scapegoats for inexplicable and frightening aspects of reality. Again, as the nightmarish living conditions afforded Albany's Irish since the Patroon's "Colonie" make inevitable, the Irish become the source of, and later the scapegoats for, the epidemic. The mature Quinn understands, and is outraged by, this victimization of his people.

The cholera that orphans Quinn plunges him into even more violent and terrifying experience. To avoid starvation, he, like scores of abandoned young men, seeks and finds employment with one of the "water rats" who run small boats on the Hudson. It is in this capacity, working with the strong and animalistic John the Brawn, that, "on a late December day in 1894," he first meets "Maud the wondrous" (p. 5) and abruptly finds himself in the middle of still more sudden death and devastation. Maud, who immediately becomes the Beatrice for Quinn's Dante, appears in the company of her aunt, "the great courtesan, Magdelena Colon, also known as La Ultima, a woman whose presence turned men into spitting, masturbating pigs," and Magdelena's maid.

Magdelena has advertised in the *Albany Chronicle* for someone to ferry her and her two associates across the ice-covered Hudson so that she can fulfill an upcoming theatrical engagement; but her reputation is so scandalous that, of all the "water rats," who themselves represent one of the lowest levels of Albany society, no one will help her "except Carrick, the rotten Scottish hunchback of syphilitic mien, no longer welcome in the Albany brothels" (p. 6). Like the Plum brothers, Carrick recalls the grotesque naturalism of Nelson Algren. La Ultima's "crossing," an absurdist pun on the idea of "crossing from life into death," becomes a public spectacle. While only Carrick, the outcast of outcasts, will come to her aid, crowds of Albany's citizens flock to a nearby bridge for a close and free glimpse of the notorious Magdelena. Inevitably their prurient curiosity results in tragedy when the inadequate bridge collapses, plunging a hundred people to death and leaving a hundred others clinging desperately to the remnants of the bridge to avoid falling into the deadly ice and water.

Moreover, the bridge collapse constitutes only the first stage of disaster. Quickly, a tidal wave of ice smashes into waterfront buildings, "mixing with and slacking the lime into chemical combustion that would set fire to a block of stores . . . fire rising out of flood—the gods gone mad" (p. 11). Incidents of massive human destruction by flood and fire, of course, recall the Old Testament, and this opening scene has a prophetic function, warning of the violent death that permeates the novel. The biblical Yahweh is a god enraged at the blasphemy and debasement of his people, while, in *Quinn's Book* as in Cormac McCarthy's *Suttree,* omnipotent power appears simply mad, randomly and carelessly spreading death among innocents and sinners alike. Quinn is as appalled at such cosmic injustice as he is at the capitalist oppression of his fellow Irish Americans. The bloodthirsty "mad gods" function in Kennedy's text as a metaphor for a violent, oppressive socioeconomic order.

He and the reader are almost exposed to a monstrous human cruelty in this opening scene. Carrick's small boat is destroyed by the ice, and an alert John the Brawn rescues Maud and retrieves what he is certain is the dead body of La Ultima, whereupon an anonymous woman, "a jungle feline," assaults the body, biting the cheek and coming away "with a blooded wad of flesh in her mouth, which she savored with a bulging smile and spat onto the dead actress's chest" (p. 13). It is hard to remember a more horrible detail than this, even in the writing of Poe, Faulkner, O'Connor, and other provocatively outrageous American writers. Clearly, it is not only the gods who are "mad" in *Quinn's Book*.

Yet, as in a polyphonic musical composition, this grotesque violence is quickly contrasted with a scene of outrageous sexuality. In fact, *Quinn's Book* is, in form, essentially contrapuntal, with its alternating motifs of violence and death and burlesque sexuality. Quinn, John the Brawn, and Maud retreat with the defiled body of La Ultima to the sanctuary of the Staats mansion and the protection of Magdelena's wealthy and philanthropic double, Hillegond. Inevitably, the "corpse" is laid to rest in the *Dood Kamer* until, in the presence of Quinn, Maud, and Hillegond, it is sexually assaulted by John the Brawn, a further defilement that has the unexpected result of reviving Magdelena. Aroused by what she sees, Hillegond rushes into the *Dood Kamer*, and John the Brawn proceeds to alternate his attentions between her and an increasingly conscious Magdelena.

There are obviously several jokes in this incredible scene. Sex becomes, instead of "the little death," a means of resurrection, and the sexually insatiable Magdelena experiences the reversal of the old male fantasy of dying while engaged in intercourse. After all this, it is hardly surprising that the gaping wound on Magdelena's face first degenerates into a hideous and foul-smelling sore until it is mysteriously healed by an African American servant who doubles as a conjure woman.

The opening scene of mass destruction with its biblical overtones foreshadows much of what is to come; throughout the text, the gods remain quite mad indeed. Racial and ethnic hatred unleash much of the worst of the subsequent death and violence, and, in his treatment of such concerns, Kennedy's ethnic consciousness is especially apparent. In one of the novel's most powerful scenes, the Irish American poverty and anger originating in "The Colonie," which Petrus Staats and Lyman Fitzgibbon have attempted to alleviate through their factory, explodes in a savage riot. The riot is sparked when a newly laid-off factory molder named Alfie Palmer gets drunk and takes out his frustration by killing an Irish worker, Toddy Ryan, with an axe. In a letter to Maud about the incident, Quinn describes the class from which Ryan emerged:

> They are the famine Irish, Maud, and they are villains in this city. . . . They are viewed not only as carriers of the cholera plague but as a plague themselves, such is their number: several thousand setting up life here in only a few years, living in hovels, in shanties, ten families to a small house, some unable to speak anything but the Irish tongue,

their wretchedness so fierce and relentless that not only does the city shun them but the constabulary and the posses meet them at the docks and on the turnpikes to herd them together in encampments on the city's great western plain. (p. 111)

Despised and exploited by the nation to which they have emigrated, Kennedy's "famine Irish" no longer even attempt communication with others except through periodic outbreaks of violence. That others of their descendants will ascend the ladder of political power in America and themselves become oppressors of African Americans is a tragic fact of history and an emphasis in *Quinn's Book.* Inevitably the murder of Toddy Ryan sparks more violence and death, specifically what comes to be known as "the battle of the Hills against the Creeks," a series of pitched battles between Albany's "native" proletariat and their Irish counterparts. Quinn witnesses the first of these and, even with his past experiences, is stunned by the savagery of what he sees: "in the [Civil] war I would see much worse, but I'd seen nothing before to equal the violence of that day" (p. 125).

In reporting the bloody confrontation, the national press simply adds to the racial and ethnic hatred, which makes impossible any saving dialogue between the combatants: "newspapers reported on the battle, calling it a feud between Papists and Americans, between the Irish and the Know-Nothings (who numbered in their political ranks the enraged nativists and assorted hybrid-haters bent on shaping a balance in this republic of equals by expelling the unequals)."[8] The Civil War, in which the adult Quinn achieves fame for his unflinchingly realistic coverage of battlefield death, was also of course a legacy of racial oppression and of one of the central and "cruelest injustices" of "the New World."

Moreover, the war indirectly sparks perhaps the novel's most unbearably savage scene, a recreation of the 1863 New York draft riot sparked by Lincoln's "conscription law," which inaugurated for the first time in American history a military draft to raise desperately needed soldiers for the Union army. Kennedy is unflinching in his analysis of the social dynamic behind the draft. For many of the urban proletariat, the idea of the emancipation of the slaves hardly represents a desired national goal. Moreover, the "conscription law" provided an exemption from military service for anyone with three hundred dollars to give the government. Quinn understands the explosive nature of the legislation: "we need not elaborate on the crystalline injustice of this to a poor man in general, and in particular to the poor Irishmen (a quarter of the entire city was Irish), marred in generational denial and humiliation as he was, and for whom free Negroes meant a swarm of competitors for the already insufficient jobs at the bottom of the world" (p. 275). Thus, even the just and necessary war to abolish slavery is compromised by exploitation of the urban poor, and especially of the Irish American urban poor.

Tragically if not surprisingly, the rioting urban white proletariat unleashes the worst of its violence on those with the least protection, the city's African American population. Among its black victims is the novel's most courageous character Joshua, an escaped slave who takes incredible risks throughout the novel in helping conduct the Underground Railroad. Kennedy uses Joshua's death to add a mythic note to the text, describing in blank verse the horrible atrocities (stabbing, stoning, evisceration, and burning) committed against his body while he is alive and afterward. The account of the mutilation and death of Joshua, introduced by the dramatically understated phrase "Here is what they did to Joshua" and elaborately set off from the rest of the page, assaults the eye; this separation, along with the language in which it is written, gives the passage a quality of orality, the appearance of a familiar legend. Joshua becomes emblematic of all the African American victims of lynching in America.[9] Indeed, the excessiveness of the mob's vicious desecration of Joshua's body conveys an unreal quality, as of an incident that has been instantaneously transformed through decades of retelling. Quinn and Kennedy both seem intent upon bestowing on the martyred African American the status of Old Testament prophet.

Moreover, it inspires a third "genealogy," which in its brevity and horror, provides its own exegesis. The text goes back only to Joshua's father, "known as Cinque" and stolen into slavery from Sierra Leone, who leads a successful rebellion aboard the slave ship on which he is being transported to America only to be betrayed afterward by a sailor who had pretended to offer support for the insurrection. Kennedy obviously intends an intertextual effect in this story, echoing as it does the real incident of the *Amistad,* the slave ship liberated by Joseph Cinque, and Melville's novella *Benito Cereno.* Kennedy's Cinque, in punishment for his rebellion, is sold to a notorious slave breaker and, after siring Joshua, attempts to escape only to be captured and "whipped until he bled to death through his face" (p. 269). One remembers, of course, that the story of the American Plums begin with Ezra, who served as Albany's official "whipper" and executioner. In *Quinn's Book,* torture and sadism are depicted as being very much a part of the American grain. It is also significant that, in sharp contrast to the Staates and even the Plums, the account of Joshua's ancestry can go back only one generation before the primal violence of enslavement uproots it from tradition and memory itself.

Yet in keeping with the contrapuntal nature of Kennedy's polyphonic text, Joshua, prior to his horrendous death at the hands of a largely Irish American mob, strikes an alliance with John the Brawn, the novel's prototype of irrepressible Irishness. After abandoning his career as a "wharf rat" for a lucrative alliance with Magdelena Colon, John becomes a successful boxer, "a bare-knuckle bard, a fistic philosopher, a poet of the poke" (p. 242).[10] (Of course, given McGee's resurrection of Magdelena, a bawdy joke is implicit in the phrase, "a poet of the poke"). Later, he converts his boxing fame into a career as an enforcer for New York City's Democratic Party machine, rounding up gangs of Irish "lads" to fight off assaults on polling places by nativist political forces. As a reward, he is allowed to open an illegal gambling house, which he parleys into "sixteen gambling hells, including the most luxurious in the city" (p. 246). In all of this, John is loyally assisted by Joshua, who still manages to spend most of his time with the Underground Railroad, ultimately helping over four hundred slaves escape, if not with his employer's actual assistance, at least with his knowledge and tacit consent.[11]

Upon escaping from slavery, Joshua first sought refuge in New York's notorious Five Points neighborhood, an actual urban nightmare that will also be explored by Caleb Carr in *The Alienist*. The very hopelessness of Five Points furnishes Joshua with security from pursuit; the area is so notoriously crime-ridden and dangerous that no one, not even slave catchers, will venture there. Kennedy's text describes Five Points as a place "where no human life was safe from the ravagements of the street and river gangs: the Daybreak Boys, the Short Tails, the Patsy Conroys" (p. 269); but, as an escaped slave, Joshua's life is already threatened and he has comparably little to fear from the human predators of Five Points. Yet, in one of the novel's most grimly pessimistic notes, the fragile racial harmony of this most desperate and vicious of places is shattered by the "conscription" laws, and much of the mob that will murder Joshua spills out of Five Points. It is in Five Points that Joshua learns the skills that will be of such assistance to the boxing career of John McGee: for instance, "how to draw blood from bare-knuckle wounds with his mouth, this taught him by an expert named Suckface, a member of the Slaughterhouse gang, who for ten cents would bite the head off a live mouse, and for a quarter off a live rat" (pp. 269–70).

Even the story of John McGee's social rise is predicated on violence and ethnic and racial acrimony. Nineteenth-century bare-knuckle boxing was an especially savage and primitive "sport." Another of the novel's polyphonic moments is an alleged report of one of John the Brawn's fights from the *Albany Telescope,* which underscores the ethnic division central to the novel. The fight story described the opponents as "John (the Brawn) McGee, also known as John of the Skiff and John of the Water (from his days on the river), and Arthur (Yankee) Barker, also known as the Pet of Poughkeepsie and The True American" (p. 242). Barker, who enters the ring with an American flag draped over his shoulders, is referred throughout the story as "the Patriot" and even after he is beaten almost beyond recognition receives tribute from the writer as "a flag himself now—red, white, and blue, and seeing the stars and stripes" (p. 244). Of course, the wedding of superpatriotism and sports writing is an old tradition in this country. The anonymous reporter ends his account with a racist allusion to Joshua, which is made even uglier by the off-handed way it is introduced: "a good time was had by all, nobody got killed that we know of, and the nigger carried off John the King on his shoulders" (p. 245).

Emphasizing the horror out of which John McGee evolved and which he transcends by *literally* capitalizing on his ability to brutalize other men is an early scene in which young Quinn observes, along with another of his mentors, Emmett Daugherty, what Daugherty refers to as "the Irish Circus." Irish immigrants who have not been able to secure even the primitive kind of housing that marks "The Colonie" are shipped west on railroad carriages where they will have to fend for themselves in the frontier wilderness. Historic echoes abound here. The forced exodus of the unwanted Irish to the west simultaneously references and undercuts the American "frontier myth" of individual freedom and regeneration. Moreover, when one remembers that *Quinn's Book* is a 1988 novel, echoes of the European Holocaust are inevitably triggered by the image of masses of people being forced into train cars.

Kennedy unites all these strands of racial and ethnic hatred with one trope, a secret "order" of white nativists called "the Society," devoted to preserving, through violence if necessary, the Dutch and Anglo-Saxon capitalist establishment from desecration by outsiders. Most obviously, "the Society" recalls the Ku Klux Klan, but on a broader level it serves as a synecdoche for the white American economic and social establishment. Because of the illegality of much of its program, it valorizes secrecy, demanding that its members take an oath of loyalty to "the Society" in which they acquiesce to a gruesome penalty for divulging information about the organization: "I agree that my stomach should be opened by a blade, and my organs and entrails exposed to the tooth and fang of ravenous rats" (p. 91). The oath has many possible origins in Gothic literature and in American popular culture from

Hollywood film versions of the Fu Manchu novels down to the Indiana Jones films.

It is hardly surprising that the Plum family is intricately tied to "the Society," serving as enforcers for it; but it is more important that Petrus Staats was one of its founders. Thus, the two genealogies that open the novel and retell, often in an absurdist manner, the American myth, merge in an organization founded on hatred and sustained by terrorism. Much more than it may appear on the surface appear to be, *Quinn's Book* is a subversive text. Yet, in keeping with the overall contrapuntal narrative strategy, the existence of "the Society" is discovered and publicized by Petrus's son Dirck who as a reward is kidnapped by the Plums, sees a man executed in the manner prescribed, and has his tongue cut out. In order to protect his revelatory work, Dirck goes so far as to invent his own language in which to write it; when he disappears, Will Canaday has to turn to "a scholar at Columbia College in Manhattan" to decode it (p. 88).

Paralleling the mutilation of Dirck, vandals destroy Will Canaday's press after he prints the expose of "the Society." Especially in the context of Dirck's self-description as "a devotee of words," it is not unlikely that Kennedy intends the incident of the secret book as a parody on literary deconstruction and its insistence upon a split between signifier and signified and on postmodernism (Borges's work, for instance, is filled with allusions to imagined languages). Kennedy's novel contains allusions to various kinds of silencings, of assaults on the word and its potential referentiality. One can at least argue that, in its stress on "the failure of advocacy journalism," Kennedy is implying that postmodernism itself constituted a kind of silencing, an end to the novel's role of social witness and reformer.[12]

Despite his awareness of the risks involved, Daniel Quinn, inspired by the courage of Dirck and Will and what they convey to him about "the power of the word" to change "the trajectory of history's arrow" (p. 77), vows to become a writer, a reporter of history. Virtually from the beginning, there are clues, most of which he manages to ignore, that Quinn's initiation as a writer will be a slow, painful, and ultimately disillusioning process. The publisher of Canaday's paper warns him that "words are flimsy things," while "type is solid and real" (p. 146). Moreover, Will offers his protégé some invaluable advice, which Quinn only begins to understand at the end of the novel: "Remember, Daniel. The only thing worth fighting for is what is real to the self. Move toward the verification of freedom, and avoid gratuitous absolutes" (p. 135). Such absolutes, such false binary oppositions, Canaday implies, often lead to violence. Only after the Civil War does Daniel realize his own inability to find, and indeed the actual impossibility of anyone's finding, words sufficient to describe all the carnage he has seen.

With this realization comes a redefinition of himself as a writer: "I knew that what was wrong with my life and work was that I was so busy accumulating and organizing facts and experience that I had failed to perceive that only in the contemplation of mystery was revelation possible; only in confronting the incomprehensible and arcane could there be any synthesis" (pp. 265–66). This epiphany constitutes a metafictional moment in what is much of the time a brutally naturalistic text. But as early as John McGee's resurrection of Magdelena, it has contained elements, often mixed with a strong degree of absurdity, of "mystery," of "the incomprehensible and arcane."

Quinn's innocence before this revelatory moment involves more than believing in the efficacy of words to change injustice and thereby redeem his people. In the optimism that he brings to his relationship with the sexually precocious Maud, he seems at times a reincarnation of Voltaire's Candide.[13] Even after Maud, following the example of her aunt, becomes socially notorious for a nearly nude theatrical performance on horseback, he remains devoted to the idea of her purity. (Kennedy is having some fun here with the tradition of courtly love.) It is only after she deserts him at a crucial moment and actually becomes engaged to someone else that he becomes disillusioned in her and attempts to forget her.

The ending of *Quinn's Book* echoes its beginning. Magdelena has become convinced that she is for the second time going to die, and John the Brawn invites everyone to come and celebrate her impending demise. The novel concludes with La Ultima very much alive and with Quinn and Maud preparing to have sexual intercourse. Its final lines celebrating the long delayed but now impending sexual union between the protagonist and his beloved echo John McGee's resurrection of La Ultima and indeed all the novel's bawdy sexuality: "The ribbon [from the bodice of Maud's dress] was long and uneven and fell the length of her torso to obscure part of her private hair. Quinn's eyes studied her with a wondrous lust and a love that was as limitless as the universe. Maud rolled backward onto the simple iron bed, her legs rising, the ribbon falling naturally between her open thighs, leaving her gift mostly secret. Quinn moved between her legs and gently lifted the ribbon to one side. And then Maud and Quinn were at last ready for love" (pp. 288–89). The last three words imply a sameness between sex and love, which in the context of John the Brawn and Magdelena is only right.

No longer believing in his ability to change "the trajectory of history" with words and horrified by all the violence and death that he has witnessed in the *Dood Kamer* of America, Quinn decides to cultivate his private garden and to abandon his project of redeeming his suffering race. He will instead merely witness its pain. From the first word of his text, William Kennedy understands what it takes his protagonist an entire novel to learn—that the best writers can describe almost unimaginable horrors and social injustice so pervasive as to discourage the most resolute of optimists while illuminating the mystery of words and the magic of storytelling.

Though depicting nineteenth-century Albany and by implication the entire nation as a death chamber, a place of pervasive and gratuitous violence and death, *Quinn's Book*, through its polyphonic virtuosity, its wonderful contrapuntal narration, transcends despair. Daniel Quinn may not be able to find the appropriate words, but William Kennedy most certainly does. With them, he evokes the origins of the systemic violence that dominates six of the other seven novels that constitute the focus of this book.

Chapter 2

The "Context" of American Innocence

Caleb Carr's *The Alienist*

In his seminal study *The Country and the City*, Raymond Williams discusses the images of London and of the recurrent characterization of the protagonist in Conan Doyle's Sherlock Holmes stories and in subsequent English detective fiction:

> London in the Sherlock Holmes stories becomes again the city of "labyrinthine obscurity and lurid fascination." Indeed the urban detective, prefigured in a minor way in Dickens and Wilkie Collins, now begins to emerge as a significant and ratifying figure: the man who can find his way through the fog, who can penetrate the intricacies of the streets. The opaque complexity of modern city life is represented by crime; the explorer of a society is reduced to the discoverer of single causes, the isolatable agent and above all his means, his technique.[1]

Caleb Carr's remarkable 1994 novel *The Alienist* is based on several important variations of the pattern described by Williams. The main plot of Carr's novel is set not in London, but primarily in the New York City of 1896, a time period that is of course roughly contemporary with Doyle's work; Carr successfully creates a mood that is reminiscent of Doyle and his successors. Certainly, crime in *The Alienist* represents "the opaque complexity of modern city life"; it in fact functions as a metaphor for the terrifying and generally disguised reality of 1896 New York and as a forecast of the essential nature of an already emerging twentieth-century urban America. Moreover, Carr's protagonist explores his society in more complex and fundamental ways than does even Sherlock Holmes.

Laszlo Kreizler in *The Alienist* is not a detective concerned with deducing clues from the surface of New York City, but a psychiatrist obsessed with probing the inner workings of the violent criminal imagination and of the essentially psychotic urban society from which it emerges.

Carr's novel succeeds on more than one level largely as a result of its focus on an inwardly tormented psychiatrist working desperately to identify and isolate the mentality behind a series of murders and mutilations of young boy prostitutes in a city where power is blatantly and perversely corrupt and where poor immigrants and children are brutally oppressed and exploited. It overtly echoes the Jack the Ripper murders of female prostitutes that terrified 1888 London; and Carr masterfully builds suspense as Kreizler and his associates work to create a psychological profile of and then identify and arrest a savage killer before he can strike again. Like Richard Wright's account of Bigger Thomas's killing of Mary Dalton, Carr's detailed descriptions of the mutilations inflicted on the bodies of the child prostitute offer support for Michael Kowalewski's theory that the sheer unfamiliarity of such horror contributes significantly to its narrative power.

On the most immediate level, *The Alienist* is an exciting read combining the popular culture elements of detective fiction, the horror story, local color, and portraits of "real" historical figures in the manner of E. L. Doctorow with psychological and social exploration. It is also a unique combination of the historical novel and critical analysis of the origins of the violence that has, from the beginning, defined American society. In addition to the gruesome fictional murders that inspire its main plot, Carr's text references the 1886 Haymarket Square bombing in Chicago in which seven policemen were killed and for which seven anarchists were arrested and three executed on little if any evidence, the notorious Five Points neighborhood in New York City, the kind of police brutality that came to be known as "the third degree" and which was associated with New York City Police Inspector Thomas Byrnes, the sanctioned sadism of Sing Sing prison, and the federal government's war with and eventual genocide of the Sioux Indians on the Great Plains. It thereby evokes a city and a nation based on violent repression of the "Other," as embodied in the immigrants crowded into the sordid tenements of New York's lower East Side, the Native Americans of the frontier, and the city's abandoned and forgotten children.

Besides Byrnes, the historical figures who appear in the novel include Jacob Riis, Lincoln Steffens, Franz Boas, the Native American expert Clark Wissler, and the notorious censor Anthony Comstock. Carr's characterizations of Riis and Steffens are especially interesting—they are depicted in the expected mode as muckrakers who exposed much of the oppression and injustice underlying New York and America, but also as men so limited by their imaginations and prejudices that they cannot challenge the repressive society in a truly fundamental way. Carr's Riis, for instance, inadvertently aids the novel's savage killer by simply refusing to admit the existence of child prostitution in New York City; Steffens is drawn as considerably more honest and imaginative, but as being primarily devoted to exposing rather than ending corruption.

In a particularly memorable scene, Kreizler and the novel's narrator, John Moore, are forcibly summoned to a meeting with J. P. Morgan, Byrnes, Comstock, and the Catholic and Episcopalian leaders of the city in Morgan's "Black Library." Morgan, after hearing objections from the others and especially from Comstock rules by fiat that the attempt by Kreizler, assisted by Moore and three representatives of the New York City Police Department, to solve the murders can continue. After realizing where he is, Moore observes to himself and to the reader that "some of the most important meetings in the history of New York—and indeed, of the United States—had taken place in this room."[2] The scene rests upon an assumption of the centrality and hegemony of capitalism in New York and American society—ultimately, Morgan, the very personification of Wall Street and of a still emerging industrial capitalism, simply rules that a serious effort will be made to stop the horrendous murders and mutilations of the child prostitutes. It is also implicit in the scene that Morgan and his capitalist associates have permitted the sadism and corruption practiced by Byrnes and the Puritanical crusade against the first amendment waged by Comstock to occur.

Yet it is important that Morgan makes the decision that he does, especially since the crucial implication of Carr's text is that Kreizler's mode of investigation represents a fundamental challenge to key assumptions underlying nineteenth-century laissez-faire capitalism. Morgan seems to realize that there are, in fact, limits even to the awesome power at his control and specifically that the insights that accompany psychological and scientific breakthroughs can be at most delayed and not finally suppressed. Such a realization is beyond Carr's intellectually shallow Comstock, the brutal Byrnes, and the two religious leaders who are compromised by the indebtedness of their churches to capitalists like Morgan.

Carr's text, in fact, assumes that, precisely because it is scientific in nature, the kind of intellectual investigation undertaken by Kreizler and his associates has a strong appeal for late-nineteenth-century and subsequent American society. The veneration of science as a new faith existing more or less in harmony with Christianity has been a central tenet of American thought during the last century and a half.[3] Thus, the fundamentally revolutionary nature of Kreizler's psychological method constitutes a central irony in the novel; Kreizler's psychological methods, supported as they are by assumptions of environmental determinism and moral relativism, will shatter the rigid and simplistic moralities of Comstock, Byrnes, the two clergymen, and even Morgan himself.

Such moral complexity and ambiguity inspires the novel's most vibrant character, Theodore Roosevelt. The novel depicts Roosevelt before he held national office, while he served as president of the Board of Commissioners of the New York City Police Department. To a degree, what emerges is the Roosevelt of popular American mythology—the amateur naturalist, the dogged foe of corruption in high places, the flamboyant man of action, and the sometimes exhausting optimist. Yet, as with Steffens and Riis, Carr depicts in the future president a man with obvious flaws. In contrast to its Steffens, the novel's Roosevelt seems incapable of cynicism, but like Riis limited in imagination and given to thinking in racist stereotypes. In fact, it is an offhand racist comment by "T. R." that makes possible a crucial step in the detection of the serial killer.

Carr's Roosevelt personifies, in his strengths as well as his weaknesses, turn-of-the-century American society. In this respect, it is important for the reader of *The Alienist* to keep in mind the distinct periods that combine to construct the text. Most obviously, there is 1896, the year during which the main plot unfolds, but also important are the early 1990s, the years in which the novel was written. Carr then has the perspective of a century from which to record and interpret the actions of his novel, and a crucial subtext of *The Alienist* is the loss of the innocence associated with the American nineteenth century and which, in many ways, Theodore Roosevelt personified. His text makes it clear that only a dangerous kind of innocence really existed in that now romanticized age. Roosevelt, for instance, seems not to have been troubled by many of the essential contradictions inherent in his ideas and actions. He could write as a naturalist even to the point of challenging the correctness of Jack London's animal lore and, as president, preside over a capitalist-industrial expansion that exploited and even destroyed irreplaceable elements of nature in America. He used the "bully pulpit" of the presidency to proclaim the superiority of American democracy, while presiding over a blatantly racist administration. In these ways, he was the very personification of a superficial and doomed national innocence.

The third time frame in the text, January 1919, is limited to an introductory framing chapter in which Moore and Kreizler meet for dinner and discuss the events of 1896 and reminisce about Roosevelt, who has just died. This chapter and thus the novel open with a thematically important one-sentence paragraph: "Theodore is in the ground" (p. 3). By giving this deliberately brutal sentence its own paragraph, Carr effectively separates it from the subsequent text and thereby assigns it the immediacy of a piece of just-breaking news and, given the emblematic role of the character Roosevelt in his novel, makes it function as the proclamation of the end of an era. In January 1919, World War I had just ended, and Carr, like so many American writers before him, envisions that international conflict as destroying American innocence and optimism. Fittingly, in this context, Roosevelt is treated as an indirect casualty of the war; Moore says that his old friend, the former president, has "been fading . . . since his son Quentin was killed in the last days of the Great Butchery" (p. 3). The text's implications are that, behind its bright democratic surface, American society has long been a "Great Butchery."

Roosevelt was a powerful voice for the last American generation that could ignore this reality and affirm that science represented a mode of transcending it. In contrast, Kreizler is the exponent of a new science of the mind devoted to exploring the darkest recesses of human consciousness. A prefatory note explains that "prior to the twentieth century, persons suffering from mental illness were thought to be 'alienated,' not only from the rest of society but from their own natures. Those experts who studied mental pathologies were therefore known as *alienists*." Kreizler's method and his central vision are moreover "alien" to the determinedly optimistic mainstream intellectual and political climate of Roosevelt's late nineteenth century, even though the reformist New York City police commissioner recruits the psychiatrist to solve the serial killings of young boy prostitutes.

For Kreizler, the violent reality of America's past promises a dark future; Moore summarizes the vision evoked by the psychiatrist during the 1919 dinner:

> We're still running, according to Kreizler—in our private moments we Americans are running just as fast and fearfully as we were then [1896], running away from the darkness we know to lie behind so many apparently tranquil household doors, away from the nightmares that continue to be injected into children's skulls by people whom Nature tells them they should love and trust, running ever faster and in ever greater numbers toward those potions, powders, priests, and philosophies that promise to obliterate such fears and nightmares, and ask in return only slavish devotion. (p. 6)

Kreizler truly speaks from a vision alien to the traditions of American optimism; he sees the nation's long-standing oppression and neglect of its children as culminating inevitably in some form of nightmarish totalitarianism. Carr writes this passage, of course, from a narrative position that allows him to evoke, without naming them, the defining moments in American history between 1919 and 1994, e.g., the Great Depression, World War II, 1950s McCarthyism, Vietnam, the 1960s counterculture, and the sanctioned greed of the Reagan era.

Kreizler's pessimism in the framing chapter rests upon a further pessimistic assumption; he grants the failure of his methods, and of the new science of psychiatry in general, to reform or change American society in any meaningful way. Looking back almost a quarter of a century, he concludes that, despite Roosevelt's recruiting him for the investigation of the serial murders and despite Morgan's allowing this investigation to continue, America, and probably humanity itself, is not, and will never be, prepared to confront the dark implications of his discoveries. Such a confrontation would mean the acknowledgment of the interlocking hegemonic systems, all based on greed and denial of the humanity of the powerless, that underlie capitalism at every level.

In order to dramatize the elaborate, if often invisible, structure of 1896 New York, Carr provides an extended tour of the city as it then existed and offers what at least always seems to be well-researched information about the places being described. As it must, the tour covers every socioeconomic level of the city. There is one lovingly detailed description of an elaborate multicourse dinner at Delmonico's Restaurant, while two important scenes take place in the still new Metropolitan Opera House, "the yellow brewery uptown" (p. 93), as it is disparaging referred to by the city's "old guard." Since it is the creation of new money derived from the entrepreneurial exploits of "men with names like Morgan, Gould, Whitney, and Vanderbilt" (p. 93), the Metropolitan is an especially effective metaphor for a changing and increasingly uncaring city. The text implies that for such men the bottom line is always related to profit—anything can be tolerated that will contribute to the acquisition and consumption of capital, while anything that might interfere with such accumulation must be suppressed. At one point events occasion Moore to make a quick trip through the city's financial and publishing districts, and he does not miss the significance of his surroundings: "I had spent much of my childhood in this part of Manhattan ...and from an early age I'd been struck by the fantastic activity that surrounded the getting and keeping of money. This activity could be alternately seductive and repellant; but by 1896 it was unarguably New York's strongest reason for being" (p. 139).

At other points, the text contains graphically detailed descriptions of some of the more "repellant" parts of the city. Late in the novel, Moore; the novel's "new woman" character, Sara Howard, a secretary in the police department and another member of Kreizler's investigative team; and the Isaacson brothers, two police inspectors whom Roosevelt assigns to aid in the apprehension of the killer, visit a bar in the center of the city's squalid and crime-ridden Five Points neighborhood. The description of what they find inside echoes the grotesque detail central to American literary naturalism from Frank Norris to Nelson Algren. Moore describes the interior of the bar and its apparently lifeless customers:

> I don't know precisely what the caves looked like that prehistoric men are said to have inhabited, but the average Five Points dive cannot have represented any great advancement—and the one we entered that night was nothing if not average. The ceiling was only eight feet or so from the dirt floor, since the space had originally been designed as a cellar for the storefront above. There were no windows: light was provided by four filthy kerosene lamps that hung above a like number of long, low tables arranged in two rows. At these tables sat and slept the customers, their differences of age, sex, and dress more than outweighed by their common air of drunken dementia. . . . There were about twenty people in the place that night, though only three . . . showed any real signs of life. They examined us with looks of glassy hatred when we came in. (pp. 427–28)

As Moore and his associates leave the bar, one of the drunken men "urinate[s] unconsciously on the floor" (p. 429).

The implications of the text are clear—the kind of degradation and dehumanization found in the Five Points bar is inextricably related to the luxury of Delmonico's and the Metropolitan Opera House. Unchecked capitalist consumption ultimately commodifies everything, even those trapped in the lower depths of society who are simultaneously objectified and forgotten about. Most New Yorkers of the socioeconomic class to which Moore and his associates belong would never venture near Five Points. Thus, the neighborhood becomes a kind of remote and even exotic colony that infringes on the consciousness of late nineteenth-century middle- and upper-class New Yorkers in much the same way that Bombay might have. The looks of "glassy hatred" directed at Moore and his companions reflect a realization by the denizens of Five Points that, in the city's complex hegemonic structure, they exist only as exotic curiosities, if they exist at all.[4]

Moore notes as he walks through Mulberry Bend that, in a significant way, the streets here are different from those in the city's other slum areas. There is very little visible activity, he observes, as if the doomed residents have retreated into "the miserable shanties and tenements that lined the streets" to enact the grim details of their lives: "death and despair did their work without fanfare in the Bend, and they did a lot of it; just walking down those lonely, decrepit streets was enough to make the sunniest of souls wonder about the ultimate value of human life" (p. 427). In fact, these dismal streets apparently never trouble the novel's "sunniest of souls," Roosevelt, if he even notices them. The threatening implications of the Five Points neighborhood cannot be reconciled with the American optimism and innocence personified by Roosevelt. In contrast, Kreizler knows exactly what its lifeless, yet still dangerous, streets portend for the future of American society.

Carr offers other graphic descriptions of the East Side tenement world, consistently providing the kind of detailed knowledge of his subject that gives the narrative its power and convincingness; for instance, he describes at one point the unique horrors of one of the smaller buildings hidden in back of many of the larger tenements: "suffice it to say that if a tenement building that fronted the street was dark, disease-ridden, and threatening, the smaller buildings that often stood behind them—in place of a yard that might have brought at least a bit more air and light to the block—were exponentially more so. . . . [H]uge barrels of ash and waste stood by the urine-soaked stoop of the structure, on which was gathered a group of filthy, rag-clad men, each indistinguishable from the next" (p. 78).

The hidden rear tenement functions as a central trope in the novel; Kreizler and his associates are explorers of a dark world hidden at the back of the city and at the back of rational consciousness. In addition, the text investigates the ways in which American optimism ignores the dark, brutal moments of the nation's history. The existence of such hidden tenements is, moreover, further evidence of the hegemonic capitalistic system of New York City and the nation. The system extends everywhere, literally reaching into the city's darkest corners. The city's rapacious landlords will allow no space to escape their relentless, dehumanizing quest for profit.

The pervasiveness of the capitalist appropriation of urban space is also emphasized in Carr's account of the city's rooftop culture:

> [R]ooftops in the New York of 1896 were secondary but nonetheless well-worn routes of urban travel, lofty counterpoints to the sidewalks below that were full of their own distinctive types of traffic. Particularly in the tenement slums, a broad but definable range of people sometimes

> did a full day's business without ever descending to the street—not only creditors seeking payment, but settlement and church workers, salesmen, visiting nurses, and others. . . . Those who had business with the poorest of the poor, rather than braving the steep and often dangerous staircases repeatedly, would simply move from one high floor to another by way of the rooftops. (p. 149)

Not only has capitalist profit claimed the streets and the suffocating buildings that rise from them, but it has appropriated the very sky above as a means of serving, observing, and ultimately controlling "the poorest of the poor." There is literally no space left to be contested, except perhaps that which lies beneath the surface of the urban streets, an underground world of darkness and dirt. The "rooftop culture" also serves as a trope in the novel and, in doing so, echoes Foucault's concept of the panoptic surveillance of capitalism—the obscure servants of capitalism can literally look down from their "lofty" space to the "distinctive types of traffic" beneath them.

Organized crime in *The Alienist*, especially that which directly exploits the children of the poor, is treated as an essential element of the capitalist structure. Carr's gift for providing supportive detail in a condensed manner is evident in his description of the city's several houses of child prostitution and their "specialties": for instance, "Paresis Hall, the Golden Rule, Shang Draper's in the Tenderloin, the Slide on Bleeker Street, and Frank Stephenson's Black and Tan, also on Bleeker, a dive that offered white women and children to black and Oriental men" (pp. 252–53). The evocative names of these temples of exploitation are chosen to simultaneously deny and tantalize with the brutal exploitation that happens inside them.

One of the novel's most fascinating figures is Paul Kelley, a powerful city vice lord. A handsome man with genuine intellectual interests and abilities, Kelley is a supreme cynic who has become expert at organizing and manipulating the city's need for such sordid activity. At one point, he summarizes his sense of morality to Kreizler and Moore: "'There you are then.' . . . 'You two gentlemen sit here talking about this city and civil unrest and all of that—but what stake do *I* have in it? What do I care if New York burns to the ground? Whoever's still standing when it's over is going to want a drink and someone to spend a lonely hour with—and I'll be here to supply those items'" (p. 283). Such profound cynicism arises in part from Kelly's understanding of the hegemonic structure of the city, his awareness that the civic and political realms of the city reinforce each other. In this same conversation, he warns Kreizler and Moore that "the big boys" will never allow their investigation to be completed. Yet Kelley understands, better than anyone in the novel except possibly Moore and Sara Howard and certainly better than Roosevelt, the threat that Kreizler's method poses for the city's controlling powers. The alienist's ideas concerning the controlling aspects of environment and the essential role of childhood experience in forming individuals will, he prophesies at the end of the novel, shatter the superficial morality advocated by those who control society.

Early in the text, Kreizler's environmental determinism and moral relativism are defined as representing philosophical opposition to William James's insistence upon free will. At Harvard, the future psychiatrist is a student of James's who inspires dislike and criticism by arguing with the popular professor:

> Though he greatly respected James's work and grew to have enormous affection for the man himself (it really was impossible not to), Laszlo was nonetheless unable to accept James's famous theories of free will, which were the cornerstone of our teacher's philosophy. . . . [James] taught that a man could, by force of will overcome all psychic (and many physical) ailments. "My first act of free will shall be to believe in free will" had been James's early battle cry, an attitude that continued to dominate his thinking in 1877. Such a philosophy was bound to collide with Kreizler's developing belief in what he called "context": the theory that every man's actions are to a very decisive extent influenced by his early experiences, and that no man's behavior can be analyzed or affected without knowledge of those experiences. (pp. 47–48)

In Carr's novel, James's devotion to free will is shown to be central to the optimism of the age. It can also clearly be placed within the overriding tradition of a distinctively American optimism—James asserts that an individual can in fact be cured through an exercise of the will, just as Emerson argued that strong individuals can partake of a process of continual renewal and redefinition through "self-reliance" and Whitman affirmed the divinity of the American common man and woman.

Not surprisingly, Kreizler's opposition to the doctrine of ongoing self-renewal offends Roosevelt, who baits the future analyst with comments about his "mystical mumbo jumbo concerning the human psyche" and then his "gypsy blood." Kreizler is so offended by the latter remark that he challenges Roosevelt to a duel, which Roosevelt transforms into a harmless boxing match after which he establishes a lifelong friendship with Kreizler. This episode reveals much about Carr's Roosevelt—his racism and intellectual superficiality, but also his irrepressible good nature and ability to co-opt threatening opposition, just as the American "Darwinicists" did with the theory of evolution. But by 1919, "Theodore is in the ground," and American optimism and innocence have been irrevocably wounded.

It is important to say that the novel does not present Kreizler as the villain in all this; rather, his views, had they been understood and transformed into social action, might, the text implies, have revolutionized and revitalized American society. But, of course, they could never have been so absorbed since they are alien to an American mythology that has succeeded in absorbing and obscuring the nation's legacy of violence and oppression. Paul Kelley, despite or perhaps because of his profitable exploitation of the dominant national ideology, comprehends the threat Kreizler's ideas pose to that ideology.

Kreizler's concept of "context" diverges from Freudianism essentially in its denial of the universality of "the family romance." The alienist believes, like Freud, that the origins of adult trauma are traceable to childhood, but denies the centrality of such Freudian universals as the Oedipus Complex. Thus, Kreizler believes that one can understand and even predict the actions of any adult if that adult's childhood can be reconstructed. His mode of comprehending the serial killer of young male prostitutes is to create "an imaginary man" from the few clues that exist: "What we must do—the only thing that *can* be done—is to paint an imaginary picture of the sort of person that *might* commit such acts" (p. 61). The investigation seems an impossibility since the defining patterns of this "imaginary picture" were necessarily drawn during the anonymous killer's childhood. Still, Moore is irresistibly drawn into it, in large part by intense intellectual curiosity: "rarely have I felt so strongly the truth of Kreizler's belief that the answers one gives to life's crucial questions are never truly spontaneous; they are embodiment of years of contextual experience, of the building of patterns in each of our lives that eventually grow to dominate our behavior" (p. 62).

Initially, recreation of the "contextual experience" of the killer is enormously complicated by the alienist's rejection of Freud's ideas concerning universal patterns in childhood and infancy, yet it is precisely this rejection that makes it ultimately possible to identify him. Gradually clues emerge that point to the unique childhood experience of one intensely troubled man, Japheth Dury. As with expansion of the nation in which he lives, Dury's conception was the result of violence. Dury's father was an immigrant who married and began a family in upstate New Paltz, New York. Tortured by the trap of poverty from which he was unable to extricate himself, he became a religious fanatic who relocated his family to Fort Ridgely, Minnesota, a military post that was attacked and briefly captured by the Sioux in

1862. He preached a harsh Calvinism to a few "curious" Sioux and dreamed of his children's carrying on his mission into the wilderness of the west.

Financial exigencies forced him, however, to return to New Paltz, where one cold winter night he raped his wife, who became pregnant with the ill-fated Japheth. At the age of eleven, Japheth is the victim of a homosexual rape committed by one George Beecham, a newly hired worker. Seemingly, though, the horrors of the boy's life have just begun. When he is a teenager, his parents are brutally murdered on the New Paltz farm; moreover, according to widely circulated reports of the case, their bodies were "most foully and savagely torn to bits'" (p. 320). The local police conclude that the murders were the actions of "several embittered Indians who had been sent east for that very purpose" and who after the massacre took the family's youngest son, Japheth, "back to live among [them] as one of their own" (pp. 320–21).

As Kreizler and his associates begin to unravel these details, Japheth's story seems easily explicable—he has been the victim of repeated victimization by males: his father, George Beecham, and the marauding Indians. Yet Kreizler feels that there are other levels of complexity in the story of Japheth Dury. The investigators are led to an awareness of Dury's existence and then the details of his past by a sequence of events. An unsigned letter from the killer to the mother of his first victim quickly proves crucial to the investigation; it contains an especially revelatory section:

> In some parts of the world such as where dirty immigrants like yourself come from it is often found that human flesh is eaten regular, as other food is scarce and people would starve without it. I have personally read this and know it to be true. Of course it is usually children what is eaten as they are tenderest and best tasting. . . .
>
> Then these people that eat come here to America and shit their little children all around, which is dirty, dirtier than a Red Injun. (p. 197)

From this, it is not difficult for Kreizler to deduce that the writer is driven by self-hatred, much of it resulting from the poverty of childhood as the son of immigrants. The phrase "dirtier than a Red Injun" is more difficult to interpret until Teddy Roosevelt, shocked by the mutilation of the body of the killer's next victim, blurts out, "I've never seen anything like it, short of a red Indian" (p. 276). Roosevelt's racist assertion leads Kreizler and Moore to the Museum of Natural History and its two Native American experts, Franz Boas and Clark Wissler. Carr creates a complex irony through the reaction of Boas especially to the alienist's questions; the anthropologist is outraged at the possibility that Kreizler's investigation will inspire even more hatred of the Native American in a society only six years removed from the massacre at Wounded Knee. Roosevelt, the future president, voices precisely this kind of hatred.[5]

After Boas and Wissler assure the two investigators that cannibalism was unknown among the American Indians as was the kind of horrendous mutilation of the dead committed against Dury's parents and the present killer's young victims, Kreizler and his team can surmise that, in fact, Japheth was never kidnapped by the Indians; rather he murdered his parents, desecrated their bodies, and then vanished. Still, some pieces of the alienist's reconstruction of Dury have not fallen into place.

The final mystery in reconstructing Japheth concerns his mutilation of the bodies and his elaborate efforts to associate that mutilation with Native Americans, especially since he was not born until his parents returned to New York from Minnesota and therefore had no contact with Indians. This mystery is also resolved. Japheth's family was in Minnesota during the Sioux uprising of 1862, and his father, with a daguerreotype camera, took pictures of "the massacred whites": "when he returned to New Paltz in 1864, he became famous—indeed infamous—for showing these pictures to large collections of the town's better-off citizens. . . . [T]he pictures of slain and mutilated corpses were so horrifying, and Dury's behavior during the presentations so feverish, that the reverend's sanity began to be questioned" (p. 330). Thus Dury, in murdering his parents and in his subsequent killings in the city, merely used his father's hideous photographs as a model.

The inclusion of Boas and Wissler in the text clarifies the truth about the 1862 Sioux uprising—that it was a desperate act of revenge and self-protection inspired by decades of white pillage and treachery. When one remembers the second crucial time frame of the novel, the 1990s, three centuries of white oppression of the Indian become a largely elided subtext in the novel.[6] This theme surfaces when Moore examines Bureau of Indian Affairs records of Native American atrocities against whites: "most of the accounts were of acts of vengeance on the part of the Sioux which, while severe, seemed at least understandable when measured against the abominable treachery of the white soldiers, Indian affairs (the Bureau of Indian Affairs was the most corrupt agency in a notoriously corrupt department), and traders in firearms and whiskey against whom they were committed" (p. 318).

The Reverend Dury's photographs also function on at least two metaphoric levels: first, they represent the coming technology of the twentieth century, and second, they symbolize capitalism's objectifying gaze, its power to dehumanize through filmed images. Through this dehumanizing technology, twentieth-century society will become devoted to the immediate, the superficial, and the impermanent.[7] These related ideas are supported by another scene in which Moore sees some primitive early films in a burlesque theater; the film images are largely threatening, e.g., "a wall of blue sea water seemingly crashing into the theater" and "pictures of the German kaiser reviewing his troops." Only from the perspective of 1919 does Moore even begin to understand the significance of the experience: "sitting there in that nondescript theater one hardly had the sense that one was witnessing the advent of a new form of communication and entertainment that would, in the hands of such modern masters as D. W. Griffith, drastically change not only New York City but the world" (p. 164). But, even in 1919, Moore's appreciation of the power of filmed images to objectify and control is limited; he perceives only the power of this new communications medium to entertain.

Sara Howard intuitively comprehends the final clue in the killer's note; she argues that a woman had to have contributed significantly to the killer's violent self-hatred, an idea that Kreizler resists for two reasons. First, his total rejection of Freud's concept of "the family romance" is threatened by any ideas that would emphasize the centrality of a mother, or for that matter of any woman, in the psychological destruction of a male child. Moreover, as a rape victim, Dury's mother initially seems as victimized as her son. Yet Howard insists that the obsessions with excrement and dirt in the killer's note hint at a traumatic toilet training, and after the investigators learn from Japheth's older brother that their mother was a cold, rejecting woman who especially resented and regularly humiliated her younger son, especially during his toilet training, Kreizler can no longer deny the obvious. In part, of course, this obsession with filth derives from the homosexual assault by Beecham, and Dury has assumed the name, John Beecham, echoing the names of his abuser and John the Baptist, "the purifier" (all of the bodies are discovered beside or above bodies of water).

In fact, Kreizler's blindness to the importance of Japheth's mother is not really convincing and constitutes therefore the weakest aspect of Carr's novel. Still, it is important to emphasize that it is his protagonist, and not Carr, who rejects the universality of Freud's "family romance." This motif seems even more forced and contrived by the revelation, late in the novel, that Kreizler and his mother were themselves assaulted regularly by his drunken, but socially respectable, father. In one of these assaults, Kreizler as a child suffered an injury to his left arm that prevented it from developing properly; he explains the damage to his arm as the result of a childhood accident. This sudden focus on the childhood abuse suffered by Kreizler explains little that is not already clear in his characterization. The most reasonable explanation for its inclusion is that Carr wants to emphasize the fact that violent abuse of children is not limited to the poor and destitute, but in fact exists at every socioeconomic level of American society.

Henry Gonshak has criticized the novel's "explanation" of the motivations of Japheth Dury on a more fundamental level:

> *The Alienist*'s clear theme is that the sole factor in the creation of a serial killer is childhood trauma. Explaining away this evil with such a psychological formula seems rather simplistic.
>
> . . . [A]s a study of the mind of a serial killer, the novel makes a strong case for the role of severe childhood trauma in the development of psychosis. Nevertheless, by explaining Dury/Beechum's [*sic*] dementia so patly, Carr misses a chance to elevate his book to another level of artistry, one in which humanity's heart of darkness is rendered in all [its] terrifying inexplicability.[8]

As long as one focuses exclusively on the overt explanation of Dury in Carr's text, Gonshak's criticism has validity. Yet, in its evocation of the brutal suppression of the Native American, its descriptions of New York's Five Points neighborhood and the degrading tenement life forced on the city's immigrants, and its emphasis upon science, photography, and other means of objectifying the human, the novel's implied analysis of Dury is much more complex and more interesting.

Kreizler's contextual psychology is suggestive of Foucault's *Mental Illness and Psychology (Maladie Mentale et Personnalité)*. In this work, originally published in 1954, Foucault writes that any diagnosis originating in such concepts as "organic totality" and "the psychological personality" will be inadequate for treating a patient: "in mental pathology, the reality of the patient does not permit such an abstraction [the psychological personality] and each morbid individuality must be understood through the practices of the environment with regard to him."[9] In his foreword to the 1987 University of California Press edition of this work, Hubert Dreyfus further clarifies Foucault's thought in this matter: "When a patient's world becomes totalized and one-dimensional, other ways of behaving endure from earlier days. These marginal stances, interpretations, and practices are not taken up into the one-dimensional clearing [of the patient's present consciousness] precisely because they are experienced as too fragmentary and trivial. The therapist must recover and focus these lost possibilities" (p. xxii).

In fact, *The Alienist* recalls Foucault in other ways, especially in its depiction of 1896 New York City as a complex, if not particularly subtle, hegemonic system. Even more frightening than the gruesome murders that drive its plot, is the novel's implicit vision of capitalism's power to destroy human beings through processes of objectification and normalization. Thus, one of the novel's most unnerving scenes does not directly involve any of the murders and very much recalls Foucault's classic study of the evolution of the penal system, *Discipline and Punish*. In that scene, Kreizler and Moore travel to the federal prison at Sing Sing to interview a notorious inmate named Jesse Pomeroy. Pomeroy is a child murderer in two ways—he killed at least two children when he was twelve years old.

The text's description of Sing Sing refers to physical torture including the beating of prisoners with clubs, submerging them in freezing water, and locking their heads into two-foot high barred cages. Still, as in Foucault's work, the most terrible aspect of Carr's Sing Sing is its combination of isolation and surveillance. In order to reach Pomeroy's cell, Kreizler and Moore are forced "to walk past dozens [of] cells, full of faces that displayed an enormous range of emotions, from the deepest anguish and sorrow to the most sullen rage. As the rule of silence was enforced at all times we heard no distinct human voices, only an occasional whisper; and the echo of our own steps throughout the cell block, combined with the unceasing scrutiny of the prisoners, soon became almost maddening" (p. 235). Thus, the prisoners are isolated into individual cells, but more important, are isolated through the denial of the possibility of speech, of communication with each other.

Pomeroy, thirty-six in 1896, is still seething with rage at the humiliation he endured from his mother and from society at large because of a facial deformity. As with all else, society has normalized human appearance and those like Pomeroy who fall outside this accepted norm are ostracized and ridiculed. Kreizler's own withered left arm evokes in him a special empathy with the tragic and frightening prisoner. Not surprisingly, Pomeroy has developed into a masochistic personality who frequently provokes the guards into physically assaulting him. As a result of the Pomeroy interview, Kreizler and Moore begin to suspect that their killer may suffer from a deformity of some sort as well, and in fact Dury, when under stress, suffers from a severe facial tic that distorts his features in an unsettling manner. He seems to have sought out the city as a refuge from the rejection that inevitably results from such momentary distortion only to encounter in New York crowds of strangers who either ignore or objectify him, as they do everyone else. This phenomenon of the objectifying urban gaze inevitably accelerates his stress and the accompanying moments of disfigurement, a process that in turn intensifies the rejecting urban gaze.

The constant in the various forms of mutilation afflicted on the corpses of the young male prostitutes is the savage removal by a sharp instrument of their eyes. The climactic moment of horror in the novel is the discovery in Dury's room in Five Points of "an enormous glass jar" in which the eyes of his victims have been preserved in a substance that Moore presumes to be formaldehyde. Moore specifies that it is "not the discovery of the condition of the eyes" that is most upsetting: instead it is their "number"; the bottle contains not just the eyes of the fourteen known victims, but "*dozens*—of eyes of more than a score of victims" (p. 432). Dury has literally tried to cut away the objectifying urban gaze, ironically by attacking some of the city's most objectified and commodified citizens, the young boy prostitutes. He begins his attack with them largely because it is relatively safe since no one reports, if they even notice, the disappearance of these exploited children.

In addition, two seemingly contradictory factors contribute to his choice of victims. First, the young prostitutes, whose value as commodities is tied directly to the degree to which they resemble a concept of "female beauty" as defined by the dominant society, enjoy a perverted valorization of their physical appearance, a kind of valorization which has always been denied to Japheth. Second, they become emblematic to him of his own innocence that was perverted by the itinerant farm worker, Beecham. Each murder is then a ritualized reenactment of the destruction of his innocence.

The Alienist is a complex and rewarding variation of the detective novel in which a psychologist, a scientist whose knowledge of the dark places of the human mind is alien to the kind of American optimism and faith in science embodied in Theodore Roosevelt, solves the crime. Its central vision is of New York, prototype of the emerging late-nineteenth-century American city, as a hegemonic system, defined by a gaze that dehumanizes and objectifies. Better than such respectable figures as Roosevelt, Comstock, and even Riis ever can, George Kelly, the unapologetic exploiter of poor and outcast women, understands the threat of Kreizler's vision and methodology to the superficial morality of American culture. Acceptance of environmental determinism and of moral relativism is incompatible with the traditions of American innocence and free will.

Perhaps the strongest aspect of Carr's novel is its thematic insistence, as revealed in the subtext of violent exploitation of the Native American, that the national innocence was compromised long before 1896. It was, in fact, an illusion from the beginning. The newly emerging industrial city of the late nineteenth century merely provided an intensified context for the nation's violent oppression of the poor, of women, and even of children. By 1919 Kreizler understands, and Moore is beginning to understand, that it is already too late to reverse the damage that such oppression has done to the national psyche; serial killers like the simultaneously terrifying and pathetic Japheth Dury merely dramatize this damage. Said's kind of contrapuntal reading provides a means of relating such apparently diverse aspects of Carr's text as industrial exploitation of the urban poor and the violent subjugation of the Native American.

Chapter 3

The Ducky Boys and the "Urban Punk Killing Machine"

Richard Price's *The Wanderers*

The twentieth-century legacy of the ethnic warfare and antagonism depicted by Carr and Kennedy is dramatized by Richard Price in his 1974 novel, *The Wanderers*. Set in the early 1960s, Price's text focuses on an Italian American street gang located in the Bronx section of New York who have named themselves "the wanderers" after a popular song and who experience life as an unending siege. The novel carried no little shock effect when it appeared two decades ago, but, in the late 1990s context of Yummy Sandifer, one reacts to major sections of it with something approaching nostalgia, even though it records numerous incidents of random and grotesque violence. In part, this is a simple matter of chronological age—a clear gulf seems, after all, to separate the seventeen-year-old protagonists of *The Wanderers* from eleven-year-old Yummy Sandifer. But there is more involved. Yummy's story is, in fact, illustrative of the dilemma of the contemporary naturalistic or realistic writer, a problem described by Philip Roth as early as 1961. In his essay "Writing American Fiction," Roth writes that American reality, especially in our cities, has become so extreme, so irrational, and so implausible as to outstrip the imagination of any mere fictionalist. He wonders therefore what the novelist who wishes to witness and record contemporary American life can do.[1] In addition, Price shows his characters undergoing some of the archetypal experiences of adolescent boys, especially sexual awakening, and as being in part the products of popular culture to which many people who grew up in the United States in the 1950s or 1960s can relate.

The nostalgia that accompanies a reading of Price's text is augmented by a shift between the 1950s and the 1960s in the national view of teenage gangs. In *October Cities: The Redevelopment of Urban Literature,* Carlo Rotella provides a concise summary of this shift. In the 1950s, Rotella argues, "juvenile delinquency" was a national obsession. Such artifacts of popular culture as the films *Rebel without a Cause* and *The Blackboard Jungle* (both released in 1955) treated the adolescent gang member as romantic prototype of rebellion against oppressive and usually hypocritical "adults." It was hard, after all, not to root for James Dean and Sidney Poitier to achieve whatever it was they were seeking. In the 1960s though, juvenile delinquency no longer seemed romantically exotic; it came to be inextricably linked with specifically black "urban crime" as deadly and menacing to the white middle class.

As a portrait of teenage boys in urban gangs, *The Wanderers* can be placed in a more specifically literary context. An early ancestor of Price's Richie Gennaro, Eugene Caputo, Joey Capra, Buddy Borsalino, Perry La Guardia, and Hang On Sloopy is Stephen Crane's Jimmie Johnson of *Maggie: A Girl of the Streets.* More recent and, not only because of race, closer to Yummy Sandifer is Bigger Thomas in Richard Wright's *Native Son* (1940). Older to be sure, Bigger is portrayed as being, like the real-life Yummy, fundamentally alone and alienated even from the other members of his gang. In this way, Bigger is comparable to Nelson Algren's Bruno "Lefty" Bicek of *Never Come Morning* (1942). Still, the novel that most obviously anticipates *The Wanderers* is Hubert Selby's *Last Exit to Brooklyn,* published a decade earlier. Harold Bloom's ideas concerning the relationship of the poetic ephebe and the strong predecessor could be applied to Price and Selby— *The Wanderers* may be said to be an especially creative misreading of *Last Exit to Brooklyn.*[2]

As in Price's text, Selby's novel focuses on a New York City white street gang; in it, Brooklyn, like Price's Bronx, is depicted as a blue-collar area with little, if any, sense of economic security. The fictional gangs in both novels are made up of isolated and alienated young men devoted to a cult of machismo and violence who view existence as a kind of perpetual warfare during which they make periodic raids against the enemy, which is finally everyone but them. Still, Price's book is, in mood, significantly different from Selby's; nostalgia is perhaps the last feeling a reader of *Last Exit to Brooklyn* might have.

Yet even with its overtones of nostalgia, Price's novel, in important ways, simultaneously looks back to *Native Son* and *Never Come Morning* and forward to the reality of Yummy Sandifer. It shows the members of the Wanderers, while committed to a violent code originating in warfare, to be at times vulnerable and frightened teenage boys, which is what, after all, they truly are; and it depicts them as seeking and sometimes finding only with each other a necessary closeness. In fact, one crucial way in which *The Wanderers* represents a departure from the "gang novels" of Wright, Algren, and Selby is that it does dramatize such emotional bonding. Frank W. Shelton has perceptively analyzed this aspect of the novel: "The genuine emotional life of the Wanderers exists not in relationship with the opposite sex but in their association with each other. Manhood is proved through women, but it is proved to other men. . . . The gang is important in the novel just because it is the focus of feeling, because it is the institution within which brotherhood can flower, and because it provides the characters with a sense of belonging."[3] The certainty that they will receive no such sustenance from the adult world, most certainly not from their parents, makes the gang even more essential to the boys. In fact, the adult world fails, even assaults, them just as it did Yummy Sandifer. And while Yummy, Cragg and Derrick Hardaway, and the other Chicago Black Disciples sought some viable form of spirituality in the language, if not the form of Christianity, Price's Wanderers have no tolerance for anything associated with organized religion, looking instead for spiritual reassurance in popular culture, especially the "teenage" music of the 1960s.

The structure of *The Wanderers* follows in the tradition of *Last Exit to Brooklyn*, but also of such distinctly nonurban fictions as Sherwood Anderson's *Winesburg, Ohio* and Ernest Hemingway's Nick Adams stories; it is divided into twelve separately titled and loosely related chapters. The first of these, "The Warlord," illustrates Price's complex mingling of horrific violence and often comic nostalgia; its opening moreover establishes the trope of irony that will dominate the entire text: "There he was in Big Playground. Richie Gennaro. Seventeen. High Warlord of the Wanderers. Surrounded by the Warlords of the Rays, Pharaohs, and the Executioners. Touchy allies. Tense convention. Issue at hand—'We gotta stop them niggers.'"[4] Terms like "High Warlord," "Pharaohs," and "Executioners" are derived from the comicbook, "B" horror movie, and television culture of America; the ironic homage that Price pays to such cultural phenomena is a further echo of Selby. In the context of Yummy Sandifer, it is interesting that "Pharaohs" has, for Price's characters, who value nothing so much as power, positive connotations; it is unlikely that the teenagers of *The Wanderers* know about the biblical account of the Pharaoh's persecution of Moses and the Hebrews. The text of the novel evokes a relentlessly secular world; in it, traditional religion is virtually nonexistent and certainly not a source of potential spirituality.

The three terse phrases that end the opening paragraph parody both American "war movies" and the language of the corporate board room, a technique that points to the novel's having a more complex point of view than appears on the surface. Richie Gennaro and the other Wanderers consciously imitate the mode and language of war movies, but know nothing, of course, about corporations. On one level, the entire text of the novel is a "Big Playground," if often a violent and even deadly one. The "issue at hand" and the language in which it is stated have comic as well as quite serious overtones. Soon after the war conference, Richie discovers that someone has painted, several times on the sidewalk outside his school, a racist and threatening slogan directed at African Americans containing the same cruel and derogatory word that he has used and then signed it "Richie Gennaro."

He is terrified and that night has a dream in which he suffers retaliation over the crude epithet. Because it is so deliberately extreme and ludicrous in its echoes of the racist stereotypes of American popular culture, Richie's nightmare seems to the reader more comic than frightening. In it, Richie is being cooked alive by "gigantic muscular blacks wearing sunglasses," while his girlfriend is forced to commit fellatio on a Chinese American with an enormous penis "with tremendous fire-breathing dragons tattooed on both sides." That the dream is, for Richie, as erotic as it is frightening is demonstrated by its aftermath: "Richie awoke with the biggest hard-on of his life, which he promptly pounded into mother-of-pearl-colored drops that flew around the room like scatter pellets" (pp. 13–14). The rapid juxtaposition of slang and mock romanticism here is illustrative of the novel's tone.

When Richie learns that the crude epithet was the work of two ten-year-old boys, his girlfriend's younger brother Dougie Rizzo and his friend Scottie Hite, he and the other Wanderers solicit a rival gang, the Zorros, to frighten and humiliate Dougie and Scottie. There is no little absurdity in Richie's being tricked by two juveniles, feeling terrified as a result, and then having others enact his revenge; he is hardly a frightening warlord. Still, the story has its quite serious ingredients as well, though their full significance may not be immediately apparent. Obviously, there is the matter of racism, which is deeply ingrained in the consciousness of virtually all of Price's characters of whatever age; moreover, for the novel's gang members, the racism is simply part of the siege mentality by which they live.

Shelton points to an important level of complexity in the gang's response to violence. Despite their warrior code and language, they are really not especially fond of conflict: "the Wanderers, while seeing violence as one avenue to manhood, are always presented as more acted upon than acting.

Rather than initiating violence, they are either victims of it or witnesses to it, so the reader can feel sympathy for them because behind their swagger one finds a fear of violence" (p. 8). The gang's reluctance to incite violence contributes to the nostalgia that one feels while reading *The Wanderers;* the members of Selby's fictional Brooklyn street gang do not, and apparently the real Yummy Sandifer and Cragg and Derrick Hardaway did not, manifest such ambivalence. Whatever their reluctance, the wanderers are beset on all sides by enemies—sometimes other gangs, and *always* the adult world of parents and indeed all authority figures. In the world of *The Wanderers,* such a pervasive threat eliminates the possibility of meaningful communication and genuine dialogue, except among the gang members themselves.

To use the categories defined by Sidney H. Bremer in *Urban Intersections,* this absence of dialogue across ethnic, gender, and chronological boundaries puts Price's novel in the tradition of the "economic" urban novel, rather than the "residential" city novel.[5] *The Wanderers* can also be viewed, like the novels of Algren and Selby, as an example of Blanche H. Gelfant's concept of "the ecological" urban novel.[6] In fact, again as in the fiction of Algren and Selby, *The Wanderers* represents a refinement of Gelfant's "ecological" urban novel; in it, the "small unit" is not only restricted by space, but by race, gender, and age as well. Typically, in their inner-city fiction, Algren, Selby, and Price heighten the claustrophobic effects of narrow segments of the city until their fictional settings become metaphors for the psychotic mental states of the characters trapped in these repressive places.

One scene from "The Warlord" communicates, in an effectively condensed fashion, the climate of conflict pervading *The Wanderers.* In it Richie draws up a "score sheet," which divides, along essentially racial lines, the Bronx's rival gangs into two broad categories of "US" and "THEM" (p. 50). Price's text is, in fact, a kind of definitive "us versus them" novel; in this way, it depicts a world that Yummy Sandifer might well recognize; and, just as it appears to have been for Yummy, some of the most dangerous "THEM" are parents. Without exception, parent-child relationships are presented in the novel as being, in some way, abusive.

This trope of parental abuse is most graphically described in the brutal relationship between Joey Capra and his vain bully of a father, Emilio. All that Joey has ever known from Emilio is physical and mental torture: "Father and son played a perpetual game of tag. When Emilio was home, Joey never sat, he crouched; he never walked, he trotted. . . . Emilio would be immobile, following Joey only with his eyes then suddenly lash out with a quick left, a quick right. Pretend to read a newspaper, and when Joey tried to sneak past, Emilio would snake out a foot—Joey would start to fall but regain his balance and dance triumphant into his bedroom. Emilio would wait for next time" (p. 47). An unexpected benefit of having to develop physical agility to avoid his father's blows is that Joey develops into an excellent athlete, the star running back of a sandlot football team (made up largely of members of the Wanderers) that plays makeshift games in different Bronx public parks. As an adolescent male, he yearns for recognition from his father of his skills as a football player, but receives cruel ridicule instead.

In every way, Emilio is a despicable character, an individual beyond redemption, feared not only by Joey, but by everyone who knows him. His wife, like her son, is regularly terrorized by him: "The only time she had defied her husband, the only time she stood up to him, he had beaten her so badly she couldn't get out of bed for a week. . . . Emilio liked to remind her of 'what happened when you got out a line that time'" (pp. 55–56). For Emilio, violence takes the place of communication, of dialogue. In this way, he becomes the personification of the adult world in *The Wanderers*. The text makes clear the roots of Emilio's violent behavior: childish vanity, fear of advancing age, and an existence saturated with boredom.

Forty-eight-year-old Emilio, a former bodybuilder who at the age of twenty-six was named **Mr. New York City**, is virtually a parody of the cult of machismo. He is described as looking "just like Kirk Douglas" with a mustache, and one wonders if this description is intended to echo Douglas's portrayal of the selfish boxer in Mark Robson's 1949 film *Champion*. Price's bully loves to look at himself naked in the mirror after a shower, admiring his genitals and amusing himself by thinking that they are larger and more imposing than his son's. In fact, Emilio is haunted by the consciousness of advancing age and its threat of impotence; assaulting those weaker than himself constitutes a safe way of reassuring himself about his virility. Without admitting it, he is ultimately terrified of death; a fireman, he transforms meals into moments of horror for his wife and son: "he would always compare somebody's burned body to something on his plate" (p. 51). As is true of characters in the fiction of Algren and Selby, Emilio seems to have been inspired by Céline—he is an embodiment of mindless human cruelty originating in moral and spiritual emptiness. His sadistic treatment of Joey is so cowardly and unrelenting that one can only be glad when the son retaliates in kind.

Still, Emilio's brutality to his wife and son functions in Price's novel as merely an extreme variation of the norm. The pattern of domestic abuse and violence that permeates the novel is quickly established in "The Warlord" when Richie comes home to a hate-filled shouting match between his parents. To dramatize this scene, Price borrows a device from Selby, recording the adult Gennaros' dialogue largely in capital letters. In the story-chapter "Buddy Borsalino's Wedding Day," the wedding of Buddy and his girlfriend Despie Carabella takes place in an epidemic of violent behavior by both of their parents. Buddy's father, Vito, returns home from his job "as night manager of Times Square transient hotels" in a savage mood and attacks his wife who is dressing for a funeral. Significantly, Price narrates the scene from the prospective of Buddy, establishing the norm for domestic relations with which the perspective groom has grown up: "Buddy heard furniture crash, slaps and snarls echo through the foyer, a grunt from Vito followed by a sharp intake of breath from his mother, the wet slap of a fist in contact with soft flesh, a crack that was either wood or bone, and then heavy breathing" (pp. 192–93). Especially since Buddy is only marrying Despie because she is pregnant, one can surmise the kind of marriage they will have.

The cult of cruel and selfish machismo is fully operative when Buddy tells Despie's father about the impending wedding and the reasons for it. After briefly berating him, Mr. Carabella extends an ironic gesture of camaraderie to Buddy: "Look, I ain't a hard guy. I was your age once an' I used to put 'em away like there was no tomorrow. But one thing . . . I never did it with nobody's daughter" (p. 195). The language here is revealing. Sexual intercourse is describing as "putting [women] away," a phrase that clearly has overtones of murder; and Mr. Carabella, like all of the adult males, has murdered his wife's pride and dignity. The comment about never having done it with anyone's daughter communicates the traditional double standard of American middle-class culture, i.e., nice girls don't, bad girls do. After bonding with Buddy, Mr. Carabella punishes his daughter by beating her naked buttocks with a belt for ten minutes each day until the wedding; of course, the implications of sadomasochistic incest are clear. The father uses the fact of Buddy's penetration of his daughter's body to appropriate it for his own perverse pleasure.

Sexual perversity is also central to seventeen-year-old Perry La Guardia's relationship with his widowed mother in "Perry—Days of Rage." The major factor in Perry's rage is the refusal of his wealthy older brother, Raymond, to take any responsibility for their mother, thus trapping the younger brother into caring for the aging, self-pitying woman who talks constantly about her pride in Raymond's success. The story culminates when Perry, who thinks of his mother as "Lou Costello in a housedress," returns home after watching pornographic films in an adult video store. Initially outraged, he is unexpectedly excited when images of male homosexual intercourse appear on the screen, and then especially aroused by images of two lesbian lovers. Leaving the store, he is abruptly overcome by feelings of shame.

Rage at his mother begins to build in Perry as soon as he returns home. His mother resumes her relentless demands on him, and he fantasizes raping her so brutally that her ribs would break. Instead of harming his mother, Perry, after yelling two profane epithets at her, allows her to take his temperature rectally. The story is a debased, and at times comic, version of Freud's "family romance": when Perry initially resists his mother's demands to take his temperature, she says that she will die soon and, after she does, she will be forced to tell her husband the words their son has yelled at her. Less brutally but perhaps no less damagingly than the male parents in the novel, Mrs. La Guardia violates her son.

Emilio Capra, Mr. and Mrs. Gennaro, Mr. Carabella, and Mrs. La Guardia are simply the most immediate examples of the abusive adult world surrounding the novel's teenage characters. All authority figures emerge as ridiculously inadequate, if not overtly cruel. After announcing "Brotherhood Week," Mr. Sharp informs his school classroom that he too was a gang member and then descends to ugly ethnic name-calling, saving the worst verbal attack for the only Jew in the room. Better-than-average bowlers, Richie, Buddy and Eugene are exploited as "hustlers" in the alleys owned and operated by the Galasso brothers, six small-time gangsters.

The characterization of the novel's only clerical figure is deliberately extreme. Like Mr. Sharp, Father O'Brian is a former gang member, in the priest's case the novel's most savage gang, the Irish Ducky Boys. O'Brian preaches, and enforces, the violent and exclusionary social beliefs and practices that appear throughout Price's text. He is, like all the novel's adults, devoted to empty forms and random brutality and obsessed with selfish regret over his vanished youth, when he was first a leader of the Ducky Boys and then a star football player at Fordham: "He didn't believe in baseball leagues or social work. He believed in confession and physical punishment. . . . He wished he was still a Ducky Boy. . . . He wished he was still a football star. He wished he was drunk" (pp. 130–31). Father O'Brian listens to the Ducky Boys' confessions of petty transactions and "[i]f he was in a particularly good or bad mood, he would march the confessor to the tiny concrete courtyard in back and administer ten lashes with a car aerial" (p. 130). Largely because the priest enforces a code with which the gang members are familiar, they idolize him. It is not difficult to imagine Joey Capra growing up to be an Italian American version of Father O'Brian.

52   The Ducky Boys and the "Urban Punk Killing Machine"

As Shelton points out, the sections of the text that focus on the Ducky Boys operate on a level of surrealism rather than traditional naturalism. The Irish adolescents are described as being abnormally small in size, legion in number, and mindlessly savage in behavior. They function on a primitive, a presocial level of existence: "They could barely communicate verbally. Conversation was unknown. The only thing they did along with the rest of the human race was go to church" (p. 130). Obviously, for such barely human figures, dialogue with others is impossible. In his creation of the Ducky Boys, Price again echoes Selby and Nelson Algren, who consistently depict gang members as existing in a state beyond redemption, and anticipates the appearance of Yummy Sandifer and the Hardaway brothers. The Ducky Boys can be seen as a surrealistic force revenging the brutal nativist oppression of Irish immigrants, which is so powerfully described by William Kennedy in *Quinn's Book*.

One extended passage in particular points to the crucial narrative function the Ducky Boys perform as a cumulative personification of the dominant environment of the text:

> They roamed their turf like midget dinosaurs, brainless and fearless. . . . They would fight anyone and everyone and they'd never lose. . . . because there were hundreds of them. Hundreds of stunted Irish madmen with crucifixes tattooed on their arms and chests, lunatics with that terrifying, slightly cross-eyed stare of the one-dimensional, semihuman, urban punk killing machine. . . .
>
> Periodically, the entire Ducky Boy nation would descend and destroy a neighborhood. Neither the Ducky Boys nor their victims knew why or when. It was more a natural calamity, an unthinking massive impulse, a quirk in gland secretions than anything thought out or even mentioned. (p. 129)

That these "terrifying" "lunatics" work in the novel as a trope for the violence and danger that threatens the Wanderers from every side is made clear in the climax of "The Game," when they swarm Bronx Park, attacking the football players and spectators with razors, car aerials, baseball bats, and tire chains. Joey Capra sees his father, Emilio, who has unexpectedly appeared at the game, join the battle, only to be hit from behind with a baseball bat.

After seeing his father fall, Joey is himself knocked to the ground where he stays until he sees his father resurrected and routing several of the Ducky Boys with a tire chain. The young Irish hoodlums retreat before the enraged Emilio and then an "elated" Joey regains his feet and rushes over to his conquering father, but "[a]t the second before contact, Emilio wheeled around, slamming him square in the gut." Joey sinks to his knees in pain, staring at Emilio with hatred and disbelief. Finally, neither Joey nor any of the other Wanderers have any real allies except each other; Emilio has been drawn to the battle not out of any desire to help his son, but rather by the opportunity to inflict physical pain on the Ducky Boys. This insane riot that originates in the surrealistic invasion of the cumulative "urban punk killing machine" and culminates in the father's instinctive assault of his son constitutes the novel's most emblematic moment.

In a chapter that pays obvious homage to "Strike," the longest segment of Selby's *Last Exit to Brooklyn,* the Ducky Boys bring about the death of nineteen-year-old James Sloop, better known as Hang On Sloopy, of the Fordham Baldies. Grotesque in appearance and psychotic in behavior, Hang On Sloopy is rejected by everyone with whom he comes in contact except the other Fordham Baldies; young women especially fear and reject him. At a dance, he tries to force himself upon a girl he does not know, terrifying her until Perry of the Wanderers physically subdues him. Afterward, he gets so drunk that he wanders accidentally into Ducky Boys territory where, in a suicidal gesture, he offers to commit fellatio on one of the leaders of the Irish gang. Just as they do in "The Game," Ducky Boys materialize as if from nowhere, chasing Hang On Sloopy until he climbs a high playground fence where they patiently wait below, "swishing the air with walking sticks, wandering around, snapping off car aerials, not seeming to pay him any attention" (p. 132). Finally, while trying to climb across to the sanctuary of the playground, he falls fifteen feet to his death on the concrete and ice below.

Immediately, the Ducky Boys gather around his fallen body, assaulting it with walking sticks for a few moments before stripping it to the waist and then abandoning it to the freezing weather. In Selby's story, the gang viciously assaults the sexually ambivalent strike-organizer Harry after he sexually approaches a young boy and then leaves the nearly dead man hanging crucified from a fence. In the context of the "Big Playground" setting of "The Warlord," the deadly frozen playground which Sloopy dies trying to reach exemplifies the subtle, and ironic, structure of *The Wanderers.* Price's text contains very little real play; instead it depicts a universe of pain and death. Just as in *Last Exit to Brooklyn,* homosexual urges are seen as signs of weakness and the failure of masculinity and inspire quick and total retribution. In the tradition of Algren and Sherwood Anderson, Hang On Sloopy is an alienated grotesque who meets a grotesque death.

Ironically, the masculine ethic of the novel is expressed most memorably and succinctly by a woman, the mother of Eugene Caputo. When Eugene discovers his girlfriend Nina being raped by a young black man holding a razor to her throat, he instinctively runs for help. Though his action saves Nina by giving the attacker a chance to flee, Eugene is tortured by guilt over his flight, and when he describes the incident to his mother, she is outraged. First Mrs. Caputo contemptuously orders her son to take a bath and then lectures him as he sits numbly in a tub of "steaming" water: "Some day, my son, you are going to learn that the two greatest joys of being a man are beating the hell out of someone and getting the hell beaten out of *you*, good night" (p. 233). The tub of hot water in this scene is clearly meant as a metaphor for the womb; the mother's message to her son is essentially that his failure to observe the communal code of masculine violence constitutes a state of infantilism out of which he must be reborn as a "real man" who glories in inflicting and receiving pain.

The wedding of Buddy Borsalino and Despie Carabella represents the end of the Wanderers. After it, the other members of the gang disperse to various destinations. Having listened to his mother, Eugene joins the Marines; and, when Richie asks him why he did, he repeats his mother's communal "wisdom." The novel's mood of nostalgia culminates in the text's description of the wedding reception, and, in keeping with the novel's irony, it is in the context of this rite of passage into adulthood that the teenage characters seem most innocent and childlike. For instance, Buddy makes a loving list of the titles of the records he collects for the wedding: "Tears on My Pillow," "Heartaches," "Lovers Who Wander," "Could This Be Magic?" "Every Beat of My Heart," "I Only Have Eyes for You," and the exercise in sustained self-pity that gave the gang its name, "The Wanderer." A few titles communicate the indulgent and "tragic" obsession with the passing of time and the end of childhood so dominant in American popular music of the 50s and 60s: "Quarter to Three," "What Time Is It?" "Any Day Now," and "The End of the World." The text nicely summarizes the preparations of Buddy and his bride for their reception: "He was bringing 287 records himself, and Despie was bringing almost 400, but it was good to have some important doubles around" (p. 202).

There are, however, no overtones of nostalgia present in "The Roof," a chapter that represents, in Bloom's terms, a "creative misreading" of *Native Son, Never Come Morning*, and especially *Last Exit to Brooklyn*, as well as prophesying the coming world of Yummy Sandifer and the Hardaway brothers. It focuses upon Dougie Rizzo and Scottie Hite, the two ten-year-olds who are scared and humiliated by the Zorros in "The Warlord." Scottie Hite has an older brother, Frank or Rockhead, who is so presocial and psychotic that the Wanderers will have nothing to do with him. The text's descriptions of the Hite brothers and of Dougie Rizzo's relationship with Scottie Hite are, in fact, marked by the same surrealism that appears in the Ducky Boy passages: "The Hite brothers were idiots. . . . The Hite boys were so blond they seemed white-haired. They always went around moving their lips wordlessly and squinting like they were figuring out a calculus problem. Only a fellow maniac, though far more evil, like Dougie Rizzo could have befriended Scottie Hite—but only so he could use Scottie as Igor for his fiendish plots. As for Frank, he was friendless although he had many enemies" (p. 74). One senses that, with the Hite brothers and the Ducky Boys, Price is deliberately indulging in cartoon characterization. In the story, Dougie finds Scottie in the Big Playground, plays a number of jokes all involving the inflicting of physical pain on his slow-witted friend, and then steals a pornographic magazine from a candy store.

After the theft of the magazine, the two boys then take an elevator to the top floor of a building in the housing projects. After showing Scottie the magazine, Dougie convinces his companion that, because they are wearing the right kind of sneakers, they can jump safely from the roof. They then prepare to leap, but of course, at the last moment Dougie pulls back to watch his "best friend" plunge to his death: "Hearing a WHAP like a splattering coconut, Dougie ran to the rail. Looking down, he saw Scottie sprawled on the pavement like a bloody Howdy Doody with cut strings. Dougie pressed his face between the cool bars of the grill and stared off to the park. After a while he trotted back to the iron door, opened it, and disappeared down the stairs" (p. 80). That Dougie Hite represents the coming generation of teenagers and thus the successors of the Wanderers emphasizes the entrapment of the novel's central characters. Richie, Eugene, Joey, Buddy, and Perry find themselves sandwiched between a coldly psychotic ten-year-old and abusive, unfeeling adults. Truly, they live a hermetic existence.

"The Roof" depicts the kind of world that Yummy Sandifer must have known, a world in which childhood is a time of homicidal impulses, human companionship is a cruel mockery, and the traditional boundaries of human decency are discarded. Moreover, the real Yummy seems to have been as completely trapped as Price's creations are. In the tradition of Hubert Selby, Price, in *The Wanderers*, does not speculate extensively about how such a savage environment came to be; instead he is content to document the dimensions of its horror.

Chapter 4

A Postmodern Children's Crusade

John Edgar Wideman's *Philadelphia Fire*

In *Philadelphia Fire* (1990), John Edgar Wideman merges his postmodernist narrative technique with an apocalyptic vision and creates a unique and powerful text. Initially, the novel is narrated through the point of view of a character named Cudjoe, but, as the dimensions of contemporary American reality unfold, Wideman's mode of narration fragments. In this work, reality is simultaneously too horribly immediate and too unreal for any conventional narrator to bear. An important implication of Wideman's text seems then to be that traditional literary realism and modernism are incapable of recording the violent and destructive nature of life in the postindustrial American city. Much is being contested in *Philadelphia Fire*, the very soul of the nation in fact, but the contest has become too one-sided, too brutal and oppressive to permit the luxury of aesthetic detachment when writing about it. Wideman has discussed his commitment to a postmodernist aesthetic as emerging out of a sense of writing as a communal endeavor: "I try to invite the reader into the process of writing, into the mysteries, into the intricacies of how things are made and so, therefore, I foreground the self-consciousness of the act of writing. And try to get the reader to experience that, so that the reader is participating in the creation of fiction. In fact I demand that and in fact scare lots of readers away, because that's not light stuff. But for me that's a funny version of call and response, my particular version of a communal work being made."[1] With his third novel, *The Lynchers* (1973), Wideman began writing out of a profoundly dialogic aesthetic, and thus he feels no hesitation in incorporating biographical events into his fiction. He offers the reader a constantly evolving self and asks in turn that the reader contribute to that evolutionary process. In *Philadelphia Fire*, he openly expresses his grief and despair over having been personally wounded by the epidemic of violence that threatens the very survival of the nation.

"Wideman" emerges as a character in the novel just as "Mailer" frequently does in Norman Mailer's work. Wideman had already described in the conventionally autobiographical *Brothers and Keepers* (1984) the arrest and imprisonment of his younger brother Robby for a murder that occurred during an armed robbery, concluding that the despair that prompted Robby to become involved in the robbery was finally understandable and might even have been alleviated by Wideman himself had he sensed it earlier. In sharp and frightening contrast is the inexplicable murder committed by his son during a camping trip, an act that haunts and ultimately deconstructs the narrative flow in *Philadelphia Fire*. His son's violent act seems so motiveless, so much a random assault upon any sense of communal stability that it cannot be transcribed in the way that Robby's tragic, but not incomprehensible mistake is.

Moreover, in its very senselessness, it parallels the event around which the novel is centered, the 1985 bombing of the MOVE house on Osage Avenue in Philadelphia ordered by African American mayor Wilson Goode in which eleven people, including women and children, died. As critic Doreatha Drummond Mbalia emphasizes, *Philadelphia Fire* is a novel very much concerned with "father-son relationships" or more specifically the ways in which fathers have failed their sons.[2] Goode was the communal father who betrayed his people and, in so doing, literally destroyed some of them; "Wideman" is attempting to discover the ways in which he unconsciously betrayed his son and destroyed much of his innocence. Mbalia modifies Henry Louis Gates's discussion in *The Signifying Monkey* of the "double-voiced narration" common to African American literature to describe the narrative structure of *Philadelphia Fire*. It is, she argues, a "triple-voiced narrative" in which "an omniscient narrator . . . becomes a character, Cudjoe, an instructor who teaches Shakespeare in a way that African children can digest him, an African-centered way . . . and reincarnates into the author who, after his son's imprisonment, finds writing impossible" (pp. 107–8).

Mbalia argues that the fragmented and shifting identity of the narrator demands such a "triple-voiced" narrative approach, which is in turn directly related to the text's "three logical parts": Cudjoe's search for Simba, a boy who supposedly survived the Osage Avenue bombardment; "Wideman's" attempt to understand his failed relationship with his son; and "the colonial father (i.e., Prospero's) relationship with the colonized . . . children (i.e., Caliban)." She cogently summarizes the cumulative effect upon the reader of all these relationships of fathers with "lost" children: "Increasingly . . . it becomes clear that it is the fathers who are lost (mentally lost), not the children. Thus, the world of the novel is topsy-turvy. The fathers, because they act like children, are the children; the children are the parents. It is the fathers who have run away from their homes; they are the runagates in need of finding (that is, discovering) themselves" (pp. 63–64). It would, in fact, be difficult to find a more comprehensive vision of the violent effects of paternal abandonment than Wideman's novel. His vision is of a selfish and irresponsible nation that has victimized its own children and thus planted the seeds of its imminent destruction.

Thus, his text is a complex mixture of cultural prophecy, self-analysis, and historical investigation. Wideman's sense of writing as communal endeavor necessitates that he warn the African American community as well as the surrounding white capitalist community of the diseases that threaten to engulf all Americans together. Especially in his more recent works, he has explored the possibilities of disease as a metaphor for the enormous problems of American society. As Wideman has stressed in an interview, his 1989 story collection *Fever* is an example of such exploration:

> *Fever* was based on an actual occurrence of yellow fever in Philadelphia, Pennsylvania, in the 1790s. Like Antonin Artaud, I think that societies, in some metaphysical sense, create the diseases they need and those diseases are metaphors for the basic problems of those societies. It's no coincidence that the yellow fever epidemic, described by many at the time as the end of the world, was allegedly brought to the Americas by slaves from the West Indies. We need to stop the wheel and look at things again, try to understand what they mean.[3]

Wideman's latest novel, *The Cattle Killing* (1996), is set in a plague-ravaged eighteenth-century Philadelphia, and, in it, the dominant white society scapegoats the slaves for the outbreak of the deadly epidemic.

His comment in the interview that it was "no coincidence" "yellow fever was *allegedly* brought to the Americas from the West Indies" contains several levels of implication, all of them relevant to *Philadelphia Fire*. The epidemic that may yet prove fatal to American society has, in Wideman's opinion, historic roots, originating in the colonial experience itself and specifically in its practices of genocide and slavery. He believes that the extermination of countless people, as well as the objectification of others, constituted an evil so vast and so total that its legacy continues to haunt us and sicken us physically and spiritually. It is also, of course, inevitable that the colonial mind would allege that the disease originated in the colonized peoples themselves. The excuse of the imperialist mind that slavery was a mode of "saving" the African "savage" rests upon an assumption of the sinfulness, the moral sickness of the African rests thus upon a view of the African as diseased "other." It was hardly surprising then that this inferior other would be identified as the source of all malignancy—the imperialist enterprise simply would not allow the colonizer to believe that the disease might be internal since such a possibility would have threatened the practice of colonization.

Now in the late twentieth century, the epidemic is no longer smallpox, but a pervasive social and cultural disease that is manifested in several interrelated ways: poverty and the absence of genuine educational opportunities for poor and marginalized Americans, the loss of communal bonds within the African American society and in the larger American society, the drug traffic in the inner city, urban street gangs, homelessness, the unshakable nightmare of Vietnam, the AIDS epidemic, etc. James Robert Saunders sees *Philadelphia Fire* as Wideman's attempt to "exorcise" these assorted "demons" by naming them.[4] It is certainly, in addition, his attempt to document the violence that is their symptom.

The text's most extensive and eloquent vision of the apocalypse that threatens Philadelphia and indeed all of urban America is relayed through another of the selves into which the initially coherent narrative consciousness fragments; J. B. is a homeless man who emerges as the narrative focus of most of the third section of the novel. These two initials, of course, recall two related Western literary sources; the Old Testament book of Job and the 1958 Archibald MacLeish play based upon it. An academic, Wideman is one of the most intellectually sophisticated of contemporary American writers and one of the most adept at using such allusions. In addition, it should be said that a variation of Said's contrapuntal reading is essential to understanding Wideman's work. In *Philadelphia Fire* Wideman looks at both the "process" of imperialism and the "process" of resistance to it, but from the perspective of the colonized rather than the colonizer as Said does with the European texts that he examines.

At any rate, J.B. has an extended vision of the city that he has known so long suddenly ravaged by flames. The Osage Avenue massacre, he believes, inaugurated the last days of a Philadelphia holocaust:

> It's almost finished now. Loud pops of automatic weapons fire scything down naked bodies lined up against walls and fences. Like taking down wash. Only these bodies are dirty and make dirty heaps where they crumble, drawing flies, dogs, crows, stirring in the hot wind of fire storms smashing whole city blocks like bowling balls scoring strikes. ... Many, many pekel falling down, falling down. Blown away because

they don't suit somebody's purposes, cut down because this is the last morning of the last day and they are victims of terminal boredom, somebody's needing something to do.[5]

The level of despair communicated by the novel's apocalyptic vision is nowhere better conveyed than in this paragraph. The destruction of the people is a mindless ritualistic act carried out by a bored authority. Afterward, the bodies are simply stacked up to begin the process of decay and disease that will infect and, in turn, destroy the living. Wideman's use of "pekel," communicates the dehumanization that has already occurred and which the holocaust will merely complete—in the eyes of the power structure, the victims have long ceased to be people.

J.B. is further shaken by his own inability to respond to the destruction of his city in a coherent manner. Moreover, his failure elides into the narrator's who discusses the loss of a traditional aesthetic mode for recording such disasters: "Philadelphia's on fire. . . . What we need is realism, the naturalistic panorama of a cityscape unfolding. . . . If we could arrange the building blocks, the rivers, boulevards, bridges, harbor, etc. etc. into some semblance of order, of reality, then we could begin disentangling ourselves from this miasma, this fever of shakes and jitters, of self-defeating selfishness called urbanization. . . . If you loved yourself less, J.B. If you loved your city more" (pp. 157–58). Yet the sheer horror represented not just by Philadelphia, but by all of urban America has become too intense and unreal for the comforting illusions of a traditional realistic or naturalistic perspective. The standard naturalistic emphases on determinism and the "plot of decline" imply that forces comprehensible on some level to someone, if not to the victims, underlie incidents of social and individual destruction. But the legacy of a selfishness so deep and so irrational that it has prevented the controlled as well as the controllers in urban America from looking closely at the implications of their social and cultural irresponsibility cannot be communicated in such a rational, if pessimistic, aesthetic. In a very real sense, every level of adult American society has abandoned the city; it is therefore irrevocably doomed. Moreover, the horror that J.B. sees everywhere in the city causes him to doubt the veracity of his own perceptions. Even Henry James's "impressionistic realism" necessitates that the observer be able to trust his or her observations while understanding that they will not be universally shared.

The adult model of selfishness and contempt for human life has, J.B. understands, infected the lives of the children: "He thinks of young black boys shotgunning other black boys, black girl babies raising black girl babies and the streets thick with love and honor and duty and angry songs running along broken curbs, love and honor and duty and nobody understands because nobody listens, can't hear in the bloody current that courses and slops dark splashes on the cracked cement, how desperate things have become" (p. 158). Some slight hope of redemption can still be found in the children's surviving capacity for "love and honor and duty," but the text warns that someone with power had better start listening to and cultivating these affirmative values before they become hopelessly distorted. Even now the children are turning to their own gangs because the adult world is not worthy to receive them.

Wideman effectively ties his Prospero-Caliban motif and the chronotope of the street gang together through J.B.'s fear of a band of young African American males who call themselves "Kaliban's Kiddie Korps" and who sometimes appear directly in the text and sometimes indirectly through their ubiquitous graffiti. For much of the novel, the gang embodies the dwindling possibility of liberation from the oppressive control of the imperialist Prospero. Wideman posits no hope in imperialist power ending in any other way than through revolution: "the saddest thing about this story is that Caliban must always love his island and Prospero must always come and steal it. Nature. Each stuck with his nature. So it ends and never ends" (p. 122). Love for space, for the "island" of one's ancestors can be, under extreme circumstances, the basis of revolution; certainly Prospero luxuriating in power and control will never change. The adults having abandoned the struggle, it is the fate of the children to continue it, to engage in a children's crusade characterized by guerilla warfare.

J.B., the despised homeless man, is tormented by other demons as well, most of them internal. Like Wideman a graduate of the University of Pennsylvania, he offers passersby "hand-printed cards" reading: *"I am a vet. Lost voice in war. Please help."* In fact, he has lost almost everything, most of all a sense of centeredness, of meaning. Yet, in a very real sense, he has not lost his voice—it is through his perceptions that Wideman communicates much of the text's encompassing vision. He is not, however, a veteran; rather than in the tropical wildness of Vietnam, he lost his way in the "jungle" of Philadelphia's inner city. As the text makes clear, the metaphoric urban jungle of the city of brotherly love, and indeed of all urban America, is closely linked, by economic realities and cultural assumptions, to the literal jungle of Vietnam: "half his crew who went to war killed over there in the jungle and half the survivors came home juiced, junkied, armless, legless, crazy as bedbugs. Fucked over good in Asian jungles while this Philly jungle fucking over J.B. and the brothers left here to run it. Casualties just as heavy here in the streets as cross the pond in Nam" (p. 173). J.B. believes that, as a casualty of urban American warfare, he is entitled to veterans' benefits or at least "to something" (p. 173).

Wideman thinks so too—J.B. gets to tell much of his story, a "benefit" that saves him from the anonymity awaiting most of the inhabitants of the urban capitalist jungle. The text's protest against the ravages of imperialism is also made manifest in J.B.'s fantasy of being a captive laborer on a tropical rubber plantation in which the women and children of the men are imprisoned "inside bamboo compounds guarded by brothers in creased khaki": "stripped to the waist, fighting back the jungle that never sleeps, that circles the compound where you've been exiled to preside over the slow death of babies and their mamas and old folks not worth saving to cultivate the rubber trees" (pp. 170–71). The prisoners are guarded by "brothers," exploited victims of colonialist power either forced or volunteering to exploit their women and children; in Vietnam, a disproportionate number of "brothers" died to protect the American imperialist enterprise. By implication the guards on the imagined rubber plantation are prototypes of Mayor Goode and his African American associates in the city government of Philadelphia, especially Timbo an associate of Cudjoe's from the University of Pennsylvania who serves as "[c]ultural attaché to the mayor" (p. 72).

J.B.'s last hours, like his life leading up to them, will be marked by random violence. He first attempts to give one of his cards to a white commuter named Richard Corey inspiring in the white man, for reasons J.B. cannot know, feelings of fear and revulsion. Wideman's naming of the white commuter is another of the literary allusions that saturate his text; "Richard Cory" is, of course, the name of the wealthy and handsome character who shocks Tilbury Town with his sudden suicide in Edwin Arlington Robinson's well-known and frequently anthologized 1896 poem. Wideman further emphasizes the parallel between his character and Robinson's in his introduction of Richard Corey into the text: "a white man, late thirties, business suit, striped silk tie, Clark Kent glasses, just in off the Chesnutt Hill local for a day at the office. J.B. doesn't know this man's name is Richard Corey today, that the pitiful sonbitch intends a swan dive at noon from the nineteenth floor of the spanking new Penn Mutual Savings and Loan Building" (p. 173). To the residents of Tilbury Town, Richard Cory's wealth, attractiveness, and sophistication make him seem, until he takes his life, safe and secure, as impregnable as the Superman of twentieth-century popular culture. The emphasis that the white commuter's name is Richard Corey *today* is another postmodern or metafictional technique; it is Wideman calling attention to the literary sophistication of his novel. It also suggests that "Corey" is a man without a coherent identity, a man who is one thing today and another tomorrow.

"Richard Corey" appears equally invulnerable to J.B., who cannot know that "the Clark Kent glasses" mask not "a man of steel," but an individual who feels that he has been assaulted and violated in the most fundamental of ways. In contrast to Robinson's poem, the motivation behind the suicide is, in Wideman's novel, explained. "Corey," while waiting with his wife in a movie queue, was mugged. It is not the loss of money or his own fear that haunts him, but the image of his wife, Cynthia, as she was knocked to the ground and lay exposing her underwear. Irrationally, "Corey" blames his wife for the indiscretion: "Cynthia's unladylike panty show as she squirmed on the sidewalk. Could a woman be raped in ten seconds? . . . Why didn't she bounce up and cover herself after the assailants fled? Boo hoo, boo-hooing, her skirt hiked up, her orange frilly underwear showing as the crowd of curious citizens gathered around her where she lay. . . . [S]he just lay where they pushed her down. . . . like she didn't mind showing her orange bloomers to anyone who cared to look" (pp. 173–74). "Corey" suffers from the kind of racial-sexual hysteria that, like Richard Wright, James Baldwin, Eldridge Cleaver, and others before him, Wideman believes haunts the white American male psyche. In a long passage centered in the account of Cudjoe's teaching Shakespeare to the children of black inner-city Philadelphia, Wideman emphasizes the sexual dynamic inherent in imperialism. Cudjoe probes the metaphoric implications of Prospero's denying Miranda the right to give herself to Caliban; such denial, he insists, is fundamentally a denial of Caliban's humanity and results ironically in an awakening of his desire for Miranda. Having her sexually would affirm his equality, his right of access to all that Prospero seeks to deny him: "that lying ass wanna be patriarch Prospero who claims to be your daddy and wants to be mine, he's capable of anything. Incest, miscegenation, genocide, infanticide, suicide, all the same to him. To him it's just a matter of staying on top, holding on to what he's got. Power. A power jones eating away at the pig knuckle he was dealt for a heart" (p. 142). Richard Wright's Bigger Thomas discovers *somewhat* accidentally the same racial-sexual dynamic of power when he kills Mary Dalton.

"Corey's" wife's sexuality, the manifestation of his personal "power jones," having been exposed, "Richard Corey" sees nothing else to do but commit suicide. Wideman's point is that an identity based upon the oppression of others, even if that oppression is not always conscious, is extremely fragile and can be abruptly shattered by the most unforeseen and unavoidable events. It is himself, not his wife, who "Corey" believes has been raped. In fact, the integrity and power of his identity have been destroyed; after he leaps to his death, his body is treated by the city as an inconvenience. Wideman's description of the aftermath of the suicide is marked by its extreme, and almost obscene, irony: "white, well dressed, a gentleman caller dropping in unexpectedly. The whole world in his hands, what's he got to go do something like this for? In the middle of the city so we have to step around him, over him" (p. 182). The implication of this passage is that the city has become so immersed in brutality and violence that it has lost its capacity for compassion. Its irony is intensified by its echoes of other more traditionally humanistic texts—Tennessee Williams's *The Glass Menagerie*, the spiritual "He's Got the Whole World in His Hands."

Finally, only J.B. and through him the reader is given the full secret of "Corey's" vulnerability. The homeless man retrieves "Corey's" briefcase after the suicide and finds in it a diary, which narrates its owner's sense of "having been born blind, under a cruel star" and then learning "to see" a vision of "the beautiful Tree of Life, Lions and lambs lying down together under the rainbow arc of its branches" (p. 174). Wideman's irony here is multilayered. The Tree of Life, a source of health and strength threatened by a diseased society, was the central vision in the preaching of King, the leader of the MOVE community, which the government of Philadelphia felt it necessary to destroy. Thus, racism, political power, and senseless urban violence destroyed the potential for saving dialogue—"Richard Corey," largely because of the mugging and what he feels to be the sexual humiliation associated with it, dies hating and fearing African Americans and especially black children. Instead of entering into King's envisioned new age of natural peace and harmony, "Corey" is assaulted by "wicked little hoodlums, kids who should have been home in bed at that hour" (p. 175).

Reading the diary, J.B. finds passages of prophecy describing the city's abandoned children rising up to enact revenge for their exploitation and abandonment, again the vision of a peculiarly perverse children's crusade:

> *It's time, my friends, to reap what's been sown. The Children's Hour now. The Kiddy Korner. What have they been up to all this time we've left them alone? Over in the shadows with Buffalo Bob. Mister Rogers. The Shadow knows. But do we? Are we ready to hear the children speak? Ready or not we shall be caught. We are pithed. Feel nothing. Children have learned to hate us as much as we hate them. I saw four*

boys yesterday steal an old man's cane and beat him with it. He was a child, lying in his blood on the sidewalk. They were old, old men tottering away. (pp. 187–88)

Senselessly, the homeless man becomes a victim of the children's demand for revenge when a gang of roving boys sets him on fire; his attempt to save himself from burning by plunging into a fountain is too late. This horrific scene confirms Kowalewski's ideas about fictional violence deriving its power from its unfamiliarity to the reader as well as John Fraser's theory that violence in art serves as a necessary means of dispelling cultural "accidie." As in Eliot's *The Waste Land,* water in *Philadelphia Fire* has lost its healing powers; on every level, the city is burning and there is no redemptive water in which to immerse oneself.

Earlier in the text, Cudjoe has heard about the malevolent gangs from Timbo. The mayor's cultural attaché describes to him pamphlets, presently being circulated throughout the city, that advertise the services of gangs as "fixers": "Fixers are these goddamned cute-little-kid-next-door death squads. Free of charge they'll take out troublesome adults. You know, abusers, pimps, dealers, derelicts [like J.B., it turns out], unreasonable teachers and parents. Fix up problems for other kiddies. Half-pint assassins. Fixers" (p. 90). Clearly, the perverse children's crusade is already well underway. Timbo also suggests the possibility of adult manipulation of the roving youths, a grotesque echo of Dickens—the specific identity of the contemporary Fagin or Fagins is never established, however. What is clear, though, is that if such adult exploitation of the gangs is occurring, it never came from King or the MOVE people, the scapegoats of Timbo's boss, Mayor Goode. Thus, senseless violence provokes more senseless violence in a never ending circle.

Cudjoe's reunion with Timbo is part of his attempted reintegration into American society, which he wants to help salvage. At the first of the novel, he has returned from an extensive retreat to the Greek island of Mykonos and has become obsessed with finding Simba, the child survivor of the Osage Avenue assault who has disappeared from public view. Several reversals of the imperialist paradigm are implicit in Cudjoe's exile and return. He is one of the colonized, a Caliban who attempts to find sanctuary and meaning in the home of the colonizer and, in fact, in the specific country from which the West has adopted many of its controlling values. His return to America represents an ironic reenactment of the archetypal colonialist voyage, ironic in large part because he finds in contemporary America not the fresh, new continent or the innocent nation of American idealism, but an old and depraved society on the verge of apocalyptic destruction. His

66   A Postmodern Children's Crusade

obsession with finding Simba, an African name for lion, is rooted in his desire to return to the unspoiled childhood of American culture, a childhood now hopelessly submerged in racism, capitalism, and violence.

Moreover, as Doreatha Drummond Mbalia points out, "Cudjoe" is also a name with African origins: "the name is a derivative of the west African name, 'Kojo,' meaning unconquerable" (p. 63). Instead of the courage and determination implied by his name, Cudjoe's life has been marked by compromise, failure, and cowardice; thus, saving Simba would be one mode of redeeming himself. He never finds the boy, though; rather part 1 of the text ends with Cudjoe having a terrifying dream of discovering a lynched boy hanging from the rim of a basketball goal on a public court where he has often played pick-up games: "it's me and every black boy I've ever seen running up and down playing" (p. 93). The hanged boy, of course, echoes Eliot's hanged man from *The Waste Land,* but, more important, it constitutes a horrific vision of the murder of Wideman's and urban America's black youth and, by extension, of the youth of the nation.

In part to cancel out his past failures and mistakes, Cudjoe wishes to save more than just Simba; he hopes to write a text that will be a powerful diagnosis of and warning about the disintegration he sees in urban America. Yet the overwhelming alienation that his native country and city evoke in him makes this task difficult if not impossible; thus "he decides he will think of himself as a reporter covering a story in a foreign country" (p. 45). Without being able to know the specific reference of his vision, Cudjoe even imagines the burning of J.B. by the street gang. For a moment he imagines the city calling out to him to articulate its voice: "you can grasp the pattern. Make sense of me. Connect the dots. I was constructed for you. . . . All you have to do is speak and you reveal me, complete me" (p. 44). Soon, though, he realizes that the only observable "pattern" is one defined by oppression and violence. What one sees by "connect[ing] the dots" is a horror, the full intensity of which cannot be communicated in any rational or coherent manner. Clearly, Philadelphia does not seem to have been "constructed" for Cudjoe. While it may at one time have been constructed for human beings, it was never built for African Americans and it is now "foreign" to any human sympathy or compassion.

Even Mayor Goode and his associates have bought into an illusionary progress that, in fact, is intent upon destroying everything that gets in its way. Timbo's justification to Cudjoe of the Osage Avenue assault is revealing:

> They [King and the MOVE people] were embarrassing, man. Embarrassing. Trying to turn back the clock. Didn't want no kind of city,

no kind of government. Wanted to live like people in the woods. . . . Mayor got tired of them mocking everything he was promising. Talk about a thorn in the side. King and them were a natural thorn halfway up his behind. A whole brier patch growing up in the mayor's chest. Sooner or later, one way or another, them and their dreadlocks had to go. (p. 81)

In fact, King and his followers did want a "kind of city," but a kind that Goode and Timbo can no longer comprehend. The MOVE people desired a city based not upon a sharp departure from nature, but upon an extension of the natural world and a humane and inclusive order, which would at times appear to be no order at all. Essentially King challenged the valorization of progress, of capitalistic expansion at the expense of the economically defenseless. Goode, ultimately of course a captive of the white power structure, was fundamentally threatened by such a challenge; for him, the homelessness of the poor was a cheap price to pay for an "urban renewal" that in actuality produced nothing new, but merely preserved and extended the capitalist agenda.

Nature itself seems now to have turned its back on the city. When Cudjoe's students tried to produce his version of *The Tempest*, it was washed away "with a [literal] tempest before it ever got started" (p. 133). For a while, Cudjoe clings to a hope that his interpretation of the play as the archetypal statement of the imperialist paradigm is still remembered by his students. At least he did not soften or compromise his interpretation of Shakespeare's text when discussing it with his students: "Today's lesson is this immortal play about colonialism, imperialism, recidivism, the royal fucking over of weak by strong, colored by white, many by few, or, if you will, the birth of the nation's blues seen through the fish-eye lens of a fee fi foe englishmon. A master Conrad. Earl the Pearl Shakespeare, you see" (p. 127). Wideman's mastery of linguistic "game-playing" is evident in this passage. "Master Conrad" emphasizes that the author of *Heart of Darkness* was a master of the English language, while also echoing the central line of Conrad's novella, "Mister Kurtz, he dead." In *Philadelphia Fire*, the "heart of darkness" has moved across the ocean to urban America. Wideman also alludes to Conrad because he was, of all the great English novelists of the late nineteenth and early twentieth centuries, the most obsessed by imperialism and its implications for colonizer and colonized. "Earl the Pearl" is the nickname of the great basketball player Earl Monroe. Throughout his work, Wideman refers to grace and dexterity on the basketball court in much the way that Hemingway alludes to bullfighting, as a trope for agility in using words, for the act of writing itself. Finally the senseless violence that he everywhere sees perpetuated on the children, and in turn perpetuated by the children, forces him to abandon the comforting illusion that his former students have remembered what he told them about the play.

Like J.B., Cudjoe is simply a mask for the narrator, for Wideman; and two of the most postmodern aspects of the text are the directness with which Wideman acknowledges that Cudjoe is a narrative device and the way in which he abandons that device for much of the text. Cudjoe's search for Simba collapses into "Wideman's" search for some meaning in the murder committed by his son. The narrative voice asks at one point: "Can this story he must never stop singing become a substitute for an integrated sense of self, of oneness, the personality he can never achieve? The son's father. Father's son" (p. 110). A recurrent trope in Wideman's work—for instance, in the prologue to *The Cattle Killing* and the brilliant autobiographical text *Fatheralong*—is the son's need for validation by the father. Here he connects this trope with the father's doomed attempt to understand the son, to grant the son the requisite independence no matter the price of that independence. The "lost Simba" is metaphor for "Wideman's" son, lost at least to the father's comprehension.

Soon the intensity of "Wideman's" need to comprehend and thereby save his son causes the narrative device of Cudjoe and indeed the essential "plan" of the novel to "unravel" (p. 115). The narrative distance, the artistic objectivity, so important to the modernists are, in *Philadelphia Fire*, revealed to be merely illusions with which the writer protects himself or herself from the pain of the process of creation and of what that process discloses. After this revelation, they are, until the last section of the novel, abandoned: "why this Cudjoe, then? . . . Why am I him when I tell certain parts? Why am I hiding from myself? Is he mirror or black hole?" (p. 122). "Cudjoe" is, in fact, both mirror and black hole—he is the author's reflection, but that reflection destroys the possibility of discovering meaning in anything external. Wideman frequently interrupts his narrative in order to quote from other writers in order to emphasize his major themes and tropes, and he turns to Paul Eluard to describe the impossibility of the artistic self's merging with an external reality: "I must not look on reality as being like myself" (p. 109). What *Philadelphia Fire* ultimately reveals is that "reality" in urban America is completely foreign to the ideal of composure and order residing at the heart of the creative process emphasized by Eliot, Stevens, and other modernists.

Wideman does return though to the narrative device of Cudjoe for the novel's conclusion. A ceremony is being held in Independence Square to honor the victims of the MOVE massacre, and during it Cudjoe imagines scenes of an 1805 riot at the same location in which African Americans were randomly assaulted and murdered by whites: "Blacks outnumbered twenty to one never had a chance. Some lie stiff where they've fallen. Others crawl off, disappear into underground bunkers. The victors repossess the square. Continue their celebration" (p. 194). In this passage, Wideman seems to be evoking a historic moment in which the space of the city was contested for the last time. In that moment, the victory of the white imperialists was inevitable and complete. Since then, the dominant white society has truly possessed the city, increasingly treating it as a kind of internal Third World colony to be simultaneously ignored and exploited. As in his evocation of the yellow fever epidemic, Wideman is emphasizing the historic roots of American racism and its symbiotic relationship with American capitalism.

Cudjoe concludes the text with a silent promise: "*Never again. Never again*" (p. 199). *Philadelphia Fire* is intended in part then as a jeremiad warning an implied white readership of the imminent holocaust that will result from continued white capitalist exploitation and neglect of the African American. Wideman is echoing the LeRoi Jones (Amiri Baraka) of the short plays *Dutchman* and *The Slave* in giving the dominant society a last chance to reject its greed and brutality and thereby attain salvation for itself and the rest of the nation before black anger and revenge explode and produce an irreparable chaos. Yet Wideman's postmodernist aesthetic necessitates that he, unlike Baraka, foreground the literariness of his warning; early in the novel, he quotes Gaston Bachelard from *The Psychoanalysis of Fire:* "at all times and in all fields the explanation by fire is a rich explanation" (p. 109). Fire is in Wideman's text a metaphor drawn from numerous sources, which proclaim the urgent need of destruction and purification.

Philadelphia Fire is a "rich" postmodernist text centered on an apocalyptic vision of a perverted children's crusade that will avenge the neglect and failures of the parents. Its setting in the "City of Brotherly Love," the cradle of American independence, contributes an additional level of irony to a novel already steeped in irony. In Wideman's vision, the seeds of the end of the American experiment were present at its beginning and are about to bear strange and tragic fruit.

Chapter 5

Nature Despoiled and Artificial

Sandra Cisneros's *The House on Mango Street*

Sandra Cisneros's *The House on Mango Street* is, in form, the most innovative text discussed in this book; Cisneros so deliberately blurs traditional literary definitions that critics disagree about whether her text should be seen as an experimental novel or a unique kind of autobiography. Maria Elena de Valdes has offered a compromise position on this question, describing it as "a fictional autobiography of the narrator and central character Esperanza Cordero"; de Valdes defines "fictional autobiography" as "a postmodern form of fiction stitching together a series of lyrical pieces, 'lazy poems' Cisneros calls them . . . into the narrativity of self-invention through writing."[1] De Valdes's approach is perceptive in more than one way. In its stress upon the act of writing as essential to first constructing and then asserting identity, *The House on Mango Street* recalls texts by other women and minority American writers. For instance, in Maxine Hong Kingston's *The Woman Warrior* (1976), the narrator "Maxine" appropriates her mother's legacy of "talk story" to (re)invent a personal and family history, often providing multiple accounts of undocumented events. When this process of reinvention is complete, "Maxine," who of course has much in common with Maxine Hong Kingston, can defy her dominating mother and assert her independence. Cisneros's paralleling of writing with identity also calls to mind Henry Louis Gates's analysis of the centrality of the "talking book" in African American literature.[2]

The innovative form of *The House on Mango Street* is reminiscent of two earlier narratives, Jean Toomer's *Cane* (1923) and Tomás Rivera's *. . . y no se lo trago la tierra* (*. . . and the earth did not swallow him*) (1971). In the former, Toomer dispenses with most of the traditions of the novel (a developed plot, recurrent characters, and consistent setting), while exploring through lyrical stories, sketches, and poems the nature of African American identity. Lacking a clear narrative center, *Cane*'s thematic focus is on communal, rather than individual, identity. Not only because of its subject matter, Rivera's text seems even more obviously to anticipate *The House on Mango Street*. Rivera's . . . *y no se lo trago la tierra* tells, in fragmentary and lyrical form, of the individual and then the cultural awakening of a young Chicano boy, the son of exploited laborers who live in Texas but travel each year to the Midwest for work. In delineating the emerging awareness of her urban female protagonist, Cisneros echoes Rivera's pattern of growth from a limiting personal to a liberating communal consciousness.

Cisneros's setting is Chicago's Chicano community, and, in keeping with its other innovative aspects, it represents a merger of Sidney H. Bremer's two categories of Chicago novels, the "standard Chicago novel," informed primarily by economic issues and a vision of technology as a dehumanizing force, and the "residential" novel, texts written by women that depict the city as a predominantly supportive environment: "As an epitome of woman's place, home was not coterminous with a physical house, as cultural critic Elizabeth Janeway . . . has explained. For these Chicago [residential] writers, however, the family house was central, implicated in civic and cultural, as well as personal and domestic, activities. . . . For [them], the family house was a domestic microcosm for—not a bulwark against—the city itself."[3]

It is crucial to point out that in *The House on Mango Street* Cisneros, unlike the earlier Chicago novelists in either of Bremer's two categories, is writing from the perspective of an exploited ethnic group. She thus could not, even if she had wanted to, view Chicago as affirmatively as Edith Franklin Wyatt, Clara Laughlin, Elia W. Peattie, and Willa Cather did. In addition, she can hardly treat the concept of ethnicity with the detachment of a middle-class writer. For Cisneros, ethnic identity is not an abstraction, but a defining aspect of her identity. Like Wyatt, Laughlin, Peattie, and Cather, a woman, she shares their sense of the centrality of "house" and "home," but, unlike them, she can only yearn for a supportive physical and emotional environment. Certainly, the house of the title does not provide anything like that.

The volume's first four sentences emphasize the transient life that Esperanza, the young narrator, and her family have led: "We didn't always live on Mango Street. Before that we lived on Loomis on the third floor, and before that we lived on Keeler. Before Keeler it was Paulina, and before that I can't remember. But what I remember most is moving a lot."[4] Recalling an incident in which "a nun from [her] school" had expressed contemptuous disbelief upon seeing the family's third-floor dwelling on Loomis Street, Esperanza describes her dream of someday having "[a] real house. [O]ne I could point to," but emphasizes that "[t]he house on Mango Street isn't it" (p. 5).

The "real house" of which Esperanza dreams functions in the novel both as a concrete place of refuge and as a metaphor for her repressed, but emerging, identity. The strong sense of self that Esperanza does ultimately succeed in constructing is firmly anchored in gender, class, and culture. Julian Olivares quotes Cisneros as acknowledging two quite different sources for *The House on Mango Street:* "She states that the nostalgia for the perfect house was impressed on her at an early age from reading many times Virginia Lee Burton's *The Little House.* . . . In a class discussion [at the Iowa Writers Workshop] of Gaston Bachelard's *The Poetics of Space,* she came to this realization: 'the metaphor of a house, *a house, a house,* it hit me. What did I know except third-floor flats? Surely my classmates know nothing about that.'"

Burton's *The Little House* is a children's book that tells the story of a house that is built in the country where it is happy until the city grows up around it and it is left to deteriorate; the little house, which is referred to as "she," is rescued from destruction only when the granddaughter of the original inhabitant notices it and has it moved back to the countryside. It is essentially urban sprawl and technology (cars and subways) that almost submerge the little house. The text assumes that urban life is unnatural:

> [P]retty soon there was an elevated train
> going back and forth above the Little House.
> The air was filled with dust and smoke,
> and the noise was so loud
> that it shook the Little House.
> Now she couldn't tell when Spring came,
> or Summer or Fall, or Winter.
> It all seemed about the same.[5]

It is possible to move the house back to the country because, despite the urban decay that surrounds it, it remains strong. Returned to the countryside, the little house is again content:

> Never again would she be curious about the city . . .
> Never again would she want to live there . . .
> The stars twinkled above her . . .
> A new moon was coming up . . .
> It was Spring . . .
> and all was quiet and peaceful in the country. (p. 40)

Thus, in Burton's book, the country is associated with life and the natural in the double sense of containing "nature" and being a human norm, while the city is viewed as being connected with death and the unnatural, an alien imposition upon the norm of nature. A not dissimilar pastoralism underlies *The House on Mango Street.*

In her essay, Olivares argues convincingly that Cisneros "reverses" Bachelard's privileged, male view of a house as "an image of 'felicitous space . . . the house shelters the daydreaming, the house protects the dreamer, the house allows one to dream in peace. . . . A house constitutes a body of images that give mankind proofs or illusions of stability.'" As an "impoverished woman raised in a ghetto," Cisneros can hardly share Bachelard's concept of a house as a "felicitous space."[6] In the world of Mango Street, women have little time or opportunity for "daydreaming," and "stability" is a dream, not a reality. For her and for Esperanza, a house as the embodiment of a secure home is in itself a dream; she only yearns for what the early-twentieth-century Chicago residential novelists could assume.

For much of her novel, Cisneros's text depicts the Chicago barrio as a terrain made dangerous and literally unnatural by poverty and violence. As in John Rechy's *The Miraculous Day of Amalia Gómez,* violence in it is the immediate legacy of class and racial oppression and of a valorization of machismo. Thus, women and female children become the perennial recipients of physical and emotional abuse. Unlike several of the novel's female characters, Esperanza is largely spared such abuse within her immediate family but encounters it virtually everywhere else. In *The House on Mango Street,* the female is thoroughly commodified, reduced to a possession without rights or voice. In fact, the struggle to claim a female voice lies at the thematic heart of the text.

As a part of her struggle for self-definition, Esperanza even desires to escape her given name and what she feels are its negative connotations: "In English my name means hope. In Spanish it means too many letters. It means sadness, it means waiting. It is like the number nine. A muddy color. It is the Mexican records my father plays on Sunday mornings when he is shaving, songs like sobbing" (p. 10). This passage is illustrative of the imaginative approach to symbolism that characterizes Cisneros's text. The traditional positive connotation of the name "Esperanza" is acknowledged, but only in order that it can be challenged; as a female of Mexican American descent living in an economically deprived neighborhood that is surrounded and controlled by a male- and Anglo-dominated society, she indeed has few reasons to feel hopeful. Outside the barrio, her name sounds foreign; it does seem to have "too many letters." The passive side of hoping is, of course, waiting, and most of the female characters in the novel are depicted as waiting, often literally, for someone to rescue them from the hopelessness in which they are trapped.

Here Cisneros's language becomes lyrical and elusive in ways that recall *Cane* and . . . *y no se lo trago la tierra*. One can feel more easily than analyze the associations of "Esperanza" with "the number nine" and "a muddy color." Esperanza is perhaps saying that, in the eyes of a racist Anglo society, her skin color is associated with images of dirt and secrecy. At any rate, the young narrator wishes to rename and thereby recreate herself: "I would like to baptize myself under a new name, a name more like the real me, the one nobody sees. Esperanza as Lisandra or Maritza or Zeze the X. Yes. Something like Zeze the X will do" (p. 11). Obviously, she has been influenced by American popular culture—"Zeze the X" sounds like the name of a male "superhero" and especially recalls Zorro, "the Mexican Robin Hood" who was given to cutting the letter "Z" with his sword on walls and curtains. The desire to be "Zeze the X" is in part, of course, an amusing indication of Esperanza's adolescence; but, more important, it indicates her early rejection of passivity, of "waiting." Finally, she will not expect a male to rescue her, but, with the help of some adult female role models, will save herself, essentially by narrating her "story."

It takes Esperanza a while to discover such positive models. She perceives instead repeated violence against innocent young women. There is Sally whose father, frightened by her beauty, attempts to imprison her in their apartment: "Her father says to be this beautiful is trouble. They are very strict in his religion. They are not supposed to dance. He remembers his sisters and is sad. Then she can't go out. Sally, I mean" (p. 81). Sally, who longs desperately for love, is usually pictured as literally "leaning" against her open window or against cars driven by young men. She becomes the very embodiment of the "waiting" against which Esperanza rebels.

Enraged in part by his daughter's innocence, Sally's father regularly and savagely abuses her. Still, Sally attempts to protect him, explaining her bruises at school by saying "she fell": "That's where all the blue places come from. That's why her skin is always scarred" (p. 92). Inevitably, the father "one day . . . catches her talking to a boy" and "just went crazy, he just forgot he was her father between the buckle and the belt" (p. 93). Not surprisingly, Sally soon runs away to get married, and, again as one might have expected, her husband, a "marshmallow salesman," proves to be abusive. In fact, her situation after her marriage is, if anything, even more desperate than it was before: "[her husband] won't let her talk on the telephone. And he doesn't let her look out the window. And he doesn't like her friends, so nobody gets to visit her unless he is working" (pp. 101–2). Now she is denied even the consolation of "leaning" out of the window. The fate of Sally illustrates the fallacy of "waiting" for the female in Cisneros's text, which emphasizes that repression and violence are the bitter fruits of such passivity. The poverty and despair of the barrio produce an unnatural environment in which men forget that they are fathers and husbands or lovers. In *The House on Mango Street,* women are possessions to be zealously guarded except during those occasions when they are proudly exhibited.

The character who is most clearly Esperanza's double, the representative of what might have happened to her, is Minerva. The short segment focusing on her is significantly entitled "Minerva Writes Poems," and its opening sentence encapsulates the young woman's desperate situation: "Minerva is only a little bit older than [Esperanza] but already she has two kids and a husband who left" (p. 84). Like the narrator, she attempts to rescue her endangered sense of self by writing poetry, seeking through language to create evidence of an identity separate from her husband and children. But her attempt is doomed—she, unlike Esperanza, will be unable to create a lasting text. The hopelessness of her situation is intensified by the fact that her husband has not truly "left"; rather he leaves repeatedly only to return. Finally, Minerva resolves to lock him out of her house and her life forever, but sadly and inevitably relents when he once again returns.

The sketch ends with a brief paragraph that utilizes internal rhyme and borrows the lyrics of an American popular song to convey the hopelessness and the triteness of the young woman's fate: "Next day she comes over black and blue and asks what can she do? Minerva. I don't know which way she'll go. There's nothing *I* can do" (p. 85). Interestingly, the song lyric echoed here asks, "What *did* I do / to be so black and blue?" Belatedly, Minerva is starting to comprehend the economic and cultural determinism in which she is trapped. The text has established the "way she'll go" or more precisely the fact that she has nowhere to go. Esperanza begins to realize that, while she is helpless to save her friend, she can and indeed must save herself through language, by writing, and that she must not allow herself to become trapped like Minerva in circumstances that would make this impossible.

It should be said that parental and spousal abuse are not the only forms that violence takes in the novel. The brutal urban environment assaults innocence in other forms as well. In one of the most powerful segments, called "Geraldo No Last Name," it appears in the guise of brutal accident and this time the central victim is male. The Geraldo of the title is a young man who is not really known by the community of Mango Street; another of Esperanza's friends, Marin, meets him at a dance and is with him when he is fatally injured in a hit-and-run accident. She then waits at the hospital while he lies dying in the emergency room. Racial prejudice and economic injustice contribute to the anonymity of Geraldo's death: "Nobody but an intern working all alone. And maybe if the surgeon would've come, maybe if he hadn't lost so much blood, if the surgeon had only come, they would know who to notify and where" (p. 66). Cisneros is calling attention in this sketch to the financial "cutbacks" that have plagued most urban public hospitals, including Chicago's, over the past decade. She is also emphasizing that, to the dominant Anglo society, the death of an unknown young Chicano man is of no significance:

> They never saw the kitchenettes. They never knew about the two-room flats and sleeping rooms he rented, the weekly money orders sent home, the currency exchange. How could they?
> His name was Geraldo. And his home is in another country. The ones he left behind are far away, will wonder, shrug, remember. Geraldo—he went north . . . we never heard from him again. (p. 66)

It is in these two brief paragraphs that Cisneros's prose most directly communicates the poetic anger at senseless and unnecessary suffering that one finds in Tomás Rivera.

In *The House on Mango Street,* poverty and violence threaten to reduce everyone to anonymity; it is therefore essential that one find models of survival wherever possible in such a dangerous and unnatural world. Perhaps the text's most symbolically important sketch describes four unlikely such models. In "Four Skinny Trees," Esperanza describes her attachment to some trees planted by the city with the apparent intention of creating the illusion of a patch of benevolent nature within the concrete harshness of the urban streets. She insists that she communicates with the trees ("They are the only ones who understand me. I am the only one who understands them" [p. 74]). She and the "skinny trees with skinny necks and pointy elbows" are alike, she believes, and, in crucial ways, they are.

As do the trees, Esperanza represents innocence, hope, and affirmation artificially grafted onto a landscape of despair. Like the trees, she is not a "natural" outgrowth of the concrete city, but, also like them, she is ultimately strengthened by the challenge of survival: "Their strength is secret. They send ferocious roots beneath the ground. They grow up and they grow down and grab the earth beneath their hairy toes and bite the sky with violent teeth and never quit their anger. This is how they keep" (p. 74). The trees, while initially a gift of city officials to the barrio, survive by sending their roots beneath, and thus outside, the city. The earth in which they secure themselves has, of course, existed infinitely longer, and is thus more natural, than the steel and concrete that have arbitrarily been imposed on it. Like *Suttree, The House on Mango Street* provides a clear illustration of Arnold L. Goldsmith's ideas about the importance of nature in urban fictions.

In "Four Skinny Trees," the affirmative self that Esperanza finally creates is, to a large extent, rooted in normally negative emotions. She too learns that she must never "quit [her] anger." In this approach, "Four Skinny Trees" recalls a poem by the Harlem Renaissance writer Claude McKay. In "The White City," McKay's African American narrator asserts that white hatred has unwittingly shaped his identity:

> Deep in the secret chambers of my heart
> I muse my life-long hate, and without flinch
> I bear it nobly as I live my part.
> My being would be a skeleton, a shell,
> If this dark Passion that fills my every mood,
> And makes my heaven in the white world's hell,
> Did not forever feed me vital blood.[7]

There is, of course, a difference between "anger" and "hate"; still, "Four Skinny Trees" and "The White City" develop similar ideas. McKay's sonnet and Cisneros's "lazy poem" emphasize the necessity of passionate resistance to oppression, in fact, of using that resistance as the cornerstone of self-awareness rather than allowing one's identity to be destroyed. The overriding message of both texts is the same: to survive, one must embrace emotions that resist oppression.

"Four Skinny Trees" concludes by stressing the importance of sheer survival: "Four who grew despite concrete. Four who reach and do not forget to reach. Four whose only reason is to be and be" (p. 75). Esperanza will soon understand that "to be" means to write, to record one's personal triumph over violence and injustice. The four trees are artificially imposed on a landscape that is itself unnatural, just as the sketch and all of *The House on Mango Street,* and indeed all works of art, are artifacts, constructs representing transcendence of the human condition. Like other marginalized writers, Cisneros and McKay pursue triumph over the ridiculous brutality of socioeconomic repression as well as over the ultimate absurdity of death.

In addition to the four seemingly fragile but deceptively strong trees, the novel describes another endangered outpost of nature in the city. "The Monkey Garden," a retelling of the archetypal garden of Eden story, describes an abandoned garden that Esperanza and her friends convert into a playground after its former owners move away. In keeping with the sketch's emphasis on lost innocence, it is narrated from the perspective of the still childlike Esperanza struggling to resist the ominous advent of adulthood. The garden got its name from an actual monkey, a pet of the people who once lived there. Esperanza and the other children inevitably remember the monkey and not the people and ascribe to the animal a very human capacity for decisive action: "The monkey doesn't live there anymore. The monkey moved—to Kentucky—and took his people with him" (p. 94). Significantly, the move described here constitutes a reversal of a familiar pattern, economically desperate people being drawn to Chicago and other northern urban centers from the South by the hope of finding work. In much of "The Monkey Garden," the reader's expectations are reversed.

Sexuality in this sketch, as well as in much of the novel, is tied strongly to violence and represents therefore a threat to the safety of female characters; "The Monkey Garden" describes, in fact, Esperanza's doomed attempt to deny her own emerging sexuality. What should be a life-affirming force is transformed by poverty and the threat of male violence into something destructive and unnatural. The dominant imagery of the sketch echoes more than one classic analysis of American literature, most obviously Leo Marx's *The Machine and the Garden: Technology and the Pastoral in America* (1964). Nature in the children's adopted playground is simultaneously luxuriant and decayed: "There were sunflowers as big as flowers on Mars and thick cockscombs bleeding the deep red fringe of theater curtains. There were dizzy bees and bow-tied fruit flies turning somersaults and humming in the air. Sweet sweet peach trees. . . . There were big green apples hard as knees. And everywhere the sleepy smell of rotting wood, damp earth and dusty hollyhocks thick and perfumy like the blue-blond hair of the dead" (pp. 94–95).

Death in the monkey garden is not solely a process of natural decay and regeneration. Human beings have infringed upon the garden in pernicious and decidedly unnatural ways; Marx's machine, or more precisely its vestiges, is present here: "Dead cars appeared overnight like mushrooms. First one and then another and then a pale blue pickup with the front windshield missing. Before you knew it, the monkey garden became filled with sleepy cars" (p. 95). The description of the dead cars appearing "overnight like mushrooms" works on at least three metaphoric levels. First, the abandoned cars are, like some mushrooms, poisonous and have polluted what was once a pristine landscape. Moreover, they quickly become so numerous as to seem the garden's natural vegetation. Finally, the rusting automobiles are emblematic of a polluting and uncaring capitalism that makes life in the barrio almost impossible.

Appropriately, it is Sally who inspires the advent of sexuality into the garden and the foreground of Esperanza's awareness. When Sally permits a group of young boys to follow her there for a kiss, Esperanza is outraged and attempts to "rescue" her older friend and evict the boys from her child's sanctuary. She is dismayed when Sally tells her to go away, that she does not want to be rescued: "And then I don't know why but I had to run away. I had to hide myself at the other end of the garden, in the jungle part, under a tree that wouldn't mind if I lay down and cried a long time" (p. 97). Just as she did with the monkey, Esperanza is attributing a power of agency to the tree that it cannot, of course, possess. She desires to preserve the bond with nature she has always felt, and, in order to do so, she tries to retreat to the innocence of her childhood.

In its perversion of sexuality into brutal oppression of the female and in its destructive pollution of the environment, the adult world has virtually destroyed any possibility of redemption through nature. In the context of the implicit Garden of Eden symbolism in "The Monkey Garden," the tree beneath which Esperanza seeks shelter can hardly offer lasting sanctuary; it is a "tree of knowledge" for Esperanza, a complex trope signifying loss of innocence and new as well as old dangers in her environment. The sketch ends with a succinct statement of the corruption of the monkey garden as a viable sanctuary for her: "And the garden that had been such a good play to play didn't seem mine either" (p. 98). The lasting and defining image of nature for Esperanza must be the artificially created one, "the four skinny trees."

Significantly, "Red Clowns," the sketch that immediately follows "The Monkey Garden," describes Esperanza's own sexual initiation and, once again, Sally is the instigating force in the incident. To convey the fear and sheer ugliness that overwhelms the young narrator, Cisneros turns to language and imagery derived from literary and popular Gothicism. In describing the setting, she echoes the bizarre unreality that characterizes Edgar Allan Poe stories such as "The Masque of the Red Death" and "The Cask of Amontillado." Sally has taken Esperanza to a carnival only to desert her when a "big boy" asks her to follow him; as she leaves she instructs her younger companion to wait for her "by the red clowns." There is a tradition of popular "horror films" and television programs that incorporate clowns as ominous, psychopathic characters, and it is natural that this tradition would inform a contemporary American initiation novel. In these cultural artifacts, garish costume as emblem of grotesque disguise is a recurrent motif: the criminal hides his deadly persona inside a costume of gaiety.

At any rate, Esperanza is herself assaulted by a group of boys, and the language describing this ugly incident effectively conveys the terror and unreality of the experience, as well as the young narrator's disillusionment with the images of sexual romance that she has derived from American popular culture: "They all lied. All the books and magazines, everything that told it wrong. Only his dirty fingernails against my skin, only his sour smell again. The moon that watched. The tilt-a-whirl. The red clowns laughing their thick-tongue laugh" (p. 100). The reference to the tilt-a-whirl metaphorically communicates that Esperanza's life has been turned upside down and that long-established perspectives of her position in the world have been perverted and thus no longer offer comfort and assurance. The boy who initiates the assault of the narrator twice calls her "Spanish girl," signaling that he has bought into the cultural stereotype of Hispanic women as sexually promiscuous, as possessing a capacity for erotic pleasure of which their Anglo counterparts are incapable.

Interestingly, the text leaves ambiguous the ethnic identity of the boy himself, communicating perhaps the widespread American acceptance of this dehumanizing view of the Hispanic woman. The strong possibility exists, of course, that he and his companions are themselves Chicanos and are expressing the machismo of the barrio. Certainly, women are reduced to sexual objects throughout Cisneros's text.

Nevertheless Esperanza comes to accept an obligation to speak for her community. In fact, Cisneros emphasizes the role of the marginalized writer as spokesperson for a community that is otherwise deprived of voice; while Esperanza for most of the novel yearns to escape Mango Street, she gradually learns that such escape is both impossible and irresponsible. While poverty and violence may threaten her personally, she discovers that by surviving them she has become inextricably bound to her environment. The process of Esperanza's coming to understand this is the focus of the four sketches that conclude the text. In "The Three Sisters," she attends a funeral for the infant sister of her friends Lucy and Rachel. Afterward, she is approached by three women whom she has never seen before and who quickly communicate to her that they possess the gift of prophecy:

"Tomorrow it will rain."
"Yes, tomorrow," they said.

"How do you know?" I asked.
"We know." (p. 104)

Echoing such other legends as that of the Hispanic rain god, the three rather eccentric sisters are contemporary incarnations of "the three fates" of classical mythology and they proceed to tell Esperanza of her future and to convey to her her responsibilities to the community: "When you leave you must remember to come back for the others. A circle, understand? You will always be Esperanza. You will always be Mango Street. You can't erase what you know. You can't forget who you are. . . . You must remember to come back. For the ones who cannot leave as easily as you" (p. 105). The words of the sisters are essential to the sense of self that the young narrator ultimately constructs. She will soon understand that, while she will leave Mango Street physically, she cannot and should not want to forget what she experienced there. In her consciousness and in her spirit, she can no more escape Mango Street that she can stop being Esperanza and, indeed, she has been fated to become the voice, the "hope" of those who will remain trapped there.

Earlier in the text, she had learned never to "quit her anger" and, now, she is beginning to realize how to convert that anger into the affirmation of writing, of art. This prophetic sketch concludes by emphasizing the supernatural identity of the three sisters—they seem to vanish almost before Esperanza's very eyes, and she never sees them again. In the next sketch, she is shown to be still resisting their message, but a friend named Alicia reinforces it and in fact clarifies its implications:

> [Alicia:] Like it or not you are Mango Street, and one day you'll come back too.
> [Esperanza:] Not me. Not until somebody makes it better.
> [Alicia:] Who's going to do it? The mayor?
>   And the thought of the mayor coming to Mango Street makes me laugh out loud.
>   Who's going to do it? Not the mayor. (p. 107)

Like the three sisters, Alicia is assuming that Esperanza will succeed in leaving Mango Street physically; but, also like the three older women, she is communicating the truth that memory cannot escape experience. She is also telling her friend why the marginalized writer has no choice but to speak for her community. Politicians as agents of an exploitative capitalism have turned their backs on the community; thus artists must give voice to the concerns of its inhabitants. Of necessity, this voice will often be one of outrage, of anger. Cisneros thus confronts directly the issue of social protest and its importance in minority writing; while accepting such protest as an inescapable obligation, her text demonstrates that it is not antithetical to lyricism or to individuality. Like McKay, she proves that poetry can express "dark" passions.

The volume's penultimate sketch, "A House of My Own," echoes and thereby pays tribute to Virginia Woolf. In two brief paragraphs, the second consisting of only one sentence, Esperanza repeats her desire to live in her own place. The novel's feminist perspective, which is often merely implicit in the text, is stated overtly here: "Not a flat. Not an apartment in back. Not a man's house. Not a daddy's. A house all my own" (p. 108). The complex metaphoric significance of the dreamed-of house, as opposed to the house on Mango Street, is succinctly expressed in the sketch's concluding sentence: "Only a house quiet as snow, a space for myself to go, clear as paper before the poem" (p. 108). The imagined house is expressed as a physical dwelling, but, more important, as the private space in which to create a work that will realize Esperanza's emerging self. Thus, the "house of [her] own" is not the house on Mango Street, but it *is The House on Mango Street*. With the help of the three sisters and of Alicia, Esperanza has created a hopeful identity that affirms her race, her class, her gender, and her individuality. The space that was the paper before the poem is a metaphor for the space she needed to construct a text and a self.

The novel's concluding sketch, "Mango Says Goodbye Sometimes," effectively ties together the major strands in the three that precede it. It opens with an short, but important assertion by Esperanza: "I like to tell stories" (p. 109). In fact, Cisneros's text can be appreciated in the context of Walter Benjamin's distinctions between the roles of the storyteller and the novelist. In his influential essay "The Storyteller," Benjamin says that, in the twentieth century, storytelling as the legacy of oral cultures is dying, that it has been superseded by the novel, the narrative form of print cultures. Storytelling, he says, has traditionally been a communal function in which usually anonymous voices shape tales for the practical and moral enrichment of others. In contrast, the modern novel is the product of an isolated artist with no immediate ties to any community: "The storyteller takes what he tells from experience—his own or that reported by others. And he in turn makes it the experience of those who are listening to the tale. The novelist has isolated himself. The birthplace of the novel is the solitary individual, who is no longer able to express himself by giving examples of his most important concerns, is himself uncounseled, and cannot counsel others."[8]

For much of Cisneros's text, events seem to be conspiring to disqualify Esperanza from being, in Benjamin's sense, a storyteller. She has not isolated herself, but she, as a woman in a marginalized culture, is initially isolated, as indicated in her desire to escape Mango Street. But the counsel that she receives from the three sisters, Alicia, and others gives birth in her to an understanding of communal responsibility that finds expression in her stories. "Mango Says Goodbye Sometimes"—and thus *The House on Mango Street*—end with Esperanza asserting again that she will leave the community of her childhood because "I am too strong" to stay there, but this time significantly qualifying her assertion: "Friends and neighbors will say, What happened to that Esperanza? Where did she go with all those books and paper? Why did she march so far away? They will not know I have gone away to come back. For the ones I left behind. For the ones who cannot out" (p. 110).

Writing the stories of her personal struggle certainly, but also of the struggles of those around her, will be a form of liberating dialogue for her. She will construct an identity through words that evolve from her developing sense of an individual *and* a communal self. Even before the four concluding sketches, the essence of this realization has been expressed. In "Born Bad," Esperanza reads her poems to a dying aunt, who warns her against abandoning her writing because it will "keep [her] free" (p. 61). While not yet understanding what her aunt means, she senses its importance. In the ultimately serious, but still amusing, "Bums in the Attic," she vows not to become like the wealthy Anglos with expensive homes in the hills whose gardens her father tends: "People who live on hills sleep so close to the stars they forget those of us who live too much on earth" (p. 86). In the house that she will someday have, she will not forget the economically oppressed, vowing to turn its attic into a shelter for hobos: "Some days after dinner, guests and I will sit in front of a fire. Floorboards will squeak upstairs. The attic grumble. Rats? they'll ask. Bums, I'll say, and I'll be happy" (p. 87). The attic of Esperanza's imagined house will be a refuge for passing bums just as Cisneros's text voices the aspirations of oppressed Chicana women.

The House on Mango Street is narrated by a strong young woman who, by clinging to the image of the "four skinny trees" and by heeding the advice of some wise female counselors expresses, transcends, and even redeems the poverty and violence of her environment. Though her innocence is violated, her faith in her community and in her art is not destroyed. By substituting her "lazy poems" for the traditional narrative techniques of the novelist and by affirming the importance of individuality and community, Cisneros effectively merges Benjamin's "storyteller" and "novelist" prototypes. Esperanza will neither be bound by Mango Street nor abandon it for an existence "close to the stars" and removed from her people.

Chapter 6

Violence and the Immanence of the "Thing Unknown"

Cormac McCarthy's *Suttree*

Cormac McCarthy's *Suttree* (1979) contrasts with the other seven novels discussed here in that it subordinates consideration of racial and ethnic injustice to a vision of a spiritually barren urban wasteland. Still, the central characters in it are economically and, in a few cases racially, marginalized. Inevitably, their marginalization makes them especially vulnerable to the violence that permeates all levels of the wasteland. Early in the novel Gene Harrogate, an innocent given to outlandish and usually criminal schemes, passes beneath the open window of a house inhabited by a deranged and "viperous" evangelist. The evangelist shouts down a curse upon the astonished Harrogate: "Die! . . . Perish a terrible death with thy bowels blown open and black blood boiling from thy nether eye, God save your soul amen."[1] The evangelist's verbal assault is, in three ways, emblematic of *Suttree* and indeed of all of McCarthy's work. First, its deliberate rhetorical excess is in keeping with McCarthy's prose style, which has frequently been compared to Faulkner's (McCarthy's first four novels are set in Tennessee and depict socioeconomic environments comparable to the ones encountered in Faulkner's *As I Lay Dying, Light in August,* and *The Town*). Moreover, such writing falls clearly into the tradition of Southern Gothicism, as practiced not only by Faulkner, but by Edgar Allan Poe, Flannery O'Connor, and Carson McCullers. Most important, in its vindictive irrationality, the evangelist's curse expresses a dominant theme in McCarthy's fiction.

Harrogate pauses in his flight from the assaultive voice to look back for a moment. What he sees only adds to his fear and amazement: "The figure had wheeled to a new window the better to see the boy past his house and he leaned now with his face pressed to the glass, his dead jaundiced flesh splayed against the pane and one eye walled up in his head, a goggling visage misshaped with hatred. Harrogate went on. Great godamighty, he said" (p. 106). Deranged ministers and self-appointed prophets appear throughout McCarthy's novels, and they frequently pronounce cruel and inhumane judgments upon central characters who are uncertain about what, if anything, they have done to deserve such condemnation. While as might be expected in the work of a Southern Gothic novelist, McCarthy's characters (for example, the murderer and necrophiliac Lester Ballard in *Child of God* [1973]) have often done plenty, the violent judgments against them seem to antedate and in fact be irrelevant to their sins. They are trapped in a fallen, and demented world, in which god can only be understood as "dead" and "jaundiced," a creator driven mad by hatred of his or her creations. The evangelist's voice descends on Harrogate from above, and he flees in consternation from it. Truly, it does not matter that it is Harrogate who walks beneath the evangelist's window; the "goggling misshapen" prophet condemns equally all passersby. Thus, McCarthy's vision is not primarily of a structural or systemic violence, but of an all-encompassing violence, the origins of which are unknown and unknowable.

Though inexplicably neglected by the academic critical establishment, McCarthy has been fortunate in the quality of what has been written about his work. Still, as is inevitable with such a complex and resolutely unfashionable writer, the handful of commentators on his work disagree strongly about certain aspects of it; the harsh and arbitrary sentences beneath which his characters struggle have, for instance, inspired debate concerning the ethical overtones of his novels. In his book on McCarthy, Vereen M. Bell discusses *Suttree* as an intensely nihilistic work in which materiality and facticity overwhelm the theoretical.[2]

While admiring much about Bell's study, Edwin T. Arnold rejects its assertion that McCarthy's work is fundamentally nihilistic and argues that the alienated title character in *Suttree*, while possessing, in the language of the novel, a "good heart," suffers primarily because he is one of McCarthy's moral "neutrals": "in McCarthy's highly moralistic world, sins must be named and owned before they can be forgiven; and those characters who most insist on the 'nothingness' of existence, who attempt to remain 'neutral,' are those most in need of grace."[3] While Arnold's reading of McCarthy is especially sensitive and perceptive, it is necessary to say that his characters can scarcely name and receive forgiveness for their sins until they understand precisely what they are and that the issue of whether they can *ever* attain "grace" seems at best uncertain.

Suttree is atypical of McCarthy's work in three ways: its urban setting (Knoxville, Tennessee, during the years 1950 to 1955), its employment of an intellectual focal character, and its affirmative ending. But its focus on violence is representative of his fiction. In fact, McCarthy is one of the most dedicated and thorough students of the nature of violence among contemporary American novelists. His approach to this subject is quite different from that of the other seven writers treated here and indeed of most realistic and naturalistic protest writers. McCarthy echoes the "romances" of Poe, Hawthorne, and Melville in his vision of violence as a nonhuman, quasi-divine force that threatens to engulf whatever barriers mere mortals try to erect against it.

A brief impressionistic chapter introduces the novel and establishes the apocalyptic tone that dominates much of it: *"The night is quiet. Like a camp before a battle. The city is beset by a thing unknown and will it come from forest or sea? The murengers have walled the pale, the gates are shut, but lo the thing's inside and can you guess his shape? . . . Dear friend he is not to be dwelt upon for it is by just suchwise that he's invited in"* (pp. 4–5). It is worth noting that, with the important exception of its considerably more moderate and less hostile tone, the anonymous voice here recalls the words of the deranged evangelist who addresses Gene Harrogate from above his head. Again, there is the message of an impending doom, of a fatal judgment that cannot be comprehended, much less resisted. The rhetoric of the passage is a fascinating combination of biblical poetry and southern colloquialism ("just suchwise"), something of a McCarthy specialty. John M. Grammar identifies the threatening "thing unknown" as "human nature, an image of ourselves presented at the gates which we are compelled to take in and worship—and which turns, immediately, into our ruin."[4] This seems simultaneously accurate and insufficient as an analysis.

Certainly, the "unknown" threat to the city is less tangible than anything like consumerism, racism, gangs, or drugs; it is perhaps so fundamental as to defy specific labeling. One critic parallels Knoxville with the southern plantation as futile and doomed attempts to escape, to wall out, the flux of nature;[5] and another notes that, because of the surrounding profligacy of nature, the sheer fact of Knoxville, its very existence, seems arbitrary and temporary:

> East Tennessee is one of the most beautiful places on earth. Once outside the city there are green fields and rolling hills. Go far enough upstream or into certain tributaries, and the water becomes pure and cold. A little further away are the peaks and coves of the Great

Smokies. Truly every prospect pleases and only man is vile. Or, more accurately, man and his works: the abandoned mines, the junked cars, the rotting shacks, the endless shopping centers that rear their ugly heads.[6]

Knoxville, with a population in 1950 of only 124,769[7] was a fragile and comparatively recent creation of human beings and thus seems a doomed and unnatural intrusion into the luxuriant permanence of nature. It is precisely this permanence from which humans are excluded; and Suttree is constantly and agonizingly aware of this exclusion. As in *The House on Mango Street,* McCarthy's text illustrates Arnold L. Goldsmith's contention that a submerged pastoralism often provides an "interior structure" for American urban novels. The "thing unknown" that threatens its fictional Knoxville is essentially human impermanence—death as the irrevocable and astonishingly unjust pronouncement of an insane god who has withdrawn his grace from the human world. Mad false prophets have rushed into the void left by god's cruel denial of grace to his or her creations.

Traditional religion is almost never a source of comfort in McCarthy's fiction, which frequently posits a vengeful and wrath-filled god. In *Suttree,* the city of Knoxville is an attempt to wall out divine retribution; such an attempt is, of course, doomed, and violence functions as a pervasive proof of the futility of attempting such an escape. Realizing this, Cornelius Suttree, the rebel and outcast son of a prominent family, chooses to confront death and impermanence by living in McAnally Flats, a former slum area of Knoxville that is being demolished at the end of the novel to make way for a new freeway. At one point late in the novel, he reads from an old newspaper "last year's someday news already foxed and yellow," while drinking a cup of coffee and realizes the inexorable nature of human existence: "he poured the coffee and stirred in milk from a can and sipped and blew and read of wildness and violence across the cup's rim. As it was then, is now and ever shall" (p. 381).

Suttree is haunted by intrusions of a past that he attempts to block from his consciousness, just as the city has tried to wall out the "thing unknown." In McCarthy's world, memory is as impossible as nature to subdue, and Suttree's past constantly intrudes on his awareness. He can never forget, for instance, that he had a twin brother who died at birth, and he often appears to be motivated by guilt over the brother's death and his own survival. Choosing to live in McAnally Flats constitutes, in part, his attempt to embrace a fate parallel with that of his dead twin's: "Mirror image. Gauche carbon. He lies in Woodlawn, whatever be left of the child with whom you shared your mother's belly. He neither spoke nor saw nor does he now. Perhaps his skull held seawater. . . . And [I] used to pray for his soul days past. Believing this ghastly circus reconvened elsewhere for alltime. He is in the limbo of the Christian righteous, I in a terrestrial hell" (p. 14). The death of his twin is a constant reminder to Suttree not only of his own mortality, but of the arbitrary and irrational murder of human innocents and of human innocence.

A critical consensus exists that Suttree's living in McAnally Flats represents, in addition to the voluntary punishment of "a terrestrial hell," an embracing of authenticity,[8] but there is less agreement about what authenticity precisely is and about the intellectual legitimacy of such a desire.[9] While Suttree's denial of his intellectual and cultural advantages is in part a rebellion against the authoritarian society of his father, it is primarily tied to his flight from his past. On a more practical level, it is an essential move in keeping open the possibility of dialogue with his decidedly unscholarly companions. He can hardly discuss Kierkegaard with individuals who are barely, if at all, literate.[10]

Indeed, Suttree, and apparently McCarthy as well, attribute a superior honesty, a higher authenticity, to the urban lumpen proletariat than they grant the capitalist middle and upper classes. McCarthy celebrates, even romanticizes, Richard H. Lehan's urban diversity. Rather than attempt to flee the Other, his protagonist hopes to merge his identity with it. Whatever the abstract viability of this position, it works in the novel largely because the destitute and outcast classes experience on an immediate and everyday level the insatiable violence emanating from the "thing unknown" that threatens to engulf the city. Suttree has chosen to submerge his very Self, his existential identity, in the concrete manifestation of a primitive and absurd divine retribution.

He survives as a fisherman, dwelling in a houseboat on the Tennessee River that flows past the city. One should not, though, attempt to force a biblical parallel here; Suttree is locked in a desperate struggle to discover some means of personal salvation and can hardly offer himself as the savior of others. Moreover, the "good heart" that Arnold correctly attributes to him would prohibit his promising others a salvation in which he cannot himself believe. The text is crowded with passages describing, often in surrealistic language, the sordid nature of life in the slums of Knoxville, and several of these passages convey a sense of impending apocalypse.

In one, Suttree awakens in an abandoned field after having passed out the night before from drunkenness: "He lifted his swollen eyes to the desolation in which he knelt, the ironcolored nettles and sedge in the reeking fields like mock weeds made from wire, a raw landscape where half familiar shapes reared from the slagheaps of trash. . . . Tottering to his feet he stood reeling in that apocalyptic waste like some biblical relict in a world no one would have" (pp. 80–81). Retreating from the scene of his disgrace, he observes the bleak environment in which he finds himself: "These quarters he soon found to be peopled with the blind and deaf. Dark figures in yard chairs. Propped and rocking in the shade of porches. Old black ladies in flowered gowns who watched impassively the farther shapes of the firmament as he went by. Only a few waifs wide eyed and ebonfaced studied at all the passage of the pale victim of turpitude among them" (p. 81). This aged world of "the blind and deaf" has, it seems, long ago abandoned all hope of salvation; the language in these two passages—"desolation," "reeking fields," "slagheaps of trash," "dark figures," "pale victim"—works in a Poe-like manner to create an overwhelming sense of doom. Here especially one is reminded of the famous opening paragraph of "The Fall of the House of Usher."

McCarthy's work is rich in allusion to other writers, and especially to T. S. Eliot.[11] The Eliot echoes are especially relevant to the thematic center of *Suttree*. Like Hemingway, Fitzgerald, and the other great American modernists, McCarthy writes out of a "Waste Land" vision of a fallen secular world in which, as Lady Brett Ashley in Hemingway's *The Sun Also Rises* says, god, if present at all, "doesn't work very well" for human beings. In contrast to the formula for human salvation that concludes Eliot's *The Waste Land,* Suttree, after great agony, discovers only a guide to his individual reconciliation with and forbearance of the world. He is a kind of Fisher King, who belatedly manages to see past the "fragments [he has] shored against [his] ruins."

As everyone notes, the river works in the novel as a major, and quite complex, symbol.[12] Certainly it represents flux and change, the primal force that prevents the establishment of lasting human order; and it is unmistakably another echo of Eliot. After the apocalyptic preface with its prophecy of a threatening "thing unknown," the novel opens with the body of a suicide being fished out of the river; in McCarthy's world, as in Eliot's, one should dread "death by water." Most important, the river in *Suttree* seems a metaphor for the protagonist's past, which he has tried to push deep into his subconscious, the extensive pollution of the river symbolizing the intellectual and spiritual waste of a life that prohibits, until the end, any clarity of vision or understanding.

As is typical of the narrative mode of the novel, McCarthy goes into considerable detail in documenting the extent of the waste that fouls the river: "[Suttree] watched idly surface phenomena, gouts of sewage faintly working, gray clots of nameless waste and yellow condoms roiling slowly out of the murk like some giant form of fluke or tapeworm. The watcher's face rode beside the boat, a sepia visage yawing in the scum. . . . A welt curled sluggishly on the river's surface as if something unseen had stirred in the deeps and small bubbles of gas erupted in oily spectra" (p. 7). According to John Lewis Longley, Jr., the actual Tennessee River in the 1950s offered McCarthy a perfect model for a degenerate past and a contaminated consciousness:

> The Tennessee River at this time was arguably one of the filthiest streams in North America. . . . It was heavily polluted by industry, and by human debris in general. Because of the dams, there are many backwaters, and the water ebbs or flows only as the river level changes. Because of this, flotsam and jetsam that backs up out of the main stream may stay around for days or even years. This includes trees, crates and boxes, discarded light bulbs, used condoms, and the random dead body. (p. 81)

In the novel's present tense, Suttree has attempted to drown his past sins and failures in his subconscious, but, like the "human debris" that floats to the top of the river, they are sometimes forced to the surface of his mind. His most painful memories are family-related, especially concerning the conflict with his father and the failure of his marriage and subsequent abandonment of his wife and son. In keeping with the image of a river so polluted that one fears to look closely at the objects floating on it, the text keeps the details of Suttree's past life obscure. For instance, we are told virtually nothing about what occasioned his break with his father; still, from what little we do know, it seems safe to assume that his father was autocratic, harsh, and judgmental, a kind of sane, secular version of the mad evangelist who condemns Harrogate.

Nevertheless, Suttree clearly feels some pain over the break, though much of it may, in fact, be displaced guilt from the failure of his marriage. He is haunted by dreams throughout the novel, and an early one effectively establishes a link between his conflict with his father and his guilt over abandoning his son:

> in a dream I was stopped by a man I took to be my father, dark figure against the shadowed brick. I would go by but he has stayed me with

his hand. I have been looking for you, he said. The wind was cold, dreamwinds are so. I had been hurrying. I would draw back from him and his bone grip. The knife he held severed the pallid lamplight like a thin blue fish and our footsteps amplified themselves in the emptiness of the streets to an echo of routed multitudes. Yet it was not my father but my son who accosted me with such rancorless intent. (p. 28)

The manner in which Suttree's failed marriage is treated exemplifies the text's shadowy account of the protagonist's past. All we know is that, until he left her, he truly loved his beautiful wife with her luxuriant black hair. When he learns of his son's death, significantly through a phone call from his father that he does not directly receive, he immediately boards a train to return to his one-time home for the funeral. The passage through "various small mountain towns" recalls, in its dominant imagery, the fiction of Thomas Wolfe, and Suttree learns quickly and painfully that he truly cannot go home again. The pain and rage that his mere presence inspires in his wife and her parents exceed any facts we are given concerning Suttree's behavior during the marriage.

His wife, appearing like an embodiment of grief itself, silently approaches him and asks that he leave immediately. As often in the novel, the language here has overt biblical overtones: "She came down the steps slowly, madonna bereaved, so grief-stunned and wooden pieta of perpetual dawn, the birds were hushed in the presence of this gravity and the derelict that she had taken for the son of light himself was consumed in shame like a torch" (p. 150). To her, Suttree seems to have transformed himself from Christ, "the son of light," to Lucifer, the "son of the morning" in Isaiah. The reactions of her parents are even more intense. Her mother literally attacks him: "her bitter twisted face looming, axemark for a mouth and eyes crazed with hatred. She tied to speak but only a half strangled scream came out. The girl was thrown aside and this demented harridan was at him clawing, kicking, gurgling with rage" (pp. 150–51). In the sheer insane excess of this reaction, the woman recalls the mad evangelist and is thus another of the novel's voices of a vindictive divinity.

After Suttree physically subdues the mother-in-law, he looks up to see her husband rushing out of the house with a shotgun and flees in fear for his life. One can surmise that Suttree's rebelliousness and his excessive drinking contribute to the emotions his mere presence evokes in this scene. But such behavior, destructive though it must have been, seems insufficient to explain the intensity of the reactions of his former wife and her parents, and critics have sought further explanation.[13] But the text does not permit a full understanding of the scene. After being forced to watch the actual funeral from a distance, he kneels before the open grave after all the other mourners have left and "[p]erhaps he addressed his God" (p. 154). If he did, there was, as usual, no affirming or healing answer.

He then rejects the assistance of the gravediggers and insists upon filling in his son's grave by himself. It is as if having been unable to prevent the intrusion of the past upon his present existence, he must attempt to bury it once again. Leaving the cemetery, he is picked up by the local sheriff, who accuses him of having "ruined" his wife's life and then tells him to leave town and never return: "You, my good buddy, are a fourteen carat gold plated son of a bitch. That's what your problem is. And that being your problem, there's not a whole lot of people in sympathy with you. Or with your problem" (p. 156). Again, we are left to guess precisely how Suttree ruined his life, but, in the present tense of the narrative, he is not a "son of a bitch," but rather, as Arnold says, a man of "good heart" who cares for and is often forced into ridiculous positions by his fellow inhabitants of the "terrestrial hell" of McAnally Flats. Suttree's "problem" is much more complex than the sheriff suggests. He has obviously sinned against his wife and son, but he has, like all of McCarthy's people, been judged with a harshness that exceeds his or anyone's capacity for sin. Returning to Knoxville, he once again embraces McAnally Flats and, until near the end of the novel, a nihilistic code best expressed by an embittered old ragman who says that, while he believes in a god, he simply does not "like him" (p. 147). One exchange of dialogue between Suttree and the ragman is especially relevant. In it, the ragman asks the protagonist what he would like to say to his creator should they ever meet and then gives his own answer: "I'd say: Wait a minute. Wait just one minute before you start in on me. Before you say anything, there's just one thing I'd like to know. And he'll say: What's that? And then I'm goin to ast him: What did you have me in that crapgame down there for anyway? I couldnt put any part of it together." When Suttree asks the ragman what he thinks god's answer would be, the embittered old man responds: "I don't believe he can answer it. . . . I don't believe there is an answer" (p. 258).

And indeed there is no final, universal answer to, no clear explanation for, the pain and alienation suffered not only by the destitute of McAnally Flats, but also by all human beings. There is only the possibility of existential choice, of confronting the sheer absurdity of death's final decay and alienation should one be strong enough to do so. Ultimately, Suttree, through his involvement with and concern for his fellow outcasts, is. His existential choice, which is in the process of being formulated throughout the novel, is essentially to escape the sins of his past by attempting to alleviate the problems of his outlandish circle of friends. According to Bell, Suttree, after freeing himself from "sentimental regret," gains "perspective, which is at least *like* transcendence" (pp. 100–101). But "like" it only in a most limited way. McCarthy's protagonist must realize that there are no permanent answers in a universe abandoned by god and then accept the fellowship that comes through bonding with those around him.

Critics have discussed *Suttree* as a naturalistic as well as an existentialist text,[14] and, in its treatment of setting and character, it recalls to a degree the work of Stephen Crane, Frank Norris, and, perhaps most of all, Nelson Algren. For the most part, it is an example of what Blanche H. Gelfant terms the urban "ecological" novel in that it focuses upon an area of a city that, for any meaningful purpose, is cut off from its immediate surroundings.[15] Certainly, the kind of dismissal of McAnally Flats and its residents articulated by Suttree's father negates the possibility of dialogue between the slum and the middle-class sections of Knoxville. Setting is intensely concrete and deterministic in McCarthy's novel. The novel contains numerous secondary characters: according to Arnold "over one hundred fifty named characters . . . some of whom appear for one time only and others who weave in and out of the story" (p. 55). Moreover, they do not always have the same names when they appear.[16] The sheer number of these supporting figures and the randomness with which they are introduced add to the sense of chaos that pervades the text.

Those who live along the polluted river are trapped in pointless and brutal lives; most of them, while not as articulate as the old ragman, share his cynicism. Daddy Watson, an old man who once worked for the railroad and also stole rides on boxcars, tells Suttree that he has given up on reading newspapers because of the stories of violence contained in them: "I never read one but what somebody aint been murdered or shot or somethin such as that. I never knowed such a place for meanness." Precisely what place the old railroader is talking about isn't clear—it might be McAnally Flats, it might be Knoxville, but most probably it is simply the world suffering under god's absurd judgment. Watson then recalls the train wrecks, the natural catastrophes, that, unlike murders, will "make ye think about things" (p. 180). He fondly remembers one specific disaster that was not a natural catastrophe, but in fact an accident that he himself caused.

During the "[d]ead of winter," Watson traveled in a boxcar through the snow-covered Colorado mountains. After lighting a cigarette, he threw the match on the floor of the car, which inexplicably caught fire. Forcing open the door, he looked out to see that "we was goin up this grade through the mountains in the snow with the moon on it and it was just blue lookin and dead quiet out there and them big old black pine trees goin by." He leapt to safety on a snowbank, and ever since has remembered the eerie beauty of the experience: "what I'm goin to tell you you'll think peculiar but it's the god's truth. That was in nineteen and thirty-one and if I live to be a hunnerd year old I don't think I'll ever see anything as pretty as that train on fire goin up that mountain and around the bend and them flames lightin up the snow and the trees and the night" (p. 182). The railroader evokes a vision of a clean white world purified even further by fire; that, however, is not "the god's truth" of his present life in an abandoned shack beside a polluted river. It is significant that, even in this treasured memory, Watson accidentally started the fire; even the most gentle of McCarthy's people carry the seeds of destruction with them everywhere.

In contrast to Daddy Watson, who lives through memory, Ab Jones lives for a just, but quixotic, cause. A proud and defiant black man, he has been fighting a private war with the white police for almost forty years. At one point, he tells Suttree about the origins of his crusade. He says that he went to work on the river at the age of twelve and, when he was about fourteen, a white man shot him "cause I whipped him. I didnt know no better." Later the white man was murdered and Jones was arrested for the crime and severely beaten while in jail: "That was my first acquaintance of the wrath of the path." He was eventually cleared of the murder, but his anger at the unjust and brutal treatment he received has not abated, even though he knows that he can never effectively avenge himself: "These bloods down here think it's somethin to whip up on police. They think that's really somethin. Shit. You aint got nothin for it but a busted head. You caint do nothin with them motherfuckers. I wouldnt fight em at all if I could keep from it" (p. 204).

But Jones cannot "keep from it," and the inevitable soon occurs. He provokes a senseless fight with two white policemen and is killed. Bell perceptively comments that "Ab's conflict with the police seems vaguely theological, as if he had displaced his resentment toward an unapparent God onto His tangible and all too willing emissaries on earth" (p. 82). In fact, Jones, like Suttree, is rebelling against a cruel sentence emanating from a vindictive god and a corrupt human society. Jones understands, but will not accept, the absurd reality that, because he is African American, he must live a life of persecution; Suttree comprehends, but rejects, the fact that, because he is human, he cannot escape suffering and death. McCarthy does not treat racism here as do most protest writers; Bell is correct in his analysis that racial hatred in the novel is not simply a matter of human ignorance and prejudice, but is even more fundamentally a manifestation of god's hatred and repudiation of human beings. There is never a shortage of vicious people to enforce the vindictive will of god and society. Suttree's bond with Jones makes sense then; they are both rebels against cruel and powerful authority.

There is much less purpose and meaning in the violent life and death of another of Suttree's McAnally Flats associates, Billy Ray Callahan, who simply likes to fight, once having in Suttree's presence subdued a dangerous killer terrorizing a roomful of men. His death is virtually a textbook example of existential absurdity. In the Moonlite Diner, he is accused by the barman of stealing money from the purses of the female customers. Billy Ray does not take the accusation seriously: "Callahan rocked back on his heels with his hooligan smile. . . . His pockets were full of the stolen change spoken, he'd drunk their drinks. You're a damned liar, he said good-naturedly" (p. 375). Then astonishingly the barman shoots him in the face, and he dies a few hours later in the hospital "unattended" (p. 377). As McCarthy's prose makes clear, Callahan's death exemplifies the kind of pointless, random violence that permeates naturalistic fiction: "Curious the small and lesser fates that join to lead a man to this. The thousand brawls and stoven jaws, the clubbings and the broken bottles and the little knives that come from nowhere. . . . These small enigmas of time and space and death" (pp. 375–76).

Callahan's devotion to brawling is obviously not an existential rebellion in the same sense as Suttree's or even Jones's; it lacks any element of the cerebral, the rational, it is simply a lust for physical conflict. Two other memorable characters are comic grotesques, recalling comparable figures in Algren's *The Man with the Golden Arm* (1949) and *A Walk on the Wild Side* (1956). Leonard, a "pale and pimpled part-time catamite," enlists Suttree's aid in disposing of his father's corpse after he and his mother have, for six months, kept the body hidden in their house in order to keep drawing the deceased man's welfare checks. Belatedly, Leonard has begun to realize the dilemma in which he and his mother have trapped themselves: "Listen Sut. We're painted into a corner anyways. I mean what if we was to just call up and say he died. I mean hell fire, you caint fool them guys. Them guys is doctors. They take one look at him and know for a fact he's been dead six months" (p. 243).

Initially, Suttree refuses his companion's request to help him dump the father's body in the river, but, when Leonard unexpectedly appears at his houseboat with the corpse in a stolen car, he feels that he has no choice but to go along with the absurd scheme. On his boat in the middle of the river, he asks Leonard if he doesn't plan to "say a few words" before dumping the corpse overboard. The hardly bereaved son is initially baffled ("This old son of a bitch never went to church in his life"), but then asks, "[w]hat about that part that goes through the shadow of the valley of death. You know any of that?" (p. 251). Truly, however comic they may at times seem, all of McCarthy's characters are trapped in "the shadow of the valley of death."

Even after the chain-wrapped body has been dumped overboard, the saga of Leonard's dead father does not end. Leonard reappears in the novel in even worse than usual physical condition ("he had gonorrhea of the colon and was otherwise covered with carbuncles") and informs Suttree that he is in legal trouble. His father's corpse somehow rose to the surface of the river and was discovered by the authorities: "He come up, Sut. Draggin all them chains with him." Suttree's response is significant: "Fathers will do that" (p. 417). After Leonard's mother bought a grave plot, the father was at last buried (without chains, one assumes). But, as Leonard informs McCarthy's protagonist, a new complication has arisen—his mother has fallen behind on her payments on the burial plot and the undertaker is threatening repossession, which would necessitate digging up his father's body. As Suttree's comment about fathers rising again signals, the difficulty in disposing of the corpse of Leonard's father is, in the tradition of black comedy, a comic symbol of Suttree's inability to suppress completely the pain of his past.

As memorable as "the part-time catamite" is, Gene Harrogate is the novel's most unforgettable comic grotesque. The text frequently refers to him as "the country mouse," and he functions as both a realistic and an emblematic figure symbolizing the innocence of Suttree and the other residents of McAnally Flats. To a degree, the concept of innocence that underlies *Suttree*, as Mark Winchell points out, echoes John Steinbeck and other social protest writers. Like the characters in Steinbeck's *Tortilla Flat* and *Cannery Row*, Harrogate is immune to the corruptions of the dominant capitalist society because he lives on its fringes and is denied full participation in it. In this way, he recalls Nelson Algren's "unincapable punk," Sparrow Saltskin of *The Man with the Golden Arm*. There is, of course, real potential for authorial condescension in this kind of approach, but, like Steinbeck and Algren at their best, McCarthy manages to avoid it. Moreover, as mentioned, the pervasive darkness of *Suttree* works to keep the text's potential sentimentality under control.

Suttree and the reader first meet Harrogate in the county workhouse to which he has been sentenced for sexually assaulting melons in an open field. After the nature of his crime has become public knowledge as well as the source of considerable entertainment among the other prisoners, he discusses the episode with Suttree:

[Harrogate:] They tried to get me for beast, beast . . .
[Suttree:] Bestiality?
[Harrogate:] Yeah. But my lawyer tole em a watermelon wasnt no beast. He was a smart son of a bitch. (p. 49)

For the rest of the novel, Suttree assumes a kind of paternal responsibility for this "convicted pervert of a botanical bent" (p. 54). This involves no small expenditure of time and energy since, like Algren's Sparrow, Harrogate conceives of one ridiculous and usually criminal scheme after another. Most memorably, Suttree has to rescue him after one of the most improbable attempts at bank robbery in American literature. Harrogate learns that a network of largely unexplored caves lies beneath the city of Knoxville and enters it armed with dynamite, planning to blow up the floor of a bank from the cave beneath it. Instead he explodes a sewer main and almost drowns in the city's waste.

Like Leonard's attempt to dispose of his father's corpse, this ridiculous episode has serious symbolic overtones. The text details in graphic fashion Suttree's search through the caves for Harrogate: "[He] pressed on, down the carious undersides of the city, through black and slaverous cavities where foul liquors seeped. He had not known how hollow the city was" (p. 276). It would be difficult to miss the origins of Suttree's journey underground in classical Western mythology, and the reference to the city's hollowness seems another of the text's many echoes of T. S. Eliot. Moreover, Harrogate's story ends on a decidedly serious note. He attempts to rob a store and is, of course, captured: "White lights crossed like warring swords the little grocery store and back, his small figure tortured there cringing and blinking as if he were being burnt. He dove headlong through a plateglass window and fetched up stunned and bleeding at the feet of a policeman who stood with a cocked revolver at his head saying: I hope you run. I wish you would run" (p. 439). We last see Harrogate staring out of the window of a train taking him away to the penitentiary, belatedly realizing the desperation of his future.

Suttree adopts Harrogate in part as a substitute for his dead son. In addition, as with Ab Jones and Leonard, his essentially compassionate nature gives a sense of responsibility for the hopeless city mouse. This inherent decency is an essential element in the protagonist's being able to make a truce with the absurdity of divine judgment during "a season [in Knoxville and McAnally Flats] of death and epidemic violence" (p. 416). Ironically, what is perhaps the novel's most senseless and cruel death is central to this resolution. Suttree falls in love and has an affair with a beautiful and innocent young woman named Wanda, the daughter of a mussel fisherman with whom Suttree briefly goes into partnership. She reminds him of his ex-wife and revives his sense of the beauty of the world. But Suttree is jarred awake one night in the fishing camp when, during a storm, a large wall of slate collapses upon and crushes Wanda. He hears her mother screaming "Oh God" and thinks "she meant for him to answer" (p. 362). There is no answer, of course, and Suttree retreats for a time to his former emotionless passivity, drifting into an affair with a prostitute until his own indifference and the madness inherent in the woman's profession destroy it.

At the end, though, he undergoes a cathartic self-examination and makes his existential truce with an absurd universe. *Suttree* echoes not only Eliot's *The Waste Land,* but his "Gerontion" as well. While hardly an old man, McCarthy's protagonist struggles "to meet [god] upon this honestly." Almost dying of typhoid, he is hospitalized and has several days of surrealistic visions; in them he encounters his old companions from McAnally Flats ("the murdered are first to embrace him" [p. 456]) and ultimately "the archetypal patriarch himself unlocking with enormous keys the gates of Hades" (p. 457). In recounting his protagonist's vision of hell, McCarthy's prose luxuriates in that richness that some critics find excessive:

> A floodtide of screaming fiends and assassins and thieves and hirsute buggers pours forth into the universe, tipping it slightly on its galactic axes. The stars go rolling down the void like redhot marbles. These simmering sinners with their cloaks smoking carry the Logos itself from the tabernacle and bear it through the streets while the absolute prebarbaric mathematick of the western world howls them down and shrouds their ragged biblical forms in oblivion. (pp. 457–58)

Yet, in the midst of his surrealistic vision of "the terrestrial hell" in which he exists, Suttree understands a central truth: "I know all souls are one and all souls lonely" (p. 459). When he awakens from the fever that has almost killed him, a priest asks if he would like to confess and he responds, "I did it" (p. 461). If Suttree is condemned by an insane divine judgment, he takes comfort in the fact that all human beings have been so unfairly judged. Released from the hospital, he returns home and, along the way, passes beneath the window of the mad evangelist, but, this time, the voice from overhead is silent: "Old broken Thersites would have called down from his high window but he was not well these latter days. . . . The eunuch was asleep in his chair and he stirred and mumbled fitfully as if the departing steps of the fisherman depleted his dreams but he did not awake" (p. 469).

The city remains threatened by the thing unknown, but Suttree's epiphany allows him at last to ignore the threat. Violence as the manifestation of divine apocalypse may overtake him at any moment, just as it does Ab Jones, Billy Ray Callahan, Wanda, and even that perennial innocent Gene Harrogate; but for now Suttree is safe. In McCarthy's world, such temporary refuge is all that is possible. The essence of Suttree's final vision is succinctly stated by a minor character in McCarthy's screenplay *The Gardener's Son:* "If men were no more just than God there'd be no peace in this world. Everywhere I look I see men trying to set right the inequities that God left them with."[17]

Chapter 7

Redemptive Landscape, Malevolent City

Scott Momaday's *House Made of Dawn*

Spiritual despair and alienation are central to N. Scott Momaday's 1968 *House Made of Dawn,* which is now widely recognized as having inaugurated a renaissance in Native American literature. Certainly its winning the 1969 Pulitzer Prize for fiction represented a major breakthrough in the critical recognition of an emerging and impressive body of writing. Yet Momaday's novel differs in important ways from those of James Welch, Louise Erdrich, Leslie Marmon Silko, and Gerald Vizenor that followed it into print; Andrew Wiget writes in his 1985 study *Native American Literature* that *House Made of Dawn* "is more European in form and style and more urban in setting than any other Native American novel."[1]

In its incorporation of existentialist and naturalist elements into an individual quest narrative, *House Made of Dawn* most clearly anticipates James Welch's *Winter in the Blood* (1974) and *The Death of Jim Loney* (1979) among major Native American novels. Yet the concluding rejection of the plot of decline and the urban setting of a large segment in Momaday's text contrasts with the two Welch fictions. As Wiget suggests, Momaday writes from the most discernible urban sensitivity of any Native American Renaissance figure, though he ultimately rejects the city, treating it as a synecdoche for white, capitalist oppression. *House Made of Dawn,* like much Native American literature, celebrates the redemptive nature of a lost pastoralism, establishing a sharp contrast between a healing natural world and the dehumanizing city. Thus, while its Western narrative and thematic elements are clearly foregrounded, a variation of Edward W. Said's concept of "contrapuntal reading" can usefully be applied to Momaday's novel.

If on an initial reading of *House Made of Dawn* one is more aware of such "Western" elements as naturalism, the quest motif of classical mythology, and existentialism, the text finally valorizes Native American values of resistance to oppression. *House Made of Dawn* can even be said to add a new level to Said's concept of contrapuntal reading—not only does it initially appear to affirm an imperialist consciousness only to negate it, but it incorporates values of two separate cultures of resistance. Momaday is of Kiowa descent, and Kiowa mythology and folklore are central to his text, but the novel's setting is the Jemez Pueblo reservation in New Mexico, where Momaday's parents taught and which he has described as "the last best home of [his] childhood."[2] Thus, Kiowa plains and Southwestern Jemez sensibilities work throughout the novel to cancel the dominant and dominating Western imperialist values.

Again, in a manner suggested by Said, geography is crucial to *House Made of Dawn;* Said writes that "imperialism and the culture associated with it affirm both the primacy of geography and an ideology about control of territory. The geographical sense makes projections—imaginative, cartographic, military, economic, historical, or in a general sense cultural. It also makes possible the construction of various kinds of knowledge, all of them in one way or another dependent upon the perceived character and destiny of a particular geography" (p. 78). Contrast and conflict between a materialistic and technological imperialist geography on one hand and a spiritual geography of resistance are central to Momaday's text.[3] Vernon E. Lattin was one of the first critics to point to the novel's depiction of a Native American vision of a healing landscape. He writes that *House Made of Dawn* and *Bless Me Ultima* (1972), by the Chicano writer Rudolfo Anaya, are seminal texts valorizing an isolated minority culture threatened by white technology and Christianity: "Anaya and Momaday have created a new romanticism, with a reverence for the land, a transcendent optimism, and a sense of mythic wholeness."[4]

As several critics have subsequently pointed out, Abel's quest for spiritual wholeness can only be successful when he realizes that the land in and surrounding the Pueblo reservation in New Mexico where he was born and grew up is restorative and indeed sacred.[5] The most extensive and perceptive discussion of landscape as a source of healing in *House Made of Dawn* can be found in a recent study by Robert M. Nelson of Momaday's novel, Leslie Marmon Silko's *Ceremony* (1977), and James Welch's *The Death of Jim Loney* (1979). In *Place and Vision: The Function of Landscape in Native American Fiction,* Nelson asserts that while "the canonized postmodern protagonist" suffers from the "disease" of "alienation," "the protagonists of these three novels (as in many other postwar American Indian texts) acquire the blessing of a cure.... [T]he antidote to alienation and its consequences in these works is . . . a rather old-fashioned-looking but still potent vaccine: geographical realism."[6]

In Momaday's text, Abel is slow to come to realize the redemptive power of the land in part because he is removed from it by two experiences involving violence and death. In both cases, he is controlled by the power of white civilization. He is initially separated from the land by the horror of World War II; the novel opens in 1945 with his return to the reservation from that bloody conflict in a state of drunken helplessness. In the war, he has been something of a hero, though the novel's only direct account of his heroism contains unmistakable overtones of a mad self-destructiveness. The text suggests that, like Silko's Tayo in *Ceremony*, he has been unable to bear the brutality and violence of the holocaust in which he has been submerged. Both Momaday and Silko treat the war with its technological horrors as a trope for the nineteenth-century genocide of the American Indian.[7] In *House Made of Dawn*, the landscape of Abel's war experiences functions, as does a comparable one for Nick Adams in "Big, Two-Hearted River," as an elided setting and a suppressed chronotope. As Alan R. Velie points out, Abel in *House Made of Dawn* is modeled in part on Ira Hayes, "the Pima Marine who became famous when he helped raise the flag on Iwo Jima but who could not readjust to life on the reservation and died of exposure while drunk" (p. 162). The fictional Abel comes very close to experiencing the same fate as the real Hayes.

Abel's second period of exile from the reservation is the result of another immersion in violence and death, his killing of the albino in the novel's most complex and surrealistic scene. This almost allegorical scene is crucial to the transition into part 2, the urban segment, of the novel, which opens with Abel's struggling to regain consciousness after having received a very real and almost fatal beating from a policeman in Los Angeles. Thus, the city is seem from the first as a violent and repressive environment.

It is necessary to say that the two parts of the text's structuring land-city dichotomy do not constitute total binary oppositions. After all, its most direct and extended episode of violence, Abel's killing of the albino, occurs on the reservation, and the protagonist does find some acceptance and even love in Los Angeles, though not enough to enable him to stay there and attain the spiritual redemption he seeks. This central ambiguity is, of course, a defining characteristic of literary modernism, and *House Made of Dawn* is a quite modernist text. Momaday, in a device reminiscent of such writers as Faulkner, tells much of his story through suspect and sometimes clearly inadequate narrative voices.

The city, in his novel, is almost entirely imperialist space, but the reservation and the surrounding countryside are spiritually, if not physically, contested spaces. Inside the reservation, one encounters the nominal control of the Catholic priest, Father Olguin, the voice of the capitalist, hierarchical Catholic Church, but quickly senses the spiritual power of Native American resistance, as personified in Francisco, Abel's grandfather. The reservation and the city are each represented by important secondary characters, with two characters, Angela Grace St. John and the albino, serving on a literal and metaphoric level respectively as figures linking the land and the city. Still, the text's underlying contrast of a benevolent and redemptive land and a destructive city is not seriously compromised by its modernist ambiguity.

House Made of Dawn opens with a brief prologue that begins with the Jemez word "dypaloh," which Momaday identifies in *The Names* as "a conventional formula for beginning a story."[8] Opening the novel with an Indian word serves more than one purpose for Momaday. It signals to the white middle-class reader a shift from a customary narrative and consequently a reversal of traditional values and expectations. The narrative perspective in this prologue, unlike much of the rest of the text, is extradiegetic and thus indicates that the text is controlled by a Native American perspective. In addition, it immediately signals that Momaday's text will be concerned with language and words, with logos, although this focus will not become overt until part 2 of the novel.

Following this brief incantation, the opening paragraph consists of a lyrical vision of the land surrounding the Jemez Pueblo reservation: "There was a house made of dawn. It was made of pollen and of rain, and the land was very old and everlasting. There were many colors on the hills, and the plain was bright with different-colored clays and sands. Red and blue and spotted horses grazed in the plain, and there was a dark wilderness on the mountains beyond. The land was still and strong. It was beautiful all around."[9] The language here conveys that the land has survived and will continue to survive the white invasion. The references to pollen and rain signal that an ongoing cycle of renewal is in effect, and the words "old" and "everlasting" convey that the land existed centuries before it was occupied by whites. A vision of redemptive pastoralism is clearly foregrounded in Momaday's text.

The first chapter of the story proper introduces Francisco, the novel's most completely sympathetic character. It will be Francisco who plays the key role in his grandson's spiritual redemption; just before he dies, he will convince Abel to run, both literally and figuratively, toward, rather than away from, his tribal legacy. Francisco's death, in fact, inspires a transformation in Father Olguin, who seems to come to a belated recognition of the limitations of his harsh and authoritarian faith. Previously, Olguin has functioned most importantly as a conduit for a voice that expresses, with no ambivalence whatsoever, the white church's, and thus the invading white civilization's, contempt for the paganism of the Indian culture. Olguin discovers a journal kept, in the late nineteenth century, by a predecessor, Fray Nicolas, in which are recorded significant events in the history of the Jemez Pueblo reservation, most important, the birth of the albino, as well as Nicolas's resentment and fear of tribal customs and traditions and his equating of Francisco with them.

After learning near the end of the novel that Nicolas is, in fact, Francisco's father, one understands that much of the old priest's bitterness was for having fathered such an unashamedly pagan offspring. Still, Francisco seems to have transcended his ancestry, as well as his father's and his own transgressions, through an absorption in Native American traditions and mythology. In contrast, Abel attempts to avoid such an immersion for most of the novel.

The information about the albino's birth contained in Nicolas's diary is needed to avoid what would be an unnecessary level of ambiguity in what is already the most complex part of Momaday's text. At no point in *House Made of Dawn* is Said's contrapuntal mode of reading more necessary than in attempting to come to grips with this complex and symbolic figure. In fact, the albino is more symbol than real, more abstraction than man. Just as Fray Nicolas did with Francisco, Abel projects his anger, confusion, and fear onto the albino, who humiliates him in the tribal ceremony of the chicken pull.

Matthias Schubnell has written informatively about the origins and significance of the chicken pull in Jemez Pueblo culture: "This activity was introduced by the Spaniards and adopted by many of the southwestern tribes. The Rio Grande Pueblos view the insertion of the rooster into the ground and its subsequent removal as a symbolic representation of planting and reaping. The scattering of the rooster's feathers and blood are representative of rain and are believed to increase the fertility of the land and the success of the harvest."[10] The essence of the ceremony is that a live rooster is buried up to its neck in sand and men on horseback compete by attempting to lean down while riding at full speed to grab the chicken's head and pull the animal from the sand. When a rider succeeds, he then beats one of the other riders with the still living rooster.

In *House Made of Dawn,* Abel fails miserably at the "chicken pull" while the albino succeeds and then chooses the protagonist as the one he beats with the rooster. To compound his initial failure, Abel is unable to defend himself when attacked. The irrational intensity of Abel's hatred for his tormentor, which seems to originate in something outside the incident of the "chicken pull," is an essential aspect of the transformation of the albino from human being to symbol. As more than one critic has pointed out, the motivations behind much of Abel's behavior in the novel are left ambiguous.[11] It is important to remember that the albino's beating of Abel with the rooster is a recognized part of the "chicken pull," not an inexplicable personal attack as the protagonist seems to perceive it.

Abel's humiliation in the game leads inexorably to the climactic scene of "The Longhair," Abel's killing of the albino, which is recounted in an extended paragraph of approximately two pages, a tour de force of modernist writing. While the implications of this scene have been discussed by every critic of the novel, no real critical consensus exists concerning its metaphoric implications. Robert M. Nelson, for instance, views it as emblematic of Abel's alienation from tribal culture. He argues that Abel, until the end of the novel, is weakened by his attempt to exist with an incomplete sense of the significance of the land. Abel, Nelson writes, wants to accept the eagle spirit of the land (a vision of floating above the landscape and possessing it), while rejecting the equally powerful snake spirit of the land (a surrender to the landscape, a willingness to be possessed by it).[12]

While also placing the albino and Abel's murder of him in a tribal context, Floyd C. Watkins denies any redemptive qualities to the albino, seeing him instead as a witch, a figure of supernatural evil.[13] Watkins points out that belief in witchcraft continues to be prevalent in Jemez culture and that Momaday based *House Made of Dawn* on an actual 1958 murder trial in which the defendant claimed that his victim had "'threatened to turn himself into a snake and bite me'" (p. 140).

In contrast, several earlier critics primarily see the albino as a personification of white cultural power,[14] while Lawrence J. Evers proposes a perceptive variation of this interpretation: "More to the point is the fact that the White Man Abel kills is, in fact, a white Indian. . . . He is the White Man in the Indian; perhaps even the White Man in Abel himself. When Abel kills the albino, in a real sense he kills a part of himself and his culture which he can no longer recognize and control" (p. 309). Evers's idea that the albino to a degree embodies Abel's considerable self-hatred originating in his alienation from tribal traditions opens up a promising avenue of interpretation.

In fact, Abel's struggle with the albino is the text's most memorable metaphor for the contested space of the reservation. As a contrapuntal reading will show, the metaphor is complex and works on several levels—it illustrates Abel's self-hatred originating in an awareness of his powerlessness and possibly in terror at latent homosexual urges, his alienation from the tribal culture as manifested in the redemptive snake spirit and the supernatural evil of witchcraft, and certainly the struggle of the Indian and the white cultures for control over the geography of the reservation.

It is worth mentioning that, in Momaday's account of the battle between the two men, the albino is called "the white man" fifteen times, and this repetition is supported by related terminology: "translucent pallor," "invisible," "white immensity of flesh," and "white, hairless arm." Momaday seems to be using repetition here much as Ernest Hemingway often does, as a means of creating emphasis. In an especially horrific moment in this brutal scene, Abel literally slices open the abdomen of the dying albino in an attempt to free himself from the death grip of his antagonist, but even this does not immediately free him: "The white hands laid hold of Abel and drew him close, and the terrible strength of the hands was brought to bear only in proportion as Abel resisted them" (p. 83). Not only is the physical space of the reservation contested by white and Native American power, but Abel's consciousness is a battleground as well, torn between allegiance to and rejection of his tribal culture on one level and resistance of and surrender to the dominant white culture on another. Significantly, he both wins and loses his struggle with the albino, conquering and even killing his enemy, but suffering imprisonment and exile as a result.

This fight scene with its surrealistic detail constitutes an especially memorable example of Michael Kowalewski's theory that descriptions of violence in fiction derive much of their power from their foreignness to readers' lives—the "unreality" of key details in the scene make it unforgettable. In its imagining of Abel's avenger it also echoes what John Fraser calls "the figure of the admirable warrior who stands at one corner of a triangle, equally distant from the dehumanizing bureaucrat and the deranged and compulsive sexual sadist . . . [and who] has always stirred men's hearts and imaginations, and will no doubt continue to do so: the continuing popularity of the Western among people of all political persuasions is testimony enough to that."[15]

At this point in the text Abel cannot simply reject white imperialist culture, because he is, to a strong degree, tempted by it. This temptation is personified by a white woman, Angela Grace St. John, who functions as the central link between the reservation and city segments of the novel. The modernist complexity of her characterization is indicated by the fact that, despite the obvious Christian associations of her name, she plays a largely negative role in the novel.[16] Rather than personifying any redemptive grace, Angela is the novel's crucial link between the superficially enticing, but inwardly dead and empty, imperialist space of the city.

Seven years elapse between the end of "The Longhair" and the second section of the novel, "The Priest of the Sun." In addition, the setting shifts abruptly to a brutal and repressive Los Angeles. Abel, who enters the novel in a state of drunken unconsciousness, is first seen in this urban section lying face down on an abandoned beach and struggling to regain consciousness after a sadistic beating by a policeman named Martinez, who personifies the racist heart of the city and its oppressive power structure and who is symbolically linked in the text to the albino. Before revealing what has happened to Abel, Momaday introduces the text's most complex narrative voice, that of the Reverend Tosamah, minister at the "Los Angeles Holiness Pan-Indian Rescue Mission" (p. 89), a peyote priest of considerable influence within the Los Angeles Native American community.

As much as the albino, Tosamah must be approached from a contrapuntal perspective to be at all comprehensible. It would, in fact, be difficult to name a more complex and ambiguous figure in modern American literature. For instance, it is Tosamah who recounts the origins of the Navaho creation myth of Tai-me and, through association with the story of his grandmother Aho, its destruction by the oppressive white culture. Tosamah is especially sympathetic and eloquent when talking about his grandmother: "Her name was Aho, and she belonged to the last culture to evolve in North America. Her forebears came down from the high north country nearly three centuries ago. The earliest evidence of their existence places them close to the source of the Yellowstone River in western Montana. They were a mountain people, a mysterious tribe of hunters whose language has never been classified in any major group" (pp. 128–29). A haunting, and clearly genuine, nostalgia for a lost culture, a vanished bond with nature and the land, dominates this and other passages in which the "priest" talks about the death of his grandmother and the white imperialist destruction of the Navaho Plains culture. In fact, his story of the origin and destruction of Tai-me is incorporated almost verbatim in Momaday's 1969 nonfiction text, *The Way to Rainy Mountain*.

The first of Tosamah's two sermons dominates the early pages of the second section of the text, and deconstructs John I of the New Testament.

It is here that Momaday introduces the novel's focus upon words, or logos. John, Tosamah proclaims, was correct in proclaiming that "in the beginning was the Word," but inevitably then he betrayed his message "because he was a preacher": "he imposed his idea of god upon the everlasting Truth. 'In the beginning was the Word. . . .' And that is all there was, and it is enough" (p. 93). Now, "in the white man's world," he argues, "language" has been so duplicated and so abused that it has lost its power and its magic. It is possible, he says, that the white man "will perish by the Word" (p. 95).

Obviously, something of a postmodernist sensibility is operative at this stage of the novel—through the peyote priest, Momaday does seem to be saying that, in modern technological society, any necessary or meaningful relationship between signifier and signified has been lost. But more important *to this text* is an implicit protest against the white man's historic betrayal of language in his dealings with Native Americans and with all oppressed peoples. Specifically in his dealings with Native Americans, the white man has used the language in treaties and other documents to deceive and oppress, the name "Indian" being itself a legacy of such deceit and oppression.

Despite his eloquent accounts of his grandmother and Navaho myth and despite his powerful analysis of the oppression made possible by the white imperialist manipulation of language, Tosamah is not an ultimately sympathetic character. An element of cynicism is inherent in everything he says and does; he is profoundly contemptuous of the members of his congregation, and especially of Abel, whom he ridicules as "a longhair" (a naive Indian fresh from the reservation). In an enlightening essay, Bernard A. Hirsch argues that just as the sadistic policeman Martinez "batters Abel's body, so Tosamah batters his spirit, and Momaday, through his narrative structure, stresses the parallel between them."[17] Above all, Tosamah personifies the superficial brilliance, but internal emptiness, of that most imperialist of spaces, the city.

In this context, it is significant that the reader is given almost no detailed information about Martinez, the principal embodiment of the soul of the city. The absence of insight into and information about Martinez metaphorically communicates the spiritual void at the heart of Momaday's city. In his treatment of Los Angeles, nothing is being contested because the imperialist triumph manifested in urbanity has been total. Consequently, the characterization of the policeman who enforces imperialism's values of necessity is largely lacking in complexity; Martinez is primarily a personification of mindless perversity and sadism. What complexity Martinez does possess is represented by his name and by a key term that Benally uses to describe him.

One can probably assume that Martinez is of Hispanic background, most probably a Chicano. If so, he exemplifies the power of the capitalist structure to pit one group of marginalized peoples against another, to maintain power by exploiting the fears and hatreds of the exploited. Thus, he becomes both victim and victimizer. No battle is being waged in the internal space of his psyche because he has so thoroughly adopted the racist values of the dominant society that he is driven by an irrational hatred for Native Americans, a group that his own scapegoated race can scapegoat in turn in order to maintain the illusion of power. He seems to have learned that, in an oppressive society, power is commonly expressed through brutality toward the helpless. Hirsch provides a nicely condensed summary of his relationship with Abel: "he acts out his own version of the American Dream with every Indian he extorts, yet his violent response to Abel's slight resistance suggests that he has paid a price for the power he enjoys" (p. 308).

After describing Martinez as "a cop, and a bad one," Benally says, "you know, they call him *culebra,*"which means snake (p. 141). Thus, he is, to a degree, an extension of the albino, an abstract force that threatens Abel's very survival. Removed to the city and thus separated from the redemptive landscape of part 1 of the novel, the serpent power has lost its complexity and become pure evil. As Nelson points out, the positive aspects of the serpent's supernatural power are tied directly to its identification with the land and cannot exist in the concrete sterility of the city. In addition, the serpent imagery in the novel, especially as personified in the albino and Martinez, evokes two distinctly Western levels of symbolic interpretation.

It calls to mind, of course, the Garden of Eden story with the serpent as the destroyer of innocence, in this case a protagonist who is dangerously unaware of the realities of an urban, technological society. In this context, Abel's name, of course, recalls the son of Adam and Eve who is killed by his jealous brother. Momaday's Abel is almost destroyed not by a brother, but by a combination of the white world and his own internal fears.[18]

Still, Martinez is, in comparison to the albino, a relatively one-dimensional figure, representing an almost allegorical mode of characterization in which the "bad cop" embodies the spiritual emptiness of the city. This vision of the city has caused Floyd C. Watkins among other critics to view part 2 of the novel as an artistic weakness, especially coming as it does after the enormous power and complexity of the first section. In fact, though, the dominant effect of the urban section of the novel is one of deliberate surrealism rather than aesthetic failure.

Because the narrative focus is kept so distant from Abel throughout the section, the things that happen to him, especially the senseless beating given him by Martinez, all seem to partake of a pervasive feeling of unreality. The city is, for Abel, truly a foreign environment in which he can find no security, nothing to anchor himself. He seeks what critic Farah Jasmine Griffin describes as "safe spaces" in Los Angeles without lasting success.[19] Two characters do attempt to guide him to such pockets of security, but both ultimately fail because of their own limitations.

Next to Tosamah, Benally is the most enigmatic figure in part 2. The narrative focus of much of this section of the novel, Benny is also "the night chanter" who sings to Abel, while both lie drunken on a hilltop overlooking Los Angeles, the tribal chant from which the title of the novel is taken. He also helps Abel on the job and serves as an intermediary for the protagonist with the dominant white culture. Still, Benny fails Abel in more than one way. First, on the night Abel seeks out Martinez in what Benally knows will be a dangerous confrontation, the night chanter has become disgusted with his protégé and refuses to stop him: "I had had about all I could take. I was tired of worrying about him all the time, and he was getting worse and something bad was going to happen and I didn't want any part of it. He just went on and it was worse and he was mad and snarling those things [Abel's angry denunciations of himself, Benny, and everyone else] at me, and I was sick of it and I told him to get out" (p. 183). More important and more ironic is Benny's final failure to understand Abel.

The night chanter is disgusted with Tosamah's habit of dismissing the protagonist as "the longhair," but his own commitment to the myth of the American Dream limits his ability to understand the import of Abel's rebellion against the capitalist order. As Hirsch perceives, Benny, despite his genuine pride in his Indianness and his knowledge of tribal traditions, has been co-opted by the dominant culture: "What Tosamah recognizes as Abel's unyielding integrity Benally sees as sheer obstinacy.... After all, Abel has a steady job, a place to live, drinking buddies—everything he needs, Ben would believe, to make it in urban America. Yet despite these advantages, he persists in being a trial to those who care for him" (p. 318). Therefore, while Benny can sing the chant that shows Abel the way to salvation, he cannot follow in the direction to which the chant points. In a fundamental way, the contest for Benally's soul and consciousness has been decided for some time.

For a time, Abel seems to find a "safe space" with Milly, the social worker from Oklahoma who becomes his lover. She, in truth, needs Abel more desperately than he finally needs her. Milly too has experienced the loneliness and spiritual emptiness of life in the city: "She had been in Los Angeles four years, and in all that time she had not talked to anyone. There were people all around; she knew them, worked with them—sometimes they would not leave her alone—but she did not talk to them, tell them anything that mattered in the least. She greeted them and joked with them and wished them well, and then she withdrew and lived her life. No one knew what she thought or felt or who she was" (pp. 121–22). Like Benny, though, Milly, despite her pain and alienation, is a believer in the capitalist system: "But Milly believed in tests, questions and answers, words on paper. She was a lot like Ben. She believed in Honor, Industry, the Second Chance, the Brotherhood of Man, the American Dream" (p. 107). Without realizing it, Milly is another agent of the destructive power of words, of logos. Her profession mandates that she work with documents created by the urban white capitalist structure to control those whom it oppresses. Since she works for the controlling urban society, it is appropriate that she has no positive feelings for the land, the Oklahoma farm on which she grew up and from which she has fled. Her lack of a sense of landscape as redemptive means that, even though she genuinely cares for him, she cannot offer Abel any lasting sanctuary. She is herself desperately in need of a "safe space" within the dead and destructive city.

Perhaps the novel's most memorable illustration of the spiritual emptiness of the city is the brief account of old Carlozini who exists in isolation in the building where Benally and Abel live. Benny has become sensitive to the woman's alienation and even to the pathetic routine of her days. On one occasion, he and Abel find her sitting out on the stairs, instead of watching them leave through her cracked door as she usually does. For the first time, Benny becomes aware of the small room in which the lonely woman spends virtually all of her time: "it was real dark and dirty-looking, and even out there on the stairs we could smell it" (p. 179). Old Carlozini further startles them by holding out to them "a little cardboard box" containing the dead body of some kind of small animal and expressing her great concern about Vincenzo: "Vincenzo is not well. . . . It is very bad this time" (p. 179).

The old woman then talks about how smart Vincenzo is and how he can do things "just like you gentlemen" (p. 180). Benny is startled to hear the old woman whom he has never heard speak before expressing such animation and feeling for the dead guinea pig. Abel then informs the old woman that the creature is, in fact, dead, and she jerks away the box and "slump[s] over a little bit": "she didn't say any more, and she wasn't crying; it was like she was real tired, you know, and didn't have any strength left" (p. 180). The city has so drained old Carlozini that she lacks even the energy for grief, and, after this one encounter, she retreats back into the isolation of her room. The reality of the city in Momaday's text is dirty, smelly, and claustrophobic. There is no spirituality to be contested in it because it has banished spirituality in favor of commodification, power, oppression, and documentation. Vincenzo, the dead guinea pig, functions as metaphor for the people trapped in the dead end of Los Angeles.

A multitribal as well as a multicultural novel, *House Made of Dawn* borrows from such Western literary classics as the Old Testament and Melville, while underscoring and sometimes even deconstructing them with Navaho and Jemez Pueblo mythology. Structured around a contrast between the redemptive landscape of the reservation and the spiritual void at the heart of the capitalist city, it rests upon a central trope of geography. Momaday continually blurs the borders between these two defining sites, only to return to and thus reinforce them. He thereby succeeds in expressing one of the most aesthetically complex visions to be found in American literature and in creating one of its most rewarding texts.

Chapter 8

Discovering a Substitute for Salvation

John Rechy's *The Miraculous Day of Amalia Gómez*

In *The Miraculous Day of Amalia Gómez* (1991), John Rechy evokes a Los Angeles, and by extension an urban America, so permeated with violence as to seem almost surrealistic. Despite this, its female protagonist, unlike Momaday's Abel, finds spiritual redemption within it. This short, powerful novel constitutes, in several ways, a shift in the writing of Rechy, who is best known as a "cult writer" committed to detailed and frank exploration of the homosexual subculture, especially the life of the gay male hustler.[1] While born in El Paso of predominately Mexican American ancestry, he had not, prior to the story of Amalia Gómez, emphasized ethnicity in his fiction, though it is certainly a subtext in *City of Night*, *Numbers*, and *The Fourth Angel* (1972).[2]

The Miraculous Day reverses the usual level of emphasis in Rechy's fiction by focusing upon twenty-four hours in the life of a Chicana maid and mother desperately seeking some protective meaning and stability in her life. While homosexual concerns are hardly ignored in it, they are subordinated to the novel's central ethnic focus. Their presence, even on a secondary level of emphasis, is evidence of Rechy's concern with four levels of discrimination undermining American society and its myth of universal affluence and well-being. His text dramatizes the corrosive effects of prejudice against Chicanos, women, the poor, and gays and the violence that such prejudice inspires. It explores the ways in which the victims of these interrelated levels of oppression are socially and psychologically marginalized in America. Like Cisneros, Rechy is especially concerned here with violence against women.

The most important departure of *The Miraculous Day in the Life of Amalia Gómez* from Rechy's earlier work is its ending. Despite the considerable pain and suffering experienced by Amalia Gómez and the novel's secondary characters, the text ends on a note of redemption and affirmation. In order to voice this concluding hopefulness, Rechy turns to "magic realism," a narrative mode found in the fiction of such twentieth-century Latin American writers as Gabriel García Márquez, Miguel Angel Asturias, Carlos Fuentes, Alejo Carpentier, and Juan Rulfo.[3] The concluding magic realism[4] in *The Miraculous Day of Amalia Gómez* is made plausible by the dialogic nature of Rechy's text. In it, dialogue evokes magic that in turn evokes affirmation. "Dialogic" is used here in a context defined primarily by Charles Taylor in his introductory essay for the volume *Multiculturalism* (1994):

> [The] crucial feature of human life is its fundamentally *dialogical* character. We become full human agents, capable of understanding ourselves, and hence of defining our identity, through our acquisition of rich human languages of expression. . . . People do not acquire the languages needed for self-definition on their own. Rather, we are introduced to them through interaction with others who matter to us. . . . The genesis of the human mind is in this sense not monological, not something each person accomplishes on his or her own, but dialogical.[5]

To further illustrate his definition of the "dialogic," he discusses George Herbert Mead's ideas concerning those "significant others," initially parents, who profoundly determine the individual's sense of a personal self. According to Mead, as we outgrow the parental influence, our individual "identities" expand through contact or dialogue with their "significant" successors. In Rechy's novel, Amalia eventually achieves salvation through dialogue with a group of secondary characters, of significant others; this extended family is made up of the protagonist's children (both living and dead) with whom she has previously been in conflict, a coworker, and two strangers who dramatically intrude upon her life in the novel's ending. Out of this mixture of children, a friend, and strangers, a redemptive concept of family is born.

The concept of family in Rechy's earlier work is rarely beneficial.[6] While a number of characters in *City of Night* play pivotal roles in shaping the identity of the "youngman" narrator, these people remain "others" who do not touch his fundamental being; in fact, his entire lifestyle is predicated on preventing anyone from becoming truly "significant" to him. Locked inside a remorseless narcissism, he views other young men as bodies who by paying him for sex will momentarily validate his existence.[7] In contrast,

Amalia Gómez, while hardly ashamed of her intense sexuality, desperately seeks validation from her society, and especially from her children, of her identity as a courageous woman and loving mother. In contrast to the anonymous narrator of *City of Night* and Johnny Rio, Amalia desires nothing more exotic than valorization of her identity as a full citizen of and equal participant in American democracy. She also wants confirmation of her identity as a beautiful woman and a loving mother.

But three of the interrelated chronotopes[8] in which she exists are the hatred for ethnic minorities that has so hideously distorted the "American Dream," contemporary urban America with its rigidly segregated areas of affluence and poverty, and the Hispanic barrio in which traditions that have historically affirmed people and the earth are threatened by violence from within and without. On one level, *The Miraculous Day of Amalia Gómez* is very much a novel about borders (borders between ethnic groups, between different sections of the city of Los Angeles, between men and women, and between parents and children) that remain largely closed, at least until the novel's miraculous final scene.[9]

As it does in the other novels discussed in this book, violence serves Rechy as the central motif around which to construct his narrative. Violence represents in *The Miraculous Day* the elaborate patterns of closure that threaten to prevent Amalia from ever recovering the self that can sustain her and give meaning to her life—it thereby makes redemptive dialogue impossible for much of the text. To depict the lifelong entrapment of his central character, Rechy calls upon a familiar novelistic structure—the central "plot" is limited to events that occur in a twenty-four-hour period, while the "story" of Amalia's past is provided through extensive flashbacks. In the "present," Amalia, a middle-aged mother of three, is seen as having been, almost without exception, victimized since childhood. Her lifelong victimization is, in fact, so thorough that, until its unexpected conclusion, *The Miraculous Day of Amalia Gómez* reads like a classic naturalistic protest novel. One early passage, in fact, identifies her as a pawn of naturalistic determinism:

> It was only that she could remember no missed opportunity to regret. She could not name a time when a desirable choice had been presented to her, something she would look back on and even suspect that it might have altered the lines of her life. Nothing. Without possibility to resist what was to come, she moved from crisis to crisis, which, finally, formed one, her life. "Change" was an intensification of the same worries. So she lived within the boundaries of her existence, and that did not include hope, real hope.[10]

As long as Amalia is depicted as a naturalistic victim, as a choiceless product of environmental determinism, the dialogic aspects of the novel cannot dominate. If "change" is not real to her, then she can hardly grow through contact with "significant others." Moreover, beginning with her father and mother, most of the "significant others" in Amalia's life, caring nothing about healing dialogue, have approached her through physical or emotional violence, or both. Eventually, a few individuals give her love and hope, but they have themselves been harmed, if not actually destroyed, by the brutal society surrounding them. As a consequence, the novel dramatizes interlinking forms of violence: familial-sexual, social-cultural, and, a familiar Rechy theme especially since *Bodies and Souls*, commodified violence and pain.

Rechy's novel echoes Cisneros's *The House on Mango Street* in its depiction of male characters as being abusive, physically and usually sexually. Amalia's father initiates the entrapment that is her existence. After immigrating to the United States from Mexico and fighting in World War II, he is unable to find meaningful or sufficient employment, drifts from one low-paying, menial job to another, becomes an alcoholic, and unleashes his frustration over his economic impotence against his family. Amalia learns early that passivity is for her the only possible response to her father's, or any male's, violence: "That was the only response she knew to violence, to become quiet, passive. Seeing no way to thwart it, she would try not to know it was occurring, even while it pulled her into its center" (p. 16).

To a degree then, Rechy is focusing on the kind of internalized marginalization that Toni Morrison dramatizes in *The Bluest Eye*. Until the magic realism of the ending, male violence threatens to exact the comparable price from her that it does from Morrison's Pecola, the negation of identity itself. Both Morrison and Rechy dramatize subcultures in which sexual assault of the female becomes simultaneously secret and accepted. With one exception (who significantly is gay), all of the men in Amalia's life are, to some degree, like her father, "violent strangers": if not immediately, they ultimately become threatening and abusive. When she is fourteen, her father's attacks become sexual and Teresa, Amalia's mother, blames her daughter for her husband's criminal advances. Amalia is actually raped not by her father, but by the son of his "drinking friend." The young man, Salvador, is the first of a series of false saviors in the novel; Amalia seeks a kind of biblical salvation through her relationships with men, seeking "handsome" ones "with holy names": in addition to Salvador, there are Gabriel and Angel. This quest for salvation through men is, of course, a central manifestation of the quietness, the internal marginalization, bequeathed to her by her father. Moreover, it negates the possibility of genuine dialogue with the men in Amalia's life; one does not converse on an equal basis with one's saviors.

Through Salvador, Rechy introduces the major unifying symbol in the novel—the young man has a distinctive tattoo on his hand, "a cross with lines that radiated from it" (p. 21). As she is by Salvador himself, Amalia is deceived by the implications of the tattoo. She believes, until the rape, that it signifies "tenderness" (p. 21). After the assault, she comes to hate the grotesque emblem, even before learning that "it was a sign of proud membership in one of the most violent gangs in the Southwest" (p. 23). Typically, her mother and father refuse to believe her account of being raped by Salvador, but move to arrange a marriage between their daughter and her rapist. The father's comment to Salvador, when the young man initially resists the idea of marriage, is especially revealing: "And it's not that bad is it? They're both young, and, after all, we're *compadres*" (p. 22). The legacy continues; women are viewed simply as property, to be assaulted whenever men so desire. It is hardly surprising that Salvador rapes Amalia a second time immediately after their wedding.

Amalia's son with Salvador, Manuel or Manny, will grow up to repeat much of Salvador's most destructive behavior, even though he is a significantly more decent and loving young man. In fact, Amalia's complex relationship with Manny is central to the novel's plot and especially to its affirmative ending. So is her relationship with her second son, Juan, the child of her second marriage, to Gabriel, "a good-looking soldier from New Mexico" (p. 33) who has been traumatized by his Vietnam experiences and who physically abuses and twice deserts Amalia (the couple also has a daughter, Gloria). The text makes clear that the heroine's fondness for soldiers results from her immersion in both Mexican American and white mainstream American culture. She seeks a warrior, a descendant of the Aztecs, who will resist the exploitative white culture, but she is also attracted to Hollywood images of heroic white soldiers and pure white women. Her dreams are compounded almost equally of the legend of Aztlán and the images of Hollywood films of the thirties and forties.[11] Again, dialogue becomes close to impossible here; it is difficult to converse meaningfully with images, with illusions.

What she consistently finds, rather than warriors or pure soldiers, are rage-filled men devoted to a cult of selfish and destructive machismo. Even in the cases of two men who seem quite different from this, appearance proves to be illusory. In the novel's present tense, she is "married" to Raynaldo, who was "a good man who had a steady job with a freight-loading company, and [who] helped generously with rent and groceries. He had been faithfully with her for five years, the only one of her men who had never hit her" (p. 5). Yet, irony, which almost equals violence as a structuring trope in the text and which is of course always a major component of naturalistic fiction, intrudes when, near the end of the novel, she discovers that Raynaldo has made sexual advances to her daughter, Gloria. In fact, there is an added level of irony here since her discovery of her husband's treacherous behavior alleviates her own guilt for a near affair with Angel, a young man whom she has met in a bar. By this point, the reader is hardly surprised when Angel abruptly turns abusive or when it is revealed that he is a "coyote," one who betrays his own people to U.S. law enforcement figures.

There is considerable complexity in Rechy's treatment of Mexican American identity. Like Cisneros, he does not soften his analysis of what he clearly considers the negative aspects of his ethnic legacy—its cult of male machismo and its obsession with a guilt-inducing Catholicism. In fact, Teresa, Amalia's mother, functions in the novel primarily as a personification of the harsh religious beliefs that help destroy her daughter's pride and confidence. She and her husband, with his drinking and cruelty, together represent Rechy's vision of the worst aspects of Chicano culture. It must be quickly said, though, that the novel posits more potential good than bad in its presentation of Mexican American life and makes clear, through plot and the kind of overt narrative editorializing that one associates with naturalistic social protest, that the drinking, male violence, and religious intolerance are the legacy of poverty, oppression, and economic injustice.[12]

The novel dramatizes the urban American street gang as a chronotope for merging its treatments of familial and social violence. Manny is dead during the novel's present tense, but the reader does not learn precisely why or how until near the end of the narrative. What is revealed earlier, though, is the novel's most pivotal scene. When Manny appears one day with the same gang insignia of the burning cross that Salvador had "worn" tattooed on his hand, Amalia is flooded with memories of past grief and, without being fully conscious of what she is doing, forces her son's already disfigured hand against the lit burner of a stove, leaving an ugly scar. The degree to which *The Miraculous Day of Amalia Gómez* can be seen as an advance in the dialogic nature of Rechy's work can be quickly realized by comparing the novel to the chapter-story entitled "Manny Gómez: 'The Frontal Christ'" from *Bodies and Souls*.[13]

The earlier piece repeats not only Manny's name, but also the incidents of the tattoo and the burning of the son's hand by the mother. In addition, details of the lives of Manny and his family in El Paso anticipate parts of *The Miraculous Day*. Still, in character emphasis, mood, and point of view, the story-chapter and the subsequent novel are quite different. In "Manny Gómez: 'The Frontal Christ,'" the narrative focus is upon Manny, an eighteen-year-old Chicano man who is proud, but deeply embittered by the poverty and oppression that control his life in East Los Angeles. Control is clearly the correct word here; in theme and technique, the story is intensely naturalistic.

Given the emphasis in *The Miraculous Day of Amalia Gómez* on the ubiquitous and implacable nature of repressive social forces, Amalia's survival is all the more impressive. In its description of her life in El Paso, the novel describes incidents reminiscent of Rivera's account of the suffering that befalls the unnamed central figure (a young boy or possibly young boys) and his family in *. . . y no se lo tragó la tierra*. Like Rivera's young boy, Amalia is regularly humiliated in school. Both child characters suffer the indignity of having their heads inspected for lice, and both are abused by bigoted teachers. Here especially Rivera's protagonist and the young Amalia suffer from the kind of racial and class oppression that assaults Morrison's Pecola in *The Bluest Eye*. Rivera's and Rechy's protagonists both escape Pecola's tragic fate, though each is constantly objectified by society's hostile external gaze. One of Amalia's teachers, for instance, mixes racial prejudice, valorization of the superficial, and Texas frontier "patriotism" in a particularly ugly way in the classroom:

> At the first of the day, they had to sing "Home on the Range" for an Anglo teacher—all the teachers were Anglos . . . [who] was always exhorting the Mexican students to pay extra attention to "grooming" because: "You're a minority, have to prove yourselves." She insisted they all change the line "where seldom is heard a discouraging word" to "where never is heard a discouraging word." Amalia thought: If all you counted were discouragements in school, this was a lie. (p. 17)

The cruelty and injustice of Amalia's El Paso childhood are crystallized in one horrible moment when, from the top of the mountain of Cristo Rey, she, her mother, and other worshippers observe the border patrol attack a group of men, women, and children attempting to cross the Rio Grande river and illegally enter the United States. "Wetbacks," someone in her group observes as a little Mexican girl and her mother drown in the muddy river (pp. 18–19).

The oppressive gaze of the dominant culture, as manifested in the border patrol and in at least one of Amalia's fellow worshipers, dehumanize, the

Mexican mother and child in life and in death. What is really being worshiped here is American colonialism.[14] The use of such dramatic narrative shifting in order to achieve irony is a staple of naturalistic social protest. Metaphorically, of course, what drowns are Amalia's youth and innocence and her hope of being able to depend on the critical, self-pitying Teresa. She learns very early that she is threatened on all sides—a drunken and abusive father, an unfeeling, judgmental mother, posturing and violent lovers, and a cold, murderous society. Thus, she is tempted to withdraw into her dreams and images, rather than seek a healing, but elusive, dialogue.

In California, she encounters the same thing, but in a more centralized way; in one sense, Los Angeles is even worse than west Texas—it tantalizes with a bright, but decaying, beauty and an illusion of possibility. She soon discovers and is drawn to the murals that decorate East L.A., unexpectedly encountering one that images all her dreams of heroic warrior-lovers: "[a] muscular Aztec prince, amber-gold-faced, in lordly feathers" (p. 45). She avoids, though, one that depicts "[a] tall, plumed Aztec [who] held a dying city boy in his arms" (p. 56). Upon seeing it, she desperately grabs Manny's hand.

But it is not long before she is forced to confront the reality of a message scrawled "in red, bleeding paint," apparently by a street gang member, on a wall: "AZTLÁN ES UNA FÁBULA" (p. 70).[15] The violent phenomenon of street gangs, which will reach out to destroy Manny just as it did his father, constitutes one of what Amalia comes to think of as the natural disasters of southern California.

The text envisions the area, and especially the city of Los Angeles, as verging on apocalypse. Violence in both human and nonhuman manifestations continually threatens the very survival of every level of society, but especially the poor. Gangs, fires, earthquakes, sadistic police and immigration agents, and Mexican American "coyotes" are continual presences in and just outside the city: "There were always sirens screaming now. At times it seemed to her that the city itself was shrieking, protesting violence everywhere, even under the earth, stirring into earthquakes" (p. 109). Throughout the novel, the characters wait for "the Big One," the ultimate earthquake that will swallow up the entire city—"the big one" works in the novel as a metaphor for the city's final consummation by random, senseless violence. In *The Miraculous Life of Amalia Gómez,* as in all his fiction, Rechy echoes T. S. Eliot's *The Waste Land* and the Old Testament with allusions to death by water and by fire. Life in East L.A. especially is described in the terminology of naturalistic determinism: "There was danger everywhere. Like living with a gun pressed to your head.... If the gun was pressed there, it intended to shoot. That meant there was nothing you could do—and there never was, was there?" (p. 147). In such an existence, dialogue, in fact any kind of meaningful contact with others (significant or not), is seriously challenged.

This has certainly been so for Amalia. She learns belatedly from a woman whom she barely knows that Manny is "one of the toughest *vatos* in 'East Ellay'—a *'vato loco,'* a gang member of extreme daring" (p. 57). Almost inevitably, he is soon arrested for attempted murder for his actions during a gang battle and is found dead after being placed in isolation—he is hanging with his shirt knotted around his neck. For Amalia, there can be no question, despite the ruling of suicide by the prison authorities, that Manny was murdered. In part because of grief over his death, Amalia has also missed the import of events transpiring in the life of her youngest son, Juan.

Her own cultural prejudices also play a crucial role in her failure of vision. Amalia views gays with horror, and Rechy lets the reader deduce, before his heroine understands it, that Juan has become a homosexual hustler. In this crucial segment of the novel, Rechy drops his emphasis upon ethnic identity in order to return to the overriding narrative focus of his earlier work. He frankly recounts the prejudice of the Mexican American community against homosexuals; he must do so, not only in the name of realism but also to express the pain of double marginalization from which he has personally suffered. Moreover, he again challenges much of his readership by treating the hustler as hero. In fact, he uses the characterization of Amalia for the purpose of narrative defamiliarization; in one scene especially, he subtly elides the identities of Amalia and an implied homophobic reader.

Observing the young male hustlers crowding Santa Monica Boulevard, Amalia can only exclaim *"Que horror!"* (p. 70). Rechy assumes that many of his readers will have the same reaction. One of the obvious implications in all his work is that such a reaction is morally wrong. In an analysis of *The Sexual Outlaw*, Rafael Pérez-Torres is especially insightful concerning the importance of Rechy's hustlers:

> He represents the image of male sexuality common to almost all of Rechy's other novels: the hustling homosexual whose actions not only address his own sexual desire, but represent a challenge to the rigid oppression of heterosexual society. Restlessly wandering the peripheries of society, the male hustler becomes for Rechy a sexual shock troop meant to disrupt and sabotage the heterosexual world. The male hustler forms a disruptive and liberating force against the repressive

and rigid social order, against its narrowly defined heterosexual identity, against the social complacency and passivity that his identity engenders. His promiscuity challenges the unexamined pieties and platitudes of the repressive heterosocial world. (pp. 204–5)

The male hustler, in Rechy, deliberately provokes and outrages a heterosexual majority devoted to the repression of difference by refusing to be invisible, by flaunting his costumed presence. The exchange of money between hustler and "john" parodies the human exploitation of capitalism.[16] With its valorization of machismo, the Chicano culture is at least as prejudiced against gays as is the dominant "Anglo" American culture.

Still, while crucial, the Juan subplot is only one part of the California section of the novel, and in it, as in the El Paso flashback sequence, Rechy's social protest is primarily directed at oppression of the Mexican American. In more than one way, Rechy is direct and unsubtle about hammering this message home. He has Amalia work in a "sewing sweatshop," in which the capitalist owners insure their being able to force squalid and unhealthy working conditions on their employees by hiring illegal immigrants. Rechy's heroine joins Stephen Crane's Maggie Johnson, Theodore Dreiser's Carrie Meeber, and Nelson Algren's Norah Egan as victims of this kind of oppressive employment.

But in her "factory," Amalia faces an added threat from which her predecessors were spared: immigration officers. These government agents are depicted as being uniformly callous, brutal, and even sadistic, looking for opportunities to intimidate all the workers, citizens or not. The sweatshop passages in Rechy's text seem hauntingly prophetic in the climate of the 1996 welfare reform bill, which denied benefits to illegal and legal immigrants alike, and California's Proposition 187, which denied health services, public education, and other benefits to undocumented immigrants. The novelist sometimes expresses his anger at the often violent repression of Chicano citizens and newly arrived immigrants in overt editorializing. Yet it is in the sweatshop that Amalia finds the friend who becomes a crucial part of her extended family and who functions in the novel as a voice of moral outrage and protest. Amalia's friend at work, Rosario, tries desperately to awaken her coworkers to the necessity of resisting what is happening to them and to their people: "And those who reach the cities? Slums! The streets! Terrorized by *gangas* and violence and the *migra* [immigration agents] always tracking them down. Illegals? Huh! How can a human being not be legal? . . . [A] human being has the right to eat, to have a home, work—" (p. 76).

Rosario especially preaches the necessity of unionization to Amalia and the others, but is thwarted by cultural prejudice against unions and by a commodification of pain and violence that the text describes as having reached its apogee in Los Angeles. Milagros (miracles), another of Amalia's coworkers is, like the heroine herself, a devoted follower of television telenovas and, while at her sewing machine, compulsively recounts the "plot" of her favorite program, "Lágrimas de Honor" ("Tears of Honor or Virtue"). The characters in this serial are relentlessly one-dimensional— "good" protagonists daily, if not hourly, threatened by supernaturally "evil" villains who consort with "godless unionists" (p. 50). The message here is crude and clear, "good" people will be delivered from evil *if* they patiently wait for miracles and do not attempt to help themselves through collective action. Consequently, Rosario is ultimately important in the novel not for her political message, but as a significant other who mentors Amalia and helps her move toward a redemptive dialogue. Amalia is prevented for a time from understanding the real importance of Rosario in part because she has embraced, through Hollywood and Mexican films, values similar to those enunciated by Milagros.

Although bothered by some of its logical inconsistencies, she loves the 1943 American film *The Song of Bernadette,* in which Jennifer Jones won an Academy Award for portraying the impossibly pure and devout peasant woman who sees a holy vision. She is equally devoted to the Mexican films of Maria Felix, especially one, *El Monje Blanco* (*The Monk in White*), in which the actress plays a mother sanctified by her Christlike child. American television has left its mark on her mind as well—in California, a neighbor, Concepción, visits Amalia to watch *Queen for a Day,* an especially odious popular "entertainment" devoted to exploiting and commodifying personal and economic suffering. For those who do not remember, poor and physically sick women competed for prizes on this program by describing their misfortunes to a simultaneously saccharine and condescending host. Concepción has discussed with her social worker the process of being chosen to appear on *Queen for a Day:* "'You have to have a really horrible life,' . . . 'I *deserve* to win'" (p. 32).

Appropriately for the home of American movies and television, the city of Los Angeles, obsessed with denying its lack of a saving past, has concocted a surreal formula of commodified suffering, death, sexuality, and violence and marketed it in numerous "tourist attractions." Rechy gives what is perhaps the definitive account of this phenomenon in *Bodies and Souls,* which takes the reader on a tour of some of the most outrageous of these settings including Forest Lawn, the Hollywood Wax Museum, and the Hollywood Walk of Fame. In *Bodies and Souls, Marilyn's Daughter,* and *The Miraculous Day of Amalia Gómez,* he emphasizes the city's ubiquitous advertisements for the tour of Universal Studios with its "earthquake attraction" as emblematic of the culture's simultaneous denial of and obsession with death and mass destruction: "Television clips and giant billboards all over the city proclaimed ominously, over scenes of fire, buildings collapsing, people running, screaming: *Earthquake! Survive it only at Universal Studios!* There were stupid people and there were even more stupid, *cruel* people, and those at Universal Studios were the *most* stupid, turning something as terrible as an earthquake into entertainment—and making money out of it. [Amalia wondered:] What next? A gang killing for tourists?" (*Miraculous Day of Amalia Gómez,* p. 122). The Universal billboards overlooking the city are proof that, in Los Angeles, one can never, in fact, escape the objectifying gaze of the dominant culture; evidences of its hegemonic power are everywhere. Thus, the city, in *The Miraculous Death of Amalia Gómez,* functions much like the prison in Foucault's *Discipline and Punish;* it is a horizontal-vertical form of the all-seeing Panopticon that Foucault argues is ubiquitous in modern Western society, valorizing violence and consumerism while outlawing privacy and imposing punishment on the soul as well as the body.

In one especially memorable scene, Amalia Gómez, while seeking a "safe space,"[17] takes a long walk through a grimly ugly and menacing Hollywood defaced by fast-food stands, strip malls, and walls covered with violent, profane gang graffiti. She comes upon a confrontation between Christian Protestant fundamentalists and Catholics, each group threatening the other with hell and both apparently oblivious to where they actually are. In its rich detail, at once graphic and surrealistic, Amalia's walk echoes Thomas Pynchon's account of Oedipa Maas's night-journey through the "unreal" streets of San Francisco in *The Crying of Lot 49.*

Yet, despite all of this surrounding horror and to the surprise of readers of Rechy's earlier work, Amalia triumphs—the novel ends by affirming the possibility of miracles, but miracles that arise from courageous self-examination, openness to and with others, and defiance of oppression, rather than from guilt and passivity. If surprising, the magic realism ending is nevertheless foreshadowed, literally from the novel's first sentence in which Amalia believes that she sees "a large silver cross in the otherwise clear sky" (p. 3). She instantly doubts her vision, telling herself that she is not worthy of receiving such a sacred sign: "no miraculous sign would appear to a twice-divorced woman with grown, rebellious children and living with a man who wasn't her husband" (p. 3). What Amalia comes finally to understand is that it is not these "sins" that separate her from grace, but her own denial of reality and the absence of frank and open dialogue with her children.

She cannot, for instance, even consider the possibility that Manny's death in prison was a suicide because that inevitably involves reliving the moment in which she forced his hand down against the burning stove. In a crucial late scene, she learns that Juan has been arrested for hustling and rejects him with the word "*maricón*," or "queer" (p. 182), and then refuses to listen to Gloria's story of Raynaldo's abuse, thereby repeating the blind insensitivity of Teresa to her. This failed attempt to communicate with her two living children reaches an ugly climax when Amalia slaps Gloria after her daughter calls her a prostitute. Still, her vision of the cross in the sky is hardly the only signal in the text of her ultimate salvation. Two others occur in a scene that happens prior to this disturbing confrontation.

As Amalia prepares to enter a church for confession, she sees the first of the two strangers who will become part of her extended family. Even though she never exchanges a word with the stranger, Amalia's brief moment of contact with her is simultaneously painful and poetically eloquent. Amalia observes "an old Mexican woman, seventy, older, draped in a heavy black shawl, dressed entirely in black . . . dropped to her knees on the sidewalk outside the church. Her face was so pale it merely looked stained brown. Dark circles rendered her eyes hollow. She proceeded to walk, on her knees, toward the steps of the church. She had lowered her black stockings just enough to expose her flesh more harshly to the chafing, hot concrete" (p. 147). The old woman is a "*beata*" making her pilgrimage to the church (Amalia has seen elderly individuals doing the same thing in South El Paso and Juárez), and she completes her journey only with genuine suffering: "Smears of blood tainted the steps behind her. Amalia flung her eyes up, to the top of the church, the cross there, impassive against the blue, still sky" (p. 148).

The symbolic significance of the old woman is complex and crucial to the thematic implications of Rechy's text. Her self-abuse is emblematic of his view of the Mexican and Chicano peoples' extreme and fruitless sacrifices to the church. Yet her persistence in completing her journey calls attention to a central motif in the novel, the individual quest for redemption. Amalia immediately senses, even if she does not consciously understand, the implicit lesson in what she has been privileged to witness. The second of the two relevant clues in this segment of the novel comes during Amalia's actual confession. Irony as trope comes into play again in this scene. Upon leaving the confessional, Amalia realizes that the priest pressed for intimate details of her night with Angel while masturbating (the reader has this epiphany earlier). During the actual exchange with the priest, Amalia thinks: "After all, . . . these holy men must have heard everything. They were themselves, in their purity, separated from certain aspects of life; but that only made them more attuned to those who turned to them. They were here to provide an immediate substitute for salvation, which you earned fully at the end of your life" (p. 156). Especially in the context of the novel's dominant critique of the Catholic Church, the reader understands that Amalia's thoughts cannot be taken with complete seriousness. In fact, the text directly refutes the false moral that salvation should be anticipated only "at the end of [one's] life."

But the phrase "immediate substitute for salvation" not only signals the direction of Rechy's aesthetic but also foreshadows the "miracle" that ends the novel. To fully understand the importance of the phrase to *The Miraculous Life of Amalia Gómez*, one needs to recall something that Rechy said in 1973: "[T]here's a phrase that appears in every one of my books and will probably appear in every book I write; that's 'No substitute for salvation.' That's one of the major themes of my writing—the search for a substitute for salvation. There isn't one, and that's the existential nightmare."[18] Indeed, the phrase does appear in every one of Rechy's books prior to *The Miraculous Day of Amalia Gómez*. In contrast, this novel ends, after its central character has engaged in frank and open dialogue with Rosario, her children, and most important, herself, finding a secular salvation.

She last talks to Rosario over the phone; when asked by Amalia if she does not believe in God, Rosario responds: "'—you're left to find your own strength, *corazón*' . . . 'you don't accept that you *must* be a victim'" (p. 177). After the traumatic scene with Juan and Gloria, she forces herself to read carefully a letter that Manny wrote her while in jail and examines the possible implications of its ending: "*Amita, if I thot I would only come out & hurt you again like I have befor I would take myself away—thats how much I love you with all my heart—allways believe that—*" (p. 192). This letter, with all its grammatical and spelling mistakes, prompts Amalia's first meaningful dialogue with Manny, and ultimately with all of her children, in years, even though that dialogue unfolds essentially within her consciousness. But before she can realize the full import of Manny's words, she is assaulted with garbage and a racist epithet hurled from a "carload of ugly young men with shaved heads" (p. 193). Enraged, she retreats to the church where, in an action that echoes her beloved Jennifer Jones and Maria Felix, she seeks solace not from the priest, but from a statue of the Madonna. This time she makes a private, but meaningful confession, reciting the real sins of rejecting Juan, slapping Gloria, and burning Manny's hand. She also understands that the young men who have just abused her are like the roving gangs whom she has seen assaulting gays. After such honesty and epiphany, she comprehends at last that her children, including Juan, have been victimized, that she must ask forgiveness of the two who are still alive, and that Manny did in fact kill himself, but out of love for her. As harsh as these truths are, they allow healing to begin, and Amalia accelerates the process with four unspoken, but nevertheless, defiant words: "*I demand a miracle*" (p. 199).

The miracle does come, but only after a second and much more shocking encounter with a stranger. Amalia wanders aimlessly through a shopping mall, the account of which, in its detailed description of a commodification so extensive and assertive as to be surreal, again recalls *Bodies and Souls* and Pynchon's *The Crying of Lot 49*. Even before she is suddenly taken hostage by an armed man, she feels lost and out of place there, precisely as one of her economic status is intended to feel. At first, the armed man seems a personification of the capitalistic culture that literally threatens her life, and, for a moment, she almost surrenders to him and to the fear and guilt that inevitably arise from her position as outsider. But she chooses instead to live, shoving the young man away, whereupon the police shoot him. Instinctively, she kneels beside him and honors his dying request by blessing him, after which she cries for the first time since Manny's death. Her tears inspire the text's concluding turn to magic realism, when she sees within "a bright light [that] smashed at her" (the light of a television camera) a vision: "Within it stood—*The Blessed Mother, with her arms outstretched*" (p. 206). By refusing to be a victim again and by accepting the role of sacred mother to the dying young man and allowing herself to grieve at last for her own dead son, Amalia has experienced a moment of secular redemption.[19] She has expanded the internal dialogue inspired by Manny's letter to include all of her children as well as the young man. Acceptance of her children for what they were and are, in spite of her own cultural prejudices, liberates her to the possibility of magic realism. Rosario, the "*beata*," and the dying young man join Manny, Juan, and Gloria to form a redemptive family, a *familia* that at last becomes more real to her than Bernadette, Maria Felix, the pathetically exploited "queens for a day," and the characters of "Lágrimas de Honor."

It is not insignificant that this occurs in a context of rampant consumerism and senseless violence. These are, after all, the realities of Rechy's America and especially of his Los Angeles. As such, they are so strong that they almost destroy the possibilities of a saving dialogue, but, after a concluding intervention of magic realism, for the first time in his fiction, they do not, and in *The Miraculous Day of Amalia Gómez* hope and secular salvation are affirmed. In contrast to the characters in his earlier work, Amalia Gómez will embrace dialogue with others and thereby find a "safe space," a substitute for salvation, transcending, at least for a moment, the sexism, racism, violence, and commodification of American culture. Her extended family transcends oppression and internalized marginalization, the capitalist urban gaze, the poverty and machismo of the Hispanic barrio, and past male assaults on her body and her sense of self.

Conclusion

Girl X and the Country of Last Things

Similar and contrasting patterns of violence inform the eight texts on which this study has focused. William Kennedy and Caleb Carr posit a peculiarly American violence as the inevitable legacy of our history of ethnic and racial antagonisms and oppression of the marginalized "other," while Richard Price depicts a 1960s inner-city New York devastated by ethnic division and hatred. John Edgar Wideman envisions inner-city Philadelphia as a metaphoric rubber plantation, an internal colony ruled by puppets of the dominant white power structure. Writing about a comparable colonized American space, Sandra Cisneros focuses upon an additional level of discrimination and oppression: the exploitation of the female in Chicago's Chicano community. In *Quinn's Book, The Alienist, The Wanderers, Philadelphia Fire,* and *The House on Mango Street,* children and adolescents are the principal victims of oppression and violence.

John Rechy, in *The Miraculous Day of Amalia Gómez,* is concerned with the triple marginalization by race, class, and gender of a female protagonist trapped in the urban spaces of the Southwest and West, while Scott Momaday in *House Made of Dawn* investigates the ways in which the alien urban landscape of Los Angeles fuels the destructive self-hatred of his Native American protagonist. *Suttree* stands out from these texts in its foregrounding of a distinctly spiritual despair. McCarthy depicts an urban wasteland that seems to have been abandoned by god to a pervasive violence; his protagonist suffers from a profound despair emanating from the absence of a redemptive spirituality, a despair fed by random moments of violence.

In part, then, *Suttree* serves a function of contrast in this study—its dominant concern is with spiritual alienation rather than with social injustice.

Yet, Suttree, Gene Harrogate, and the other residents of Knoxville's Mc-Anally Flats do constitute an urban lumpenproletariat into which anyone might fall. They are invisible and voiceless to the dominant capitalist society of Knoxville unless and until they happen to violate its rules. To a degree, the spiritual wasteland that McCarthy imagines seems an inevitable result of the legacy of injustice and oppression depicted by Kennedy and Carr.

Cumulatively, these eight fictions bear witness to the suffering of individuals threatened by spiritual and physical annihilation in America's inner cities. Tragically no fiction, Yummy Sandifer's life and death exemplified the enormity of this threat. In some ways, another young victim of random violence in Chicago illustrates it even more. Once again in early April of 1997, the front pages of the *Chicago Tribune* seemed to offer convincing evidence of David Bell's epiphany in DeLillo's *Americana* of "a casual savagery [being] fed by [the] mute cities" of America. The front page of the April 6 edition of the *Tribune* was dominated by two stories recapitulating the horrific attack on a nine-year-old girl identified only as Girl X; the stories shared a common headline, "The Tragic World of Girl X." The child's tragedy had been detailed in a *Tribune* story published two days earlier in connection with the arrest of a suspect three months after the attack.

On January 9 the girl, sometime after leaving her grandmother's apartment in a Chicago high-rise public-housing building, suffered a savage attack. According to police, the suspect, identified as Patrick Sykes, first sexually assaulted Girl X and, when she began to scream, strangled her "until she lost consciousness": "he then carried her to the stairwell, where he allegedly forced a poisonous liquid down her throat, scrawled with a marker on her stomach and left her."[1] The longer of the two April 6 stories followed the standard format of news stories about such horrible crimes. After describing the ongoing struggle of the young girl to regain full consciousness three months after the attack, it focuses on excerpts from interviews with relatives and neighbors of the victim, searching for some redemptive meaning in the incident while adding new details in a tone of grim irony.

Subtitled "Her Life: Joy of Childhood Torn Away," the story begins by pointing to the innocence of Girl X's life prior to the assault. The child had spent the night of January 8 with a ten-year-old friend, Shavontay Fluker, in the Cabrini-Green complex: "[the two girls] had spent the evening watching cartoons and playing Girl X's favorite game: school."[2] Shavontay told the *Tribune* reporter that "that night, she was the student, and I was the teacher." Another poignant detail was contributed by another child, who was apparently the last person to see Girl X before the attack: "Shatonya Edwards, also 9, was heading down the stairs at 8:30 on her way to school when she saw Girl X bent over in the 6th-floor landing, tying her gym shoes. 'We said "hi" and I kept going,' said Shatonya."

Later, in a phrase that could have been intended as a capsule summary of a recurrent trope in most of the novels analyzed in this book, reporter Dahleen Glanton ascribes symbolic importance to Girl X. After emphasizing that even those so moved by the incident as to have sent cards, flowers, and money to the unconscious victim and her grandmother cannot appreciate the "personality," the "sense of humor," and "the little-girl exuberance" of the victimized child, Glanton writes that these things make the Girl X case "emblematic of innocence lost by so many children in the violence of urban America." Glanton then quotes Beverly Reed, herself a survivor of childhood rape, who argues that the very anonymity of the victim inspired the outpouring of gifts from strangers: "In the name Girl X, they realize this could have been anybody's child. They don't attach a face to her, and it makes her that much more real. . . . She has given people an opportunity to transcend race, class and everything else to help an innocent child."

Reed had, in fact, transformed the case into something of a personal crusade, having discussed it on television talk shows including *Geraldo, Oprah,* and *Leeza* while raising $264,000 for Girl X's medical expenses. The *Tribune* emphasized that Reed's crusade had roots in her own suffering: at the age of eight, she was sexually assaulted "by a teenage neighbor," who continued to abuse her for four years. She tells Glanton that, throughout this period, "she never told anyone, least of all her parents, who worked hard to provide a decent life for her and her siblings." Still her pain had to find some outlet, and she later turned to alcohol, prostitution, and cocaine abuse. "The sexual abuse is the thing that destroyed me. . . . It just made me think this is what I deserved. I don't know why because I was a happy little brown kid up until that point," she says. Helping Girl X is a means of furthering her own redemption, Reed believes.

After describing the architectural layout of Cabrini-Green, Glanton, in one of those comments that appear frequently in such accounts and can only astonish a middle-class reader, writes that its "residents have learned how to cope with the gunfire, drug-dealing and even murders that occasionally occur in public housing. But this crime, unsolved for three months, took an extraordinary toll." One remembers that the back windows of the Hardaway house "had often been shot out." Zater Bohlar, the grandmother of the victim, tells the *Tribune* reporter that she now intends to move out of

Cabrini-Green: "I want to be on my own. I never have before because I always had children. . . . I raised 11 children and two grandchildren here."

The second April 6 story essentially recounts the facts of the police investigation, but it does contain one astonishing detail. The Gangster Disciples, the street gang that claimed Yummy Sandifer and the Hardaway brothers as members, aided the police in their search for the missing girl's assailant because they "were so incensed that their letters were scrawled on the girl's stomach": "but the gang made at least one mistake. In the hours after the attack, gang members severely beat a man whom they suspected of raping Girl X, sending him to the hospital, police said."[3] In a final irony, the police revealed that the scrawls on the child's abdomen had no relation to gang symbols or to anything else that anyone could understand.

In keeping with the neglect that characterized her life, Girl X had been shoved off the front page of the April 5 edition of the *Tribune* by a story of two other, and unrelated, cases of assaults on children. Titled "2 Drive-bys, 2 Innocents Lost," the story tells of two fatal drive-by shootings in the Chicago metropolitan area. In the first instance, a two-year-old girl was shot from a car "while standing in a breezeway near her apartment" in the city; the child later died in the hospital.[4] At virtually the same time as the murder of the two-year-old girl, a seven-year-old child was fatally shot and another child and two adults were wounded in a near western suburb. Grotesque irony characterized the second incident: the seven-year-old and the other child were waiting to buy ice-cream from a truck that made regular stops in the neighborhood. One of the two wounded "adults" was the seventeen-year-old driver of the ice-cream truck; the other, twenty-four years old, was simply driving by in his car. The story begins with a description of the funeral of the two-year-old at which one saw "a collection of stuffed bunnies, teddy bears, candles and an open Bible" and concludes with the comments of a neighborhood witness of the ice-cream truck shooting: "'this was a beautiful day, and why does there have to be all the shooting?' . . . 'How do I know this won't be my child?'" The answer to this plaintive question is, of course, that she cannot know. As stories of Girl X and the two drive-by shootings continued to dominate the news, the trials of Cragg and Derrick Hardaway, the young killers of Yummy Sandifer, were progressing.

Ten months after the initial Girl X articles, the *Tribune* carried another story by Dahleen Glanton concerning controversy involving Beverly Reed and the Girl X fund. It recorded Reed's responses to charges by the mother of Girl X that Reed had been remiss, if not worse, in distributing the fund: "In an interview last week, Reed acknowledged that she has paid herself a

$20,000 administrative fee from the Girl X fund, which at one point totaled $264,000, and that only about $1,000 had been spent on the child." She claims that the tense relationship that later developed between her and Girl X's mother has interfered with distributing the funds. Almost as an afterthought the story reports that Girl X had made "little progress" in her medical treatment: "she will likely need substantial medical care and therapy for the rest of her life."[5] The Girl X fund scandal was a lead story of local Chicago television for several nights.

Girl X, the still unnamed and silenced child, had, it seemed, been violated again. At least in media accounts, her suffering had been subordinated to controversy over the fund established in her name. Ironically, even in the cruel April of her assault, media attention had shifted to other young victims of violence in Chicago. Again as with Yummy Sandifer, the *Tribune* brought home the degree to which violence had assumed a terrifying ordinariness in parts of Chicago—even a simple purchase of ice cream abruptly turned murderous. In the past two decades, at least in part because of such media coverage, violent crime has become an obsession with voters not just in Chicago, but throughout the nation. Tragically, most middle-class voters seemed to have lost interest in alleviating the socioeconomic conditions that inspire urban violence; increasingly perceiving the inner city as deadly space rather than exotic internal colony, they were interested only in increasing the numbers of police officers patrolling it.

In such a national climate, the appearance of an urban dystopian novel was probably inevitable.[6] Paul Auster's *In the Country of Last Things* (1987) is reminiscent of Orwell's *1984* in its depiction of a society ruled by an invisible dictatorship that functions on the laws of individual greed, dwindling sources of food, clothing, shelter, and corrupt political repression. While the specific setting of *In the Country of Last Things* is never identified, it is not difficult to deduce, from the text's descriptions of geography, that it is a surrealistically realized New York City. One can also surmise some specific inspirations for Auster's horrific vision, for example, homelessness in urban America, New York's desperate and crumbling slums in the 1980s, turf wars between urban gangs in any number of American cities, *and* the Holocaust.

Many of the details of everyday life in his unnamed city echo the accounts by Primo Levi, Elie Wiesel, and others of existence in the Nazi concentration camps; and Auster seems to perceive the deterioration of New York and urban America as constituting a kind of domestic holocaust. He writes movingly about the incomprehensible tragedy of the Holocaust from the specific perspective of his Jewish ancestry in his memoir *The Invention of Solitude* (1982), at one point recounting a visit to the Amsterdam attic in which Anne Frank and her family were hidden from the Nazis:

> From the window of that room, facing out on the backyard, you can see the rear windows of a house in which Descartes once lived. There are children's swings in the yard now, toys scattered in the grass, pretty little flowers. As he looked out the window that day, he wondered if the children those toys belonged to had any idea of what had happened thirty-five years earlier in the spot where he was standing. And if they did, what it would be like to grow up in the shadow of Anne Frank's room.[7]

This is a richly evocative paragraph. It constitutes something of an introduction into the postmodern world to which World War II and the Holocaust gave birth. As a result of this horrendous legacy, the illusory world defined by Descartes's rationalism is long gone. Truly, we live now "in the shadow of Anne Frank's room." Still, children continue to be born and, for a time at least, innocence reappears, an innocence made possible by the absence of historical knowledge and memory.

As the female protagonist and narrator of *In the Country of Last Things* informs us,[8] violence and savagery are the norms in Auster's dystopia, and the sheer act of walking down its streets has become an unavoidable danger:

> The rubble is a special problem. You must learn how to manage the unseen furrows, the sudden clusters of rocks, the shallow ruts, so that you do not stumble or hurt yourself. And then there are the tolls, these worst of all, and you must use cunning to avoid them. Wherever buildings have fallen or garbage has gathered, large mounds stand in the middle of the street, blocking all passage. Men build these barricades whenever the materials are at hand, and then they mount them, with clubs, or rifles, or bricks, and wait on their perches for people to pass by. They are in control of the street. If you want to get through, you must give the guards whatever they demand. Sometimes it is money; sometimes it is food; sometimes it is sex. Beatings are commonplace, and every now and then you hear of a murder.[9]

Moreover, the text offers a subtle explanation for the deterioration of the city. A woman the narrator befriends at one point dresses her in overly large and shapeless clothing and shoes in order to disguise her gender and thus protect her from potential assault on the streets. Afterward, the narrator comments about the success of her disguise: "it would have taken a strong imagination to see what was really there, and if anything is in short supply in the city, it's imagination" (pp. 60–61). It seems that the cause of the cataclysmic deterioration of Auster's unnamed city has been a pervasive failure of the imagination.

Yet as the sheer narrative virtuosity of *In the Country of Last Things* illustrates, the imaginations of America's urban novelists have not failed, and even while committed to an unflinching witnessing of the worst of the nation's urban horrors, they have not allowed their witnessing to destroy affirmation. Auster's protagonist finds love, however fleetingly, in his doomed city just as Daniel Quinn does in *Quinn's Book*. One remembers Caleb Carr's vibrant depiction of the color and diversity of nineteen-century New York City in *The Alienist* as much as his graphic accounts of the murders of child prostitutes. Cormac McCarthy's incomparable prose and gift for making the most absurd plot details real are evident on virtually every page of *Suttree*.

Similarly, John Edgar Wideman's *Philadelphia Fire* is characterized by a succession of rich and uninhibited verbal riffs, and Sandra Cisneros's *The House on Mango Street* is narrated in a uniquely lyrical prose and innovative poetic structure. Scott Momaday's multilayered *House Made of Dawn* evokes the magic of Native American tradition, and John Rechy's *The Miraculous Day of Amalia Gómez* finds affirmation in the Latin American and Chicano fictional legacy of magic realism. Finally, Richard Price, in an otherwise naturalistic text, evokes the nostalgic popular culture of the 1960s. An abundance of creative imagination is evident in the structural innovations to be found in these novels: Kennedy's incorporation of naturalistic detail and bawdy absurdist humor into a historical novel; Carr's innovative merger of the historical novel and the detective novel; Price's flights of surrealism and Rechy's concluding turn to magic realism in otherwise naturalistic texts; McCarthy's wedding of the spiritual quest narrative with an elaborately detailed naturalistic setting; Wideman's postmodernist narration emanating from a fragmenting central consciousness; Cisneros's "lazy poems" and lyrical, episodic narration; and Momaday's experiments with orality.

Thus, while they take what is useful from the realism and the naturalism of earlier American urban fiction, the creators of these innovative and powerful texts refuse to be limited by these traditions. They assuredly witness violence, but they refuse to surrender to it. They record the violations of the Girl Xs, the deadly struggles of gangs over contested turfs, and the desire of the relatives of victims of violence to flee the cities. But, as Beverly Reed at least *said* she wanted to do, they also strive to "transcend race, class, and everything else." For them "everything else" includes an inner-city culture in which violence has become the norm and a spiritually barren wasteland ruled by a mad god.

Notes

Preface

1. Arthur Redding, *Raids on Human Consciousness: Writing, Anarchism, and Violence* (Columbia: University of South Carolina Press, 1998), pp. 4–5; all subsequent references to this work are cited parenthetically in the text.
2. Carlo Rotella, *October Cities: The Redevelopment of Urban Literature* (Berkeley and Los Angeles: University of California Press, 1998).
3. Richard Lehan, *The City in Literature: An Intellectual and Cultural History* (Berkeley and Los Angeles: University of California Press, 1998), p. 8.
4. Kevin R. McNamara, *Urban Verbs: Arts and Discourses of American Cities* (Berkeley and Los Angeles: University of California Press, 1996).
5. Edward W. Said, afterword to *Orientalism* (New York: Vintage, 1994), p. 347.
6. Said, *Culture and Imperialism* (New York: Random House Vintage, 1994), p. 66.
7. See for instance my *The Naturalistic Inner-City Novel in America: Encounters with the Fat Man* (Columbia: University of South Carolina Press, 1995).

Introduction: Innocence Dying Younger

1. Peter Kendall and John W. Fountain, "An Ignominious Death: Boy Shot Twice in Head in Graffiti-scarred Tunnel," *Chicago Tribune*, September 1, 1994.
2. John W. Fountain and Joseph A. Kirby, "DEATH AT AN EARLY AGE: 2 Boys from Robert's Gang Charged in His Execution," *Chicago Tribune*, September 3, 1994.
3. George Papajohn, "DCFS Files Show Boy Sought in Slaying Scarred by Abuse," *Chicago Tribune*, September 1, 1994.
4. George Papajohn and Peter Kendall, "Law Opened the Door for Boy, 11, to Go Free," *Chicago Tribune*, September 1, 1994, 1:29.
5. Fountain and Kirby, "DEATH AT AN EARLY AGE."
6. Don DeLillo, *Americana* (New York: Penguin, 1989), p. 124.
7. DeLillo, *Great Jones Street* (New York: Penguin, 1973), p. 263.
8. DeLillo, *Mao II* (New York: Penguin, 1992), p. 174.
9. Tom LeClair, *In the Loop: Don DeLillo and the Systems Novel* (Urbana: University of Illinois Press, 1987), p. 87.
10. Rotella's term, borrowed from Nelson Algren.

Chapter 1: Dedalus in the *Dood Kamer*

1. Michael Kowalewski, *Deadly Musings: Violence and Verbal Form in American Fiction* (Princeton, N.J.: Princeton University Press, 1993), p. 11.
2. J. K. Van Dover, *Understanding William Kennedy* (Columbia: University of South Car-

olina Press, 1991), p. 117; all subsequent references to this work are to this edition and are cited parenthetically in the text.

3. F. Scott Fitzgerald, *The Great Gatsby* (New York: Scribner's, 1925), p. 217.

4. William Kennedy, *Quinn's Book* (New York: Viking, 1988), p. 22; all subsequent references to this work are to this edition and are cited parenthetically in the text.

5. Edward W. Said, *Culture and Imperialism* (New York: Random House Vintage, 1994), pp. 66–67.

6. Reilly, *William Kennedy* (Boston: G. K. Hall, 1991), p. 88; all subsequent references to this work are to this edition and are cited parenthetically in the text.

7. Reilly establishes in an interview with Kennedy that the man who is struck down with the plank is Bailey from *The Ink Truck* (*William Kennedy*, p. 102).

8. After Pat Buchanan's 1996 presidential campaign, one can read *Quinn's Book* only with a profound sense of irony. The Irish American Buchanan campaigned tirelessly and viciously against African Americans and "immigrants."

9. For a description of the horrific and ritualistic nature of many of these lynchings and of the reaction of African American writers to them, see Trudier Harris, *Exorcising Blackness: Historical and Literary Lynching and Burning Rituals* (Bloomington: Indiana University Press, 1984).

10. Reilly sees a possible prototype for John the Brawn in one James Morrissey, described in *The Big Book of Irish Culture* as "the first great Irish-American heavyweight." Reilly, "John the Brawn McGee in *Quinn's Book:* A Probable Source," *Notes on Contemporary Literature* 19 (May 1989): 4–5.

11. In an interesting essay, Tramble T. Turner sees the John the Brawn–Jacobus alliance as illustrative of "a bridge-building dynamic" that characterizes the novel. For me, Turner's argument makes the novel more affirmative than I believe it is, but it is nevertheless intriguing. Turner, "*Quinn's Book:* Reconstructing Irish-American History," MELUS 18 (Spring 1993): 31–45.

12. In the ongoing debate concerning the American novel's mimetic function and its role as witness and participant in social conflict, Kennedy seems to fall somewhere close to the middle position outlined by Amy Kaplan in her discussion of the American realistic novels of the 1880s and 1890s. Kaplan, *The Social Construction of American Realism* (Chicago: University of Chicago Press, 1988).

13. There seem, in fact, to be several potential literary models for Daniel Quinn. Van Dover describes him as "the nineteenth-century boy protagonist, a David Copperfield uncertain whether he will be the hero of his own story" (p. 106). Van Dover's comparison is given credence by Reilly, who establishes Dickens as one of the writers Kennedy first came to love (*William Kennedy*, p. 3). Since Kennedy is always a consciously literary writer, it is hardly surprising that critics can find so many prototypes for Quinn.

Chapter 2: The "Context" of American Innocence

1. Raymond Williams, *The Country and the City* (New York: Oxford University Press, 1973), p. 227.

2. Caleb Carr, *The Alienist* (New York: Random House, 1994), p. 297; all subsequent references to this work are to this edition and are cited parenthetically in the text.

3. In his *American Literary Naturalism and Its Twentieth-Century Transformations* (Athens: University of Georgia Press, 1994), Paul Civello provides a nicely condensed summary of the thought of such nineteenth-century Darwinicists as Herbert Spencer, Joseph LeComte, and Asa Gray.

4. Significantly, Carr's sequel to *The Alienist*, *The Angel of Darkness*, even though it is again concerned with violence against children, is not as powerful a work as its predecessor, in part because, for a significant interval, it takes place in upstate New York and thus loses the sense of the city as a claustrophobic and controlling presence.

5. Angie Debo captures the tragic hypocrisy of Roosevelt and the America he embodied toward the Native American in one beautifully condensed sentence: "presidents of Western sympathy, like Andrew Jackson and Theodore Roosevelt, who took a personal interest in Indian affairs and even cultivated a boyish romantic friendship with chiefs, consistently directed an anti-Indian policy." Debo, *A History of the Indians of the United States* (Norman: University of Oklahoma Press, 1970), p. 332.

6. In addition to the Wounded Knee massacre, the motif of a white character mutilating bodies in order to blame Indians is probably meant to evoke the Sioux attack on Fort Ridgely and the hideous 1864 Sand Creek massacre of almost two hundred Indians. The white perpetrators of Sand Creek, led by Colonel John Chivington, after the massacre, "returned to Denver, where they exhibited more than one hundred scalps and were lauded as heroes" (Debo, p. 195).

7. Cathy N. Davidson gave a fascinating lecture called "Photographs of the Dead" in which she emphasized corpses as a frequent subject in daguerreotypes and the supernatural belief that photography destroys the soul while preserving an image of the body. Davidson, "Photographs of the Dead," at Northern Illinois University, March 1, 1997.

8. Henry Gonshak, "'The Child Is Father to the Man': The Psychopathology of Serial Killing in Caleb Carr's *The Alienist*," *Notes on Contemporary Literature* 25 (1995): 13.

9. Michel Foucault, *Mental Illness and Psychology*, trans. Alan Sheridan (Berkeley and Los Angeles: University of California Press, 1987), p. 12; all subsequent references to this work are to this edition and are cited parenthetically in the text.

Chapter 3: The Ducky Boys and the "Urban Punk Killing Machine"

1. Philip Roth, "Writing American Fiction," *Commentary* 31 (March 1961): 223–33.

2. Harold Bloom, *The Anxiety of Influence: A Theory of Poetry* (Oxford: Oxford University Press, 1973).

3. Frank W. Shelton, "Family, Community, and Masculinity in the Urban Novels of Richard Price," *Critique* 21 (1979): 8–9; all subsequent references to this article are cited parenthetically in the text.

4. Richard Price, *The Wanderers* (New York: Avon, 1974), p. 1; all subsequent references to this work are to this edition and are cited parenthetically in the text.

5. Sidney H. Bremer, *Urban Intersections: Meetings of Life and Literature in United States Cities* (Urbana: University of Illinois Press, 1992).

6. Blanche H. Gelfant, *The American City Novel* (Norman: University of Oklahoma Press, 1954), pp. 12–13.

Chapter 4: A Postmodern Children's Crusade

1. James W. Coleman, "Appendix: Interview with John Edgar Wideman, 12 August 1988," in his *Blackness and Modernism: The Literary Career of John Edgar Wideman* (Jackson: University Press of Mississippi, 1989), pp. 159–60; all subsequent references to this work are to this edition and are cited parenthetically in the text.

2. Doreatha Drummond Mbalia, *John Edgar Wideman: Reclaiming the African Personality* (Selinsgrove, Pa.: Susquehanna University Press, 1995), p. 63; all subsequent references to this work are to this edition and are cited parenthetically in the text.

3. Charles H. Rowell, "An Interview with John Edgar Wideman," *Callaloo* 13 (Winter 1990): 57.

4. James Robert Saunders, "Exorcizing the Demons: John Edgar Wideman's Literary Response," *Hollins Critic* 29 (December 1992): 1–10.

5. John Edgar Wideman, *Philadelphia Fire* (New York: Random House Vintage, 1991), p. 156; all subsequent references to this work are to this edition and are cited parenthetically in the text.

Chapter 5: Nature Despoiled and Artificial

1. Maria Elena de Valdes, "In Search of Identity in Cisneros's *The House on Mango Street*," *Canadian Review of American Studies* 23 (Fall 1992): 68–69.

2. Especially as developed in Gates's *The Signifying Monkey* (New York: Oxford University Press, 1988).

3. Sidney H. Bremer, *Urban Intersections: Meetings of Life and Literature in United States Cities* (Urbana: University of Illinois Press, 1992), pp. 97–98.

4. Sandra Cisneros, *The House on Mango Street* (New York: Random House Vintage, 1991, p. 3; subsequent references to this work are cited parenthetically in the text.

5. Virginia Lee Burton, *The Little House* (Boston: Houghton Mifflin, 1942), p. 25; all subsequent references to this work are to this edition and are cited in the text. I am indebted to my student Kathi Strong for introducing me to Burton's text.

6. Julian Olivares, "Sandra Cisneros' *The House on Mango Street*, and the Poetics of Space," *Americas Review* 15 (Fall-Winter 1987): 160; all subsequent references to this article are cited parenthetically in the text.

7. Claude McKay, "The White City," in *Selected Poems of Claude McKay* (New York: Bookman Associates, 1953), p. 74.

8. Walter Benjamin, "The Storyteller: Reflections on the Works of Nikolai Leskov," in *Illuminations: Essays and Reflections*, ed. Hannah Arendt (New York: Schocken Books, 1969), p. 87.

Chapter 6: Violence and the Immanence of the "Thing Unknown"

1. Cormac McCarthy, *Suttree* (New York: Random House Vintage, 1979), p. 106; all subsequent references to this work are cited parenthetically in the text.

2. Vereen M. Bell, *The Achievement of Cormac McCarthy* (Baton Rouge: Louisiana State University Press, 1988), p. 76. John Lewis Longley, Jr., takes a comparably existential approach in his "Suttree and the Metaphysics of Death," *Southern Literary Journal* 17 (Spring 1985): 82; all subsequent references to this article are cited parenthetically in the text.

3. Edwin T. Arnold, "Naming, Knowing and Nothingness: McCarthy's Moral Parables," in *Perspectives on Cormac McCarthy*, ed. Arnold and Luce, p. 52; all subsequent references to this article are cited parenthetically in the text.

4. John Ditsky, "Further into Darkness: The Novels of Cormac McCarthy," *Hollins Critic* 18 (April 1981): 9.

5. John M. Grammar, "A Thing against Which Time Will Not Prevail: Pastoral and History in Cormac McCarthy's South," in *Perspectives on Cormac McCarthy*, ed. Arnold and Luce, p. 29; all subsequent references to this work are cited parenthetically in the text.

6. Longley, pp. 81–82.

7. John L. Andriot, *Population Abstract of the United States* (McLean, Va.: Andriot Associates, 1980), p. 771.

8. See, for instance, Bell, p. 72.

9. Mark Rydell Winchell, for instance, regards Suttree's choice of residence as an example of the kind of sentimental embracing of the social outcast that one finds in John Steinbeck's *Cannery Row*. Winchell, "Inner Dark; or, The Place of Cormac McCarthy," *Southern Review* 26 (April 1990): 306. For Ditsky, Suttree is largely a 1960s cultural rebel at war with his father: "[Suttree] is nearly a stereotype of the Sixties—a gifted and conscious dropout (as they used to be called) from a rotten society" (p. 9).

10. Frank W. Shelton offers a convincing interpretation of Suttree's decision to live in the lower depths. After comparing McCarthy's protagonist to Camus's evocation of humanity in "The Myth of Sisyphus," he suggests that Knoxville's slums are a concrete manifestation of existential absurdity: "If, as Camus maintains, in an absurd universe all usual codes lack meaning, no locale would better mirror that situation than the chaotic slums of the modern city." Shelton, "Suttree and Suicide," *Southern Quarterly* 29 (Fall 1990): 75.

11. Faulkner, O'Connor, Poe, Steinbeck, and Eliot are hardly the only writers whom critics have seen as having influenced *Suttree*. Bell points to several other literary sources for McCarthy's text: for instance, James Joyce's *Portrait of the Artist as a Young Man* and *Ulysses*, the fiction of Dickens, and the poetry of Walt Whitman. In the opinion of Grammar, Suttree's name is meant to recall "another famous East Tennessean in our literature, George Washington Harris's Sut Lovingood" (pp. 38–39). Winchell also discusses McCarthy's novel in the context of the nineteenth century "southwestern humorists," but argues that it represents a significant departure from that body of work: "[Suttree's] entire life, and McCarthy's entire novel, is as much a social and political statement as the work of the southwest humorists. The difference is that McCarthy's vision is radical and proletarian rather than conservative and aristocratic" (p. 305). It should also be said that McCarthy's fiction is intensely intertextual; Thomas D. Young, Jr., for instance, notes more or less overt allusions in *Suttree* to works by W. H. Auden, Robert Frost, and e. e. cummings, in addition to Faulkner. Young, "The Imprisonment of Sensibility: *Suttree*," *Southern Quarterly* 30 (Summer 1992): 80. For discussions of McCarthy's borrowing from Eliot, see Arnold, pp. 49–50; Shelton, p. 74; and Ditsky, p. 11.

12. Young believes that Suttree chooses to live on the river because its "facticity" "is for him the symbolic equivalent of the world of the spirit." Bell stresses the ambivalent nature of the river as metaphor, arguing that it represents the polarities of hope and despair that war within Suttree's consciousness. For Grammar, "the river is, to put it mildly, a symbol: of life . . . and of death . . . and ultimately (as for Heraclitus) of the mysterious flux at the heart of existence, of everything that Knoxville attempts to deny" (p. 40).

13. Longley, for instance, suggests the possibility that the parents' rage might have originated in a "shotgun marriage" (p. 82).

14. See, for instance, Winchell, p. 295, and Bell, p. 78.

15. Gelfant, pp. 12–13.

16. Arnold also points out that the novel "mixes real and fictional characters. An example is John Randolph Neal, Jr., who was indeed chief counsel for John T. Scopes. Suttree meets him on the streets of Knoxville in 1952, seven years before Neal's death" (p. 65).

17. Cormac McCarthy, *The Gardener's Son* (Hopewell, N.J.: Ecco Press, 1996), p. 67.

Chapter 7: Redemptive Landscape, Malevolent City

1. Andrew Wiget, *Native American Literature* (Boston: Twayne, 1985), p. 82; subsequent references to this work are cited parenthetically in the text.

2. Quoted in Alan R. Velie's biographical-critical essay about Momaday in *American Novelists since World War II*, ed. James R. Giles and Wanda H. Giles, vol. 143 of *The Dictionary of Literary Biography* (Detroit: Bruccoli Clark Layman/Gale, 1994), pp. 159–70.

3. As Lawrence J. Evers points out, references to "mechanical sounds are associated with Abel's disorientation" throughout the novel. Evers, "Words and Place: A Reading of *House Made of Dawn*," *Western American Literature* 11 (1977): 303.

4. Vernon E. Lattin, "The Quest for Mythic Vision in Contemporary Native American and Chicano Fiction," *American Literature* 50 (1979): 637–38; all subsequent references to this article are cited parenthetically in the text.

5. Carole Oleson, for instance, emphasizes that, in Momaday's text, "the landscape is of central importance, holy in itself." She further argues that *House Made of Dawn* "is not a short novel about Abel, but a long prose poem about the earth, about the people who have known how to love it, and who can survive as a people if they cling to that knowledge." Oleson, "The Remembered Earth: Momaday's *House Made of Dawn*," *South Dakota Review* 11 (1973): 59–78. A comparable stress is inherent in the title of Susan Scarberry-Garcia's extensive study of Momaday's use of a "multitribal mythic context" to ground his text; in *Landmarks of Healing*, she asserts that "healing is the process of achieving wholeness or a state of physical and spiritual balance, both within a person and between the person and his or her social and natural environment. In *House Made of Dawn* healing occurs when the characters internalize images of the land by means of the symbolic acts of singing and story-telling." Scarberry-Garcia, *Landmarks of Healing: A Study of "House Made of Dawn"* (Albuquerque: University of New Mexico Press, 1990), p. 2.

6. Robert M. Nelson, *Place and Vision: The Function of Landscape in Native American Fiction* (New York: Peter Lang, 1993), p. 6; all subsequent references to this work are cited parenthetically in the text.

7. In part because more than one Native American writer and/or critic of Native American literature prefers the term "Indian," I will use "Native American" and "Indian" interchangeably throughout this chapter. The argument is that "Native American" is no less a white-created term than is "Indian."

8. N. Scott Momaday, *The Names: A Memoir* (Tucson: Sun Tracks/University of Arizona Press, 1976), p. 168; all subsequent references to this work are cited parenthetically in the text.

9. Momaday, *House Made of Dawn* (New York: Harper & Row, 1989), p. 1; all subsequent references to this work are to this edition and are cited parenthetically in the text.

10. Matthias Schubnell, *N. Scott Momaday: The Cultural and Literary Background* (Norman: University of Oklahoma Press, 1985), p. 114; all subsequent references to this work are cited parenthetically in the text.

11. S. K. Aithal, for instance, writes that "Momaday probably seems to suggest that one has to go beyond the experience of any single individual Indian to find a satisfactory explanation for his behavior—one has to go to historical experiences of the whole race in order to understand it." Aithal, "The Redemptive Return: Momaday's *House Made of Dawn*," *North Dakota Quarterly* 53 (Spring 1985): 161.

12. In the division that W. H. Frohock makes between the "novel of erosion" and "the novel of destiny," *House Made of Dawn* clearly falls into the second catagory. Frohock writes that the "hero" in "the novel of destiny" "finds himself in a predicament such that

the only possible exit is through inflicting harm on some other human" (p. 6). Frohock makes another distinction between his two types of the novel of violence that is relevant to Momaday's text: "[the hero of the novel of destiny] will probably not belong to the middle class, because the middle class resorts less often to violence than to due process of law" (pp. 9–10). Frohock, *The Novel of Violence in America* (Dallas: Southern Methodist University Press, 1974) pp. 9–10.

13. Floyd C. Watkins, "Culture versus Anonymity in *House Made of Dawn*," in his *In Time and Place: Some Origins of American Literature* (Athens: University of Georgia Press, 1977), p. 139; all subsequent references to this work are cited parenthetically in the text.

14. Oleson, for instance, writes that "there are signs that [the albino] stands for White Man; he is large, powerful, very skillful and brutal in contest; there is something unnatural about him, something repulsive to the point of horror in his huge face and lax lips." Oleson then points to a crucial sentence in the account of Abel's deadly confrontation with the albino ("Abel was not used to the game, and the white man was too strong and quick for him") as evidence that the albino embodies the historic white oppression of the Indian (pp. 64–65). Wiget correctly argues that the albino cannot be "pure symbol" since he has, "as Fray Nicolas's journal tells us, historical precedents in the community," but adds that Abel's antagonist "certainly represents the impersonal, malicious force of white power as prejudicial fate" (p. 85). Finally, Schubnell, in his reading of the novel, argues for a merger of the interpretations of the albino as witch doctor and embodiment of white power.

15. John Fraser, *Violence in the Arts* (Cambridge: Cambridge University Press, 1974), p. 108.

16. It should be said that some critics do not agree with this assessment. Harold S. McAllister writes that "*House Made of Dawn* may be a Christian morality play; its subject is spiritual redemption in a squalid, hellish temporal world" (p. 117) and argues that Angela is an "analogue of the Virgin" who aids Abel in finding salvation: "[Her] role . . . is not to provide salvation, but to aid and comfort Abel as he seeks it. . . . [S]he demonstrates for him the sustaining power of mythic perspective, the redeeming strength of sacramental vision" (p. 123). McAllister, "Incarnate Grace and the Paths of Salvation in *House Made of Dawn*," *South Dakota Review* 12 (1974–75): 115–25. In addition, Robert Nelson views her as "a second, female avatar of the [redemptive] snake spirit informing also the spirit of the albino" (p. 60).

17. Bernard A. Hirsch, "Self-Hatred and Spiritual Corruption in *House Made of Dawn*," *Western American Literature* 17 (1983): 311; all subsequent references to this article are cited parenthetically in the text.

18. Schubnell sees parallels in Momaday's novel with Melville's *Billy Budd*, believing that Momaday like Melville finds in the Old Testament an extensive symbolic pattern with which to anchor his narrative. For Schubnell, the albino and Martinez correspond to Melville's Claggert as figures who provoke an inarticulate protagonist into acts of self-destructive violence. He also emphasizes the "homosexual innuendo" that permeates *Billy Budd* and *House Made of Dawn*, arguing that the two texts contain a parallel emphasis on perversity. Alan R. Velie, among other critics, sees *Moby Dick* as a probable source for *House Made of Dawn*. Velie, *Four American Indian Literary Masters: N. Scott Momaday, James Welch, Leslie Marmon Silko, and Gerald Vizenor* (Norman: University of Oklahoma Press, 1982), p. 57.

19. Farah Jasmine Griffin, *"Who Set You Flowin'?": The African-American Migration Narrative* (New York: Oxford University Press, 1995).

Chapter 8: Discovering a Substitute for Salvation

1. See, for instance, Marcus Cunliffe, *The Penguin History of Literature: American Literature since 1900* (London: Penguin/Sphere, 1975); Malcolm Bradbury, *The Modern American Novel* (New York: Oxford University Press, 1983); and Tony Hilfer, *American Fiction since 1940* (London: Longman, 1992). Rechy, in fact, is discussed from three perspectives in *The Columbia History of the American Novel*, ed. Emory Elliott (New York: Columbia University Press, 1991): Thomas J. Ferraro, in his chapter entitled "Ethnicity in the Marketplace," lists him as a writer "from the Caribbean Rim including Mexico" (p. 406); James H. Maguire views him as a Western writer; while David Leer, in "Society and Identity," describes Rechy as a writer who along with William Burroughs has held "positions of authority in the counterculture" (p. 502). Rechy is also the subject of a brief sketch in the end section called "Biographies of American Authors" (p. 802).

An amusing bit of evidence of Rechy's "cult status" can be found in Felice Picano's 1995 novel *Like People in History* (New York: Viking). At one point in this "Gay American Epic," the middle-aged narrator Roger Sansarc tells a group of younger homosexual friends about having written a series of interviews with the "forebears" of contemporary gay literature. His listeners interestingly have no awareness of any major overtly gay American writers before Andrew Holleran and Edmund White. Sansarc then proceeds to educate them: "John Rechy was the youngest.... He was sweet really." Next, Sansarc tells about an episode in which he observed Rechy, now himself middle-aged, hustling on a West Hollywood street corner: "There was Rechy on a street corner near this porno theater, wearing boots, tight jeans, no shirt, dark glasses. Upper torso naked, but all oiled up. He was standing indirectly under this streetlight so you couldn't see his face" (p. 293). There is more than one in-joke embedded in this passage. First, John Rechy, while in truth a nice, sensitive man, went to great lengths to develop a hustler persona rooted in performance, which valorized qualities quite different from "sweetness." Moreover, his early fiction, in its existential obsession with the dread and inevitability of death, is devoted to a mystique of youth.

2. It is worth noting that Rechy published several pieces of short nonfictional protest, for instance, an exposé of brutal and degrading conditions in the El Paso, Texas, Juvenile Detention Home, "All It Does Is Make You Hate," *Texas Observer*, January 8, 1971, pp. 9–11. Ethnicity is a related, but not a central, concern in this piece. In a recent interview in the *Advocate*, Rechy talks about "the restriction of being labeled a gay writer" and says that "*The New York Times* stopped reviewing me when I stopped writing about homosexuals." Charles Isherwood, "Beyond the Night," *Advocate*, October 15, 1996, p. 63.

3. Joseph Sommers is one of several critics to point out Rulfo's influence on Rivera. See Sommers, "Interpreting Tomás Rivera," *Modern Chicano Writers*, ed. Sommers and Tomás Ybarra-Frausto (Englewood Cliffs, N.J.: Prentice-Hall, 1979), pp. 94–107.

4. For a good discussion of the development of magic realism in Latin American fiction, see Amaryll Chanady, "Introduction: Latin American Imagined Communities and the Postmodern Challenge," in *Latin American Identity and Constructions of Difference*, ed. Chanady, Hispanic Issues (Minneapolis: University of Minnesota Press, 1994), pp. ix–xlvi.

5. Charles Taylor, "The Politics of Recognition," in *Multiculturalism*, ed. Amy Gutman (Princeton, N.J.: Princeton University Press, 1994), p. 32; all subsequent references to this work are to this edition and are cited parenthetically in the text.

6. One still does not find a great deal of serious criticism about Rechy's work. Not surprisingly, the best of what has appeared focuses primarily, if not exclusively, on *City*

of Night: for example, Stanton Hoffman, "The Cities of Night: John Rechy's *City of Night* and the American Literature of Homosexuality," *Chicago Review* 17 (1964): 195–206; Bruce-Novoa, "In Search of the Honest Outlaw: John Rechy," *Minority Voices* 3 (1979): 37–45; Charles M. Tatum, "The Sexual Underworld of John Rechy," *Minority Voices* 3 (1979): 47–52; Carlos Zamora, "Odysseus in John Rechy's *City of Night:* The Epistemological Journal," *Minority Voices* 3 (1979): 53–62; Stephen Adam, "Terminal Sex: JOHN RECHY and William Burroughs," in *The Homosexual as Hero in Contemporary Fiction* (New York: Barnes and Noble, 1980), pp. 83–105; Ben Satterfield, "John Rechy's Tormented World," *Southwest Review* 67 (Winter 1982): 78–85; E. S. Nelson, "John Rechy, James Baldwin and the American Double Minority Literature," *Journal of American Culture* 6 (1983): 70–74. See also the chapter "'Hey, World': John Rechy's *City of Night*" in my *The Naturalistic Inner-City Novel in America: Encounters with the Fat Man* (Columbia: University of South Carolina Press, 1995), pp. 139–59. In addition, Rafael Pérez-Torres has published an essay about Rechy's highly controversial 1977 nonfictional exploration of the gay subculture, *The Sexual Outlaw: A Documentary,* "The Ambiguous Outlaw: John Rechy and Complicitous Homotextuality," in *Fictions of Masculinity: Crossing Cultures, Crossing Sexualities,* ed. Peter F. Murphy (New York: New York University Press, 1994), pp. 204–25. More recently, Lawrence Birken has given us an interesting analysis of Rechy's early fiction from the perspective of Foucault's critique of capitalism, "Desire and Death: The Early Fiction of John Rechy," *Western Humanities Review* 51 (Summer 1997): 236–45. It is doubtless safe to assert that a crucial factor in the relative neglect of Rechy's work has been the historic homophobia of academia. By referencing Jeffrey Meyers's *Homosexuality and Literature, 1890–1930* (Montreal: McGill-Queen's University Press, 1977), Mark Lilly demonstrates the hostility not uncommonly manifested toward writers like Rechy and Hubert Selby who write frankly about homosexual acts ("The Homophobic Academy," *Gay Men's Literature in the Twentieth Century* [Houndsmills, England: Macmillan, 1993]). As a heterosexual male who not only taught *City of Night* in the early 1970s but insisted upon bringing John to my university for a lecture, I could also cite my personal experience. Still, it must be acknowledged that Rechy's depiction of the persona and code of the hustler offended and indeed seemed counterrevolutionary to some critics who were and are sympathetic to gay writing.

7. Especially since allusions to mirrors and windows dominate the text, a Lacanian approach to *City of Night* would seem to offer real promise.

8. In discussing the concept of the chronotope, I am depending to a great deal on Michael Holquist's analysis of the literary theory of Mikhail Bakhtin. Bakhtin's concept, as summarized by Holquist, of the "adventured novel of everyday life" is also useful here: generally "realistic" novels dramatize the effects of a specific "chronotope," or convergence of time and space, upon an individual character: "These changes may be abrupt metamorphoses, similar to mere adventures, but they do more than articulate an abstract pattern of rearrangeable events: they create a pattern of development in the biography of the hero as he moves from guilt through punishment to redemption." Michael Holquist, *Dialogism: Bakhtin and His World* (London: Routledge, 1990), p. 110.

9. Easily the best critical discussion of *The Miraculous Day of Amalia Gómez* published thus far can be found in José David Saldívar's *Border Matters: Remapping American Cultural Studies* (Berkeley and Los Angeles: University of California Press, 1997). Saldívar approaches Rechy's novel as part of an emerging United States–Mexico border writing: "Another phrase that recurs throughout this work is 'U.S.–Mexico border

writing,' by which I mean the writer's strategies of representation whereby *frontera* subjects such as Americo Parades, John Rechy, and Helena Viramontes produce a theory of culture as resistance and struggle, not coherence and consensus" (p. 14).

10. John Rechy, *The Miraculous Day of Amalia Gómez* (New York: Arcade, 1993), p. 13; all subsequent references to this work are to this edition and are cited parenthetically in the text.

11. Characters whose intellects are saturated by American films of this period are a Rechy staple. Most memorably perhaps, there are Miss Destiny of *City of Night*, the flamboyant drag queen who fantasizes a big Hollywood wedding and ultimately just may have one, and Lisa, one of the young "angels" from *Bodies and Souls*, who can barely think except in the context of such films that she calls "my all-times."

12. When Wanda H. Giles and I interviewed Rechy in El Paso in 1972, his cultural ambivalence manifested itself in several ways. He took us sightseeing first to the fifty-foot-tall statue of Christ on top of the mountain of Cristo Rey outside El Paso. This statue and this mountain function consistently in Rechy's work, and most crucially in *The Fourth Angel* (1972), as emblems of a primitive, more vital faith. Then he drove us across the border to Juárez, where he stopped first at the street market and interacted in a modest and friendly manner with the vendors. Next, he took us to one of those ornate, gold-filled churches with elaborate and visceral carvings that one finds throughout Mexico. John refused to join us inside the church, explaining that, while its beauty should be seen, he was always enraged at the enormous expenditures that might have gone to the betterment of the Mexican people in *this* world. When we crossed the bridge to return to El Paso, John was stopped and his car searched for drugs. Justly angry, he rather quickly attained sufficient perspective to laugh about it, commenting that he didn't know whether he had been stopped because of his ethnicity or because of his long hair (this *was* Texas in the early seventies, after all) and dramatic, carefully costumed appearance (shirt open nearly to the waist and skin-tight pants).

13. Rechy, *Bodies and Souls* (New York: Carroll & Graf, 1983). *Bodies and Souls*, like *City of Night*, is structured in a manner reminiscent of John Dos Passos's *U.S.A.* and John Steinbeck's *The Grapes of Wrath*—a sequence of more or less independent stories linked by the recurring presence of central characters in both of Rechy's novels.

14. In an introductory essay for the Bilingual Press's 1990 reissue and translation of Aristeo Brito's *El diablo en Texas*, Charles Tatum briefly discusses Rechy as one of the few Chicano writers of fiction who have extensively depicted the Mexico–U.S. border culture. He writes that Rechy views this transitional world "ambivalently": "This is nowhere more clearly set forth than in his first novel, *Cities of Night* [sic], in which the young male protagonist leaves his native city of El Paso to embark upon his search for a place in which he can escape intense self-examination. El Paso is at once a source of fond nostalgia and the cause of his unhappiness" (p. 16). In addition to Brito and Rechy, Tatum mentions Antonio Villarreal, Richard Vásquez, Rolando Hinojosa, Miguel Méndez, and Estela Portillo-Trambley as other fictionalists who have emphasized border culture in their writing. Tatum, "Stasis and Change along the Rio Grande," in Aristeo Brito, *The Devil in Texas/El diablo en Texas* (Tucson, Ariz.: Bilingual Press, 1990), pp. 1–19.

15. In addition to the vision of Aztec Emperor Motecuhzoma of a fabled city to arise in "the land to the north," Rechy is probably referencing here "el plan espiritual de Aztlán," the document of Chicano pride drawn up at the Chicano Liberation Youth Conference in Denver in 1969. This document, as well as a brief description of the legend of the mythical northern kingdom, can be found in *Aztlan: An Anthology of*

Mexican American Literature, ed. Luis Valdez and Stan Steiner (New York: Vintage, 1972), pp. 401–6.

16. Birken argues that Rechy "is caught between an emerging culture of impersonal consumption and a dying culture of production" (p. 237).

17. In her study of the African American migration novel *"Who Set You Flowin'?"* Griffin discusses the pattern of African American newcomers to the urban north seeking, after an initial period of bewilderment and alienation, areas of reassurance and sometimes even nostalgia for a rural home within the city, areas that Griffin calls "safe spaces" (pp. 61–64).

18. James R. Giles and Wanda H. Giles, "An Interview with John Rechy," *Chicago Review* 25 (1973): 20.

19. Saldívar argues that "'The Blessed Mother' who appears to Amalia is Guadalupe—the Mexican people's version of the Virgin Mary who, as Norma Alarcón suggests, 'substituted for the Aztec goddess Tonantzin.'" Thus, Saldívar adds, "to argue over whether Rechy's denouement is 'unbelievable' is downright silly, and misses the social message of the author's fable-making, for Guadalupe . . . always represents in Mexican folktales 'mother, food, hope, life; supernatural salvation from oppression'" (p. 121).

Conclusion: Girl X and the Country of Last Things

1. Eric Ferkenhoff and Dahleen Glanton, "Suspect Arrested in Girl X Assault," *Chicago Tribune,* April 4, 1997; all subsequent references to this article are cited parenthetically in the text.

2. Dahleen Glanton, "Her Life: Joy of Childhood Torn Away," *Chicago Tribune,* April 6, 1997; all subsequent references to this article are cited parenthetically in the text.

3. Andrew Martin and John O'Brien, "The Investigation: This Was a Case That Cops Just Had to Solve," *Chicago Tribune,* April 6, 1997.

4. Heather Lally, "2 Drive-bys, 2 Innocents Lost," *Chicago Tribune,* April 5, 1997; all subsequent references to this article are cited parenthetically in the text.

5. Glanton, "Complaints Have State Looking at Girl X Fund," *Chicago Tribune,* November 23, 1997.

6. Another recent dystopian novel, this time set in Los Angeles, is Cynthia Kadohata's *In the Heart of the Valley of Love* (New York: Viking/Penguin, 1992).

7. Paul Auster, *The Invention of Solitude* (New York: Penguin, 1982), p. 83.

8. She is actually something of an indirect narrator since the text consists of a detached observer summarizing the contents of a letter she wrote.

9. Auster, *In the Country of Last Things* (New York: Penguin, 1988), pp. 5–6; all subsequent references to this work are to this edition and are cited parenthetically in the text.

Bibliography

Adam, Stephen. "Terminal Sex: JOHN RECHY and William Burroughs." In *The Homosex-ual as Hero in Contemporary Fiction*. New York: Barnes and Noble, 1980.
Aithal, S. K. "The Redemptive Return: Momaday's *House Made of Dawn*." *North Dakota Quarterly* 53 (Spring 1985): 160–72.
Andriot, John L. *Population Abstract of the United States*. McLean, Va.: Andriot Associates, 1980.
Arnold, Edwin T. "Naming, Knowing and Nothingness: McCarthy's Moral Parables." In *Perspectives on Cormac McCarthy*, ed. Arnold and Diane Luce, pp. 43–67. Jackson: University Press of Mississippi, 1993.
Auster, Paul. *In the Country of Last Things*. New York: Penguin, 1982.
———. *The Invention of Solitude*. New York: Penguin, 1982.
Bawer, Bruce. "Don DeLillo's America." In *Diminishing Fictions: Essays on the Modern American Novel and Its Critics*. St. Paul, Minn.: Graywolf Press, 1988.
Bell, Vereen M. *The Achievement of Cormac McCarthy*. Baton Rouge: Louisiana State University Press, 1988.
Benjamin, Walter. "The Storyteller: Reflections on the Works of Nikolai Leskov." In *Illustrations: Essays and Reflections*, ed. Hannah Arendt, pp. 83–109. New York: Schocken Books, 1969.
Birken, Lawrence. "Desire and Death: The Early Fiction of John Rechy." *Western Humanities Review* 51 (Summer 1997): 236–45.
Bloom, Harold. *The Anxiety of Influence: A Theory of Poetry*. Oxford: Oxford University Press, 1973.
Bradbury, Malcolm. *The Modern American Novel*. New York: Oxford University Press, 1983.
Bremer, Sidney H. *Urban Intersections: Meetings of Life and Literature in United States Cities*. Urbana: University of Illinois Press, 1992.
Bruce-Novoa. "In Search of the Honest Outlaw: John Rechy." *Minority Voices* 3 (1979): 37–45.
Burton, Virginia Lee. *The Little House*. Boston: Houghton Mifflin, 1942.
Carr, Caleb. *The Alienist*. New York: Random House, 1994.
Chanady, Amaryll. "Introduction: Latin American Imagined Communities and the Postmodern Challenge." In *Latin American Identity and Constructions of Difference*, ed. Chanady, pp. ix–xlvi. Hispanic Issues. Minneapolis: University of Minnesota Press, 1994.
Cisneros, Sandra. *The House on Mango Street*. New York: Random House Vintage, 1991.
Civello, Paul. *American Literary Naturalism and Its Twentieth-Century Transformations*. Athens: University of Georgia Press, 1994.

Coleman, James W. *Blackness and Modernism: The Literary Career of John Edgar Wideman.* Jackson: University Press of Mississippi, 1989.
Cunliffe, Marcus. *The Penguin History of Literature: American Literature Since 1900.* London: Penguin/Sphere, 1975.
Davidson, Cathy N. "Photographs of the Dead." Lecture, Northern Illinois University, March 1, 1997.
Debo, Angie. *A History of the Indians of the United States.* Norman: University of Oklahoma Press, 1970.
DeLillo, Don. *Americana.* New York: Penguin, 1989.
———. *Great Jones Street.* New York: Penguin, 1973.
———. *Mao II.* New York: Penguin, 1992.
de Valdes, Maria Elena. "In Search of Identity in Cisneros's *The House on Mango Street.*" *Canadian Review of American Studies* 23 (Fall 1992): 55–72.
Ditsky, John. "Further into Darkness: The Novels of Cormac McCarthy." *Hollins Critic* 18 (April 1981): 1–11.
Elliott, Emory, ed. *The Columbia History of the American Novel.* New York: Columbia University Press, 1991.
Evers, Lawrence J. "Words and Place: A Reading of *House Made of Dawn.*" *Western American Literature* 11 (1977): 297–320.
Ferkenhoff, Eric, and Dahleen Glanton. "Suspect Arrested in Girl X Assault." *Chicago Tribune,* April 4, 1997.
Fitzgerald, F. Scott. *The Great Gatsby.* New York: Scribner's, 1925.
Foucault, Michel. *Mental Illness and Psychology.* Trans. Alan Sheridan. Berkeley and Los Angeles: University of California Press, 1987.
Fountain, John W., and Joseph A. Kirby. "DEATH AT AN EARLY AGE: 2 Boys from Robert's Gang Charged in His Execution." *Chicago Tribune,* September 3, 1994.
Fraser, John. *Violence in the Arts.* Cambridge and London: Cambridge University Press, 1974.
Frohock, W. H. *The Novel of Violence in America.* Rev. ed. Dallas, Tex.: Southern Methodist University Press, 1957.
Gates, Henry Louis, Jr. *The Signifying Monkey.* New York: Oxford University Press, 1988.
Gelfant, Blanche H. *The American City Novel.* Norman: University of Oklahoma Press, 1954.
Giles, James R. *The Naturalistic Inner-City Novel in America: Encounters with the Fat Man.* Columbia: University of South Carolina Press, 1995.
Giles, James R., and Wanda H. Giles. "An Interview with John Rechy." *Chicago Review* 25 (1973): 19–31.
Glanton, Dahleen. "Her Life: Joy of Childhood Torn Away." *Chicago Tribune,* April 6, 1997.
———. "Complaints Have State Looking at Girl X Fund." *Chicago Tribune,* November 23, 1997.
Goldsmith, Arnold L. *The Modern American Urban Novel: Novel as "Interior Structure."* Detroit, Mich.: Wayne State University Press, 1991.
Gonshak, Henry. "'The Child Is Father to the Man': The Psychopathology of Serial Killing in Caleb Carr's *The Alienist.*" *Notes on Contemporary Literature* 25 (1995): 12–13.
Grammar, John M. "A Thing against Which Time Will Not Prevail: Pastoral and History in Cormac McCarthy's South." In *Perspectives on Cormac McCarthy,* ed. Edwin

L. Arnold and Diane Luce, pp. 27–42. Jackson: University Press of Mississippi, 1993.
Griffin, Farah Jasmine. *"Who Set You Flowin'?": The African-American Migration Narrative.* New York: Oxford University Press, 1995.
Hilfer, Tony. *American Fiction since 1940.* London: Longman, 1992.
Hirsch, Bernard A. "Self-Hatred and Spiritual Corruption in *House Made of Dawn.*" *Western American Literature* 17 (1983): 307–20.
Hoffman, Stanton. "The Cities of Night: John Rechy's *City of Night* and the American Literature of Homosexuality." *Chicago Review* 17 (1964): 195–206.
Holquist, Michael. *Dialogism: Bakhtin and His World.* London: Routledge, 1990.
Hurm, Gerd. *Fragmented Urban Images: The American City in Modern Fiction from Stephen Crane to Thomas Pynchon.* New York: Peter Lang, 1991.
Isherwood, Charles. "Beyond the Night." *The Advocate,* October 15, 1996, pp. 58–60, 62–64.
Kadohata, Cynthia. *In the Heart of the Valley of Love.* New York: Viking/Penguin, 1992.
Kaplan, Amy. *The Social Construction of American Realism.* Chicago: University of Chicago Press, 1988.
Kendall, Peter, and John W. Fountain. "An Igniminious Death: Boy Shot Twice in Head in Graffiti-scarred Tunnel." *Chicago Tribune,* September 1, 1994.
Kennedy, William. *Quinn's Book.* New York: Viking, 1988.
Keesey, Douglas. *Don DeLillo.* New York: Twayne, 1993.
Kowalewski, Michael. *Deadly Musings: Violence and Verbal Form in American Fiction.* Princeton, N.J.: Princeton University Press, 1993.
Lally, Heather. "2 Drive-bys, 2 Innocents Lost." *Chicago Tribune,* April 5, 1997.
Lattin, Vernon E. "The Quest for Mythic Vision in Contemporary Native American and Chicano Fiction." *American Literature* 50 (1979): 625–40.
LeClair, Tom. *In the Loop: Don DeLillo and the Systems Novel.* Urbana: University of Illinois Press, 1987.
Lehan, Richard. *The City in Literature: An Intellectual and Cultural History.* Berkeley and Los Angeles: University of California Press, 1998.
Lilly, Mark. *Gay Men's Literature in the Twentieth Century.* Houndsmill, England: Macmillan, 1993.
Longley, John Lewis, Jr. "Suttree and the Metaphysics of Death." *Southern Literary Journal* 17 (Spring 1985): 79–90.
Lynch, Honora M. *Patterns of Anarchy and Order in the Works of John Rechy.* Ph.D. diss., University of Houston, 1976.
Martin, Andrew, and John O'Brien. "The Investigation: This Was a Case That Cops Just Had to Solve." *Chicago Tribune,* April 6, 1997.
Mbalia, Doreatha Drummond. *John Edgar Wideman: Reclaiming the African Personality.* Selinsgrove, Pa: Susquehanna University Press, 1995.
McAllister, Harold S. "Incarnate Grace and the Paths of Salvation in *House Made of Dawn.*" *South Dakota Review* 12 (1974–75): 115–25.
McCarthy, Cormac. *The Gardener's Son.* Hopewell, N.J.: Ecco Press, 1996.
———. *Suttree.* New York: Random House Vintage, 1979.
McKay, Claude. "The White City." In *Selected Poems of Claude McKay.* New York: Bookman Associates, 1953.
McNamara, Kevin R. *Urban Verbs: Arts and Discourses of American Cities.* Stanford, Calif.: Stanford University Press, 1996.

Momaday, N. Scott. *House Made of Dawn.* New York: Harper & Row, 1989.
———. *The Names: A Memoir.* Tucson: Sun Tracks/University of Arizona Press, 1976.
Nelson, E. S. "John Rechy, James Baldwin and the American Double Minority Literature." *Journal of American Culture* 6 (Summer 1983): 70–74.
Nelson, Robert M. *Place and Vision: The Function of Landscape in Native American Fiction.* New York: Peter Lang, 1993.
Oleson, Carole. "The Remembered Earth: Momaday's *House Made of Dawn.*" *South Dakota Review* 11 (1973): 59–78.
Olivares, Julian. "Sandra Cisneros' *The House on Mango Street,* and the Poetics of Space." *Americas Review* (Fall-Winter 1989): 160–70.
Papajohn, George. "DCFS Files Show Boy Sought in Slaying Scarred by Abuse." *Chicago Tribune,* September 1, 1994.
———. "Innocence Dying Younger: Kids Fall for Deadly Code Despite Gangs' Bloody Past." *Chicago Tribune,* September 4, 1991.
Papajohn, George, and Peter Kendall. "Law Opened the Door for Boy, 11, to Go Free." *Chicago Tribune,* September 1, 1994.
Pérez-Torres, Rafael. "The Ambiguous Outlaw: John Rechy and Complicitous Homotextuality." In *Fictions of Masculinity: Crossing Cultures, Crossing Sexuali-ties,* ed. Peter F. Murphy, pp. 204–25. New York: New York University Press, 1994.
Picano, Felice. *Like People in History.* New York: Viking, 1995.
Price, Richard. *The Wanderers.* New York: Avon, 1974.
Rechy, John. "All It Does Is Make You Hate." *Texas Observer,* January 8, 1971, pp. 9–11.
———. *Bodies and Souls.* New York: Carroll & Graf, 1983.
———. *The Miraculous Day of Amalia Gómez.* New York: Arcade, 1993.
Redding, Arthur. *Raids on Human Consciousness: Writing, Anarchism, and Violence.* Columbia: University of South Carolina Press, 1998.
Reilly, Edward C. "John the Brawn McGee in *Quinn's Book:* A Probable Source." *Notes on Contemporary Literature* 19 (May 1989): 4–5.
———. *William Kennedy.* Boston: Twayne, 1991.
Rotella, Carlo. *October Cities: The Redevelopment of Urban Literature.* Berkeley and Los Angeles: University of California Press, 1998.
Roth, Philip. "Writing American Fiction." *Commentary* 31 (March 1961): 223–33.
Rowell, Charles H. "An Interview with John Edgar Wideman." *Callaloo* 13 (Winter 1990): 47–61.
Said, Edward W. *Culture and Imperialism.* New York: Random House Vintage, 1994.
———. *Orientalism.* New York: Routledge, 1994.
Saldívar, José David. *Border Matters: Remapping American Cultural Studies.* Berkeley and Los Angeles: University of California Press, 1997.
Satterfield, Ben. "John Rechy's Tormented World." *Southwest Review* 67 (Winter 1982): 78–85.
Saunders, James Robert. "Exorcizing the Demons: John Edgar Wideman's Literary Response." *Hollins Critic* 29 (December 1992): 1–10.
Scarberry-Garcia, Susan. *Landmarks of Healing: A Study of "House Made of Dawn."* Albuquerque: University of New Mexico Press, 1990.
Scruggs, Charles. *Sweet Home: Invisible Cities in the Afro-American Novel.* Baltimore, Md.: Johns Hopkins University Press, 1993.
Schubnell, Matthias. *N. Scott Momaday: The Cultural and Literary Background.* Norman: University of Oklahoma Press, 1985.

Shelton, Frank W. "Family, Community and Masculinity in the Urban Novels of Richard Price." *Critique* 21 (1979): 5–15.

———. "Suttree and Suicide." *Southern Quarterly* 29 (Fall 1990): 71–83.

Sommers, Joseph. "Interpreting Tomás Rivera." In *Modern Chicano Writers*, ed. Sommers and Tomás Ybarra-Frausto, pp. 94–107. Englewood Cliffs, N.J.: Prentice-Hall, 1979.

Tatum, Charles M. "Stasis and Change along the Rio Grande." In Aristeo Brito, *The Devil in Texas/El diablo en Texas*. Tucson, Ariz.: Bilingual Press, 1990, pp. 1–19.

———. "The Sexual Underworld of John Rechy." *Minority Voices* 3 (1979): 47–52.

Taylor, Charles. "The Politics of Recognition." In *Multiculturalism*, ed. Amy Gutman, pp. 25–73. Princeton, N.J.: Princeton University Press, 1994.

Turner, Tramble T. "*Quinn's Book:* Reconstructing Irish-American History." *MELUS* 18 (Spring 1993): 31–45.

Valdez, Luis, and Stan Steiner, eds. *Aztlan: An Anthology of Mexican-American Literature*. New York: Vintage, 1972.

Van Dover, J. K. *Understanding William Kennedy*. Columbia: University of South Carolina Press, 1991.

Velie, Alan R. "*House Made of Dawn:* Nobody's Protest Novel." In *Four American Indian Literary Masters: N. Scott Momaday, James Welch, Leslie Marmon Silko, and Gerald Vizenor*. Norman: University of Oklahoma Press, 1982.

———. "N. Scott Momaday." In *American Novelists since World War II*, ed. James R. Giles and Wanda H. Giles, pp. 159–70. Vol. 143 of *The Dictionary of Literary Biography*. Detroit: Bruccoli Clark Layman/Gale, 1994.

Watkins, Floyd C. "Culture versus Anonymity in *House Made of Dawn*." In *In Time and Place: Some Origins of American Literature*. Athens: University of Georgia Press, 1977.

Wideman, John Edgar. *Philadelphia Fire*. New York: Random House Vintage, 1991.

Wiget, Andrew. *Native American Literature*. Boston: Twayne, 1985.

Williams, Raymond. *The Country and the City*. Oxford: Oxford University Press, 1971.

Winchell, Mark Rydell. "Inner Dark: or, The Place of Cormac McCarthy." *Southern Review* 26 (April 1990): 293–309.

Young, Thomas D., Jr. "The Imprisonment of Sensibility: *Suttree*." *Southern Quarterly* 30 (Summer 1992): 72–92.

Zamora, Carlos. "Odysseus in John Rechy's *City of Night*." *Minority Voices* 3 (1979): 53–62.

Index

Adam, Stephen: "Terminal Sex: JOHN RECHY and William Burroughs," 145n. 6
AIDS epidemic, 59
Aithal, S. K.: "The Redemptive Return: Momaday's *House Made of Dawn*," 142n. 11
Alden, Priscilla, 14
Algren, Nelson, 14, 17, 33, 46, 48, 52, 53, 93; *The Man with the Golden Arm*, 95, 96; *Never Come Morning*, 45, 54; *Somebody in Boots*, 122; *A Walk on the Wild Side*, 95
Alienist, The (Carr), 6, 15, 21; analyzed, 26–43, 129, 135; Franz Boas as character in, 27, 37, 38; Thomas Byrnes as character in, 27, 28, 29; Anthony Comstock as character in, 27, 28, 29, 42; consumerism theme in, 32; Delmonico's Restaurant in, 31, 32; Five Points neighborhood in, 27, 32–33, 40, 42; Fort Ridgely (Minnesota) raid (1862) in, 36–37, 38; Haymarket Square riot (1886) in, 27; Metropolitan Opera House in, 31, 32; J. P. Morgan as character in, 28, 31; photography in, 38–39; Jacob Riis as character in, 27, 29, 42; Theodore Roosevelt as character in, 29–30, 33, 35–36, 42; Lincoln Steffens as character in, 27–29; tenement life in, 33–34, 40; Clark Wissler as character in, 27, 37, 38
Amistad (slave ship), 20
Anaya, Rudolfo: *Bless Me Ultima*, 101
Anderson, Sherwood: *Winesburg, Ohio*, 46, 53

Angel of Darkness (Carr), 138–39n. 4
Arnold, Edwin T.: "Naming, Knowing and Nothingness: McCarthy's Moral-Parables," 85, 88, 91
Artaud, Antonin, 58
Asturias, Miguel Angel, 114

Bachelard, Gaston: *The Poetics of Space*, 72; *The Psychoanalysis of Fire*, 69
Baldwin, James, 63
Baraka, Amiri: *Dutchman*, 69; *The Slave*, 69
Bell, Vereen M.: *The Achievement of Cormac McCarthy*, 85, 93
Benjamin, Walter: "The Storyteller: Reflections on the Works of Nikolai Leskov," 82–83
Birken, Lawrence: "Desire and Death: The Early Fiction of John Rechy," 145n. 6
Blackboard Jungle, The (film), 45
Black Disciples (street gang), 1, 3
Bloom, Harold: *The Anxiety of Influence: A Theory of Poetry*, 45, 54
Bodies and Souls (Rechy), 116, 118, 123–24, 127
Borges, Jorge Luis, 23
Bradbury, Malcolm: *The Modern American Novel*, 144n. 1
Bremer, Sidney H.: *Urban Intersections: Meetings of Life and Literature in United States Cities*, 48, 71
Brito, Aristeo: *El diablo in Texas*, 146n. 14
Brothers and Keepers (Wideman), 57
Bruce-Novoa: "In Search of the Honest Outlaw: John Rechy," 145n. 6

156   Index

Buchanan, Pat, 138n. 8
Burroughs, William, 144n. 1, 145n. 6

Camus, Albert, 16; *The Plague,* 16
Carpentier, Alejo, 114
Carr, Caleb, 6, 7, 129, 130. *See also* Alienist, The; Angel of Darkness
Cather, Willa, 71
Cattle Killing, The (Wideman), 58, 68
Céline, Louis-Ferdinand, 49
Champion (film), 49
Chanady, Amaryll: "Introduction: Latin American Imagined Communities and the Postmodern Challenge," 144n. 4
Chicago Tribune, 1, 2, 3, 130, 131, 132, 133
Child of God (McCarthy), 85
Cinque, Joseph, 20
Cisneros, Sandra, 6, 129. *See also* House on Mango Street, The
City of Night (Rechy), 113, 114–15
Civello, Paul: *American Literary Naturalism and Its Twentieth-Century Transformations,* 138n. 3
Cleaver, Eldridge, 63
Coleman, James W.: *Blackness and Modernism: The Literary Career of John Edgar Wideman,* 139n. 1
Conrad, Joseph, 67; *Heart of Darkness,* 67
conscription law (Lincoln), 19–20, 21
Costello, Lou, 50
counterculture (1960s), 31
Crane, Stephen, 93; *Maggie: A Girl of the Streets,* 45, 122
Cunliffe, Marcus: *The Penguin History of Literature: American Literature since 1900,* 144n. 1

Dante, *The Divine Comedy,* 16
Davidson, Cathy N.: "Photographs of the Dead," 139n. 7
Dean, James, 45
Debo, Angie: *A History of the Indians of the United States,* 139n. 5
DeLillo, Don, 8; *Americana,* 4, 5–6, 130; *Great Jones Street,* 4–5; *Mao II,* 5; *Underworld,* 5

Descartes, René, 134
detective fiction, 6, 42
de Valdes, Maria Elena: "In Search of Identity in Cisneros's *The House on Mango Street,*" 70
Dickens, Charles: *Oliver Twist,* 65
Ditsky, John: "Further into Darkness: The Novels of Cormac McCarthy," 140n. 4
Doctorow, E. L., 27
Douglas, Kirk, 49
Dreiser, Theodore: *Sister Carrie,* 122
Dreyfus, Hubert, 40

Eliot, T. S., 68, 89, 97; "Gerontion," 98; *The Waste Land,* 65, 66, 89, 98, 120
Elliott, Emory: *The Columbia History of the American Novel,* 144n. 1
El Monte Blanco (film), 123
Eluard, Paul, 68
Emerson, Ralph Waldo, 35
Erdrich, Louise, 100
"el plan espiritual de Aztlán" (document of Chicano pride, 1969), 146–47n. 15
Evers, Lawrence J.: "Words and Place: A Reading of *House Made of Dawn,*" 105

Fatheralong (Wideman), 68
Faulkner, William, 18, 102; *As I Lay Dying,* 14–15, 84; *Light in August,* 84; *The Town,* 84
Felix, Maria, 123, 127
Ferkenhoff, Eric, and Dahleen Glanton: "Suspect Arrested in Girl X Assault," 147n. 1
Ferraro, Thomas J., 144n. 1
Fever (Wideman), 58
Fitzgerald, F. Scott, 89; *The Great Gatsby,* 10
Foucault, Michel, 34, 41; *Discipline and Punish,* 41, 124; *Mental Illness and Psychology,* 40
Fountain, John W., and Joseph A. Kirby: "DEATH AT AN EARLY AGE," 137n. 2
Fourth Angel, The (Rechy), 113

Frank, Anne, 134
Fraser, John: *Violence in the Arts,* 65, 106
Freud, Sigmund, 36, 39, 50
Frohock, W. H.: *The Novel of Violence in America,* 142–43n. 12
Fuentes, Carlos, 114

García Márquez, Gabriel, 114
Gardener's Son, The (McCarthy), 99
Gates, Henry Louis: *The Signifying Monkey,* 57–70
Gelfant, Blanche H.: *The American City Novel,* 48, 93
Geraldo (television series), 131
Giles, James R.: "'Hey, World': John Rechy's *City of Night,*" 145n. 6; *The Naturalistic Inner-City Novel in America,* 145n. 6
Giles, James R., and Wanda H. Giles: "An Interview with John Rechy," 147n. 18
Girl X, 130–33, 135. *See also* Ferkenhoff, Eric, and Dahleen Glanton; Glanton, Dahleen
Glanton, Dahleen, 131–33; "Complaints Have State Looking at Girl X Fund," 147n. 5
Goldsmith, Arnold L.: *The Modern American Urban Novel: Novel as "Interior Structure,"* 77, 87
Goode, Wilson, 62, 65, 66–67
Gonshak, Henry: "'The Child Is Father to the Man': The Psychopathology of Serial Killing in Caleb Carr's *The Alienist,*" 40
Gould, Jay, 31
Grammar, John M.: "A Thing against Which Time Will Not Prevail: Pastoral and History in Cormac McCarthy's South," 86
Great Depression, 31
Griffin, Farah Jasmine: *"Who Set You Flowin'?" The African-American Migration Narrative,* 110
Griffith, D. W., 39

Harris, George Washington, 141n. 11
Harris, Trudier: *Exorcising Blackness:* *Historical and Literary Lynching and Burning Rituals,* 138n. 9
Hawthorne, Nathaniel, 86
Hayes, Ira, 102
Hemingway, Ernest, 67, 89, 106; "Big, Two-Hearted River," 102; Nick Adams stories, 46; *The Sun Also Rises,* 89
"He's Got the Whole World in His Hands" (spiritual), 64
Hilfer, Tony: *American Fiction since 1940,* 144n. 1
Hinojosa, Rolando, 146n. 14
Hirsch, Bernard A.: "Self-Hatred and Spiritual Corruption in *House Made of Dawn,*" 108–9, 110
historical novel, 27
Hoffman, Stanton: "The Cities of Night: John Rechy's *City of Night* and the American Literature of Homosexuality," 145n. 6
Holleran, Andrew, 144n. 1
Holmes, Sherlock (Doyle character), 26
Holocaust: and Auster's *In the Country of Last Things,* 133–34
Holquist, Michael: *Dialogism: Bakhtin and His World,* 145n. 8
House Made of Dawn (Momaday), 6; analyzed, 100–12, 113, 129; Catholic Church in, 103–4; character of Tosamah in, 107–8; chicken pull ritual in, 104–5; inadequacy of language as theme in, 107–8, 110; Kiowa and Jemez influences in, 101, 107, 112; as modernist text, 102; Pulitzer Prize for, 100; repetition as device in, 106; technology in, 101, 102; World War II in, 102
House on Mango Street, The (Cisneros), 6; analyzed, 70–83, 116, 129, 135; commodification of the female in, 73, 74–75; as "fictional autobiography," 70; influence of Bachelard's *The Poetics of Space* on, 72–73; influence of Burton's *The Little House* on, 72–73; nature in, 76–79; popular culture in, 75; storytelling in, 82–83

158   Index

Indiana Jones films, 23
Ink Truck, The (Kennedy), 138n. 7
In the Country of Last Things (Auster), 133–35
Invention of Solitude, The (Auster), 133–34
Irving, Washington: *Knickerbocker's History of New York*, 14
Isherwood, Charles: "Beyond the Night," 144n. 2

Jackson, Andrew, 139n. 5
Jack the Ripper, 27
James, Henry, 60
Joyce, James: *Portrait of the Artist as a Young Man, A*, 9
James, William, 35
jeremiad, 6
Jones, Jennifer, 123, 127

Kadohata, Cynthia: *In the Heart of the Valley of Love*, 147n. 6
Kendall, Peter, and John W. Fountain: "An Ignominious Death," 137n. 1
Kennedy, William, 6, 7, 129, 130. See also *Ink Truck, The*; *Quinn's Book*
Kingston, Maxine Hong: *The Woman Warrior*, 70
"Know-Nothing" political party, 19
Kowalewski, Michael: *Deadly Musings: Violence and Verbal Form in American Fiction*, 8, 27, 65, 106
Ku Klux Klan, 22

Lally, Heather: "2 Drive-bys, 2 Innocents Lost," 147n. 4
Lattin, Vernon E.: "The Quest for Mythic Vision in Contemporary Native American and Chicano Fiction," 101
Laughlin, Clara, 71
LeClair, Tom: *In the Loop: Don DeLillo and the Systems Novel*, 137n. 9
Leer, David, 144n. 1
Leeza (television series), 131
Lehan, Richard H.: *The City in Literature: An Intellectual and Cultural History*, 8, 88

Levi, Primo, 133
Lilly, Mark: "The Homophobic Academy," 145n. 6
London, Jack, 29
Longley, John Lewis, Jr.: "Suttree and the Metaphysics of Death," 90
lost generation, 9
Lynchers, The (Wideman), 56
lynching of African Americans, 20

MacLeish: *J.B.*, 59
Marx, Leo: *The Machine in the Garden: Technology and the Pastoral in America*, 78
Maguire, James H., 144n. 1
Mailer, Norman, 4, 57
Manchu, Fu (Rohmer character), 23
Martin, Andrew, and John O'Brien: "The Investigation: This Was a Case That Cops Just Had to Solve," 147n. 2
Mbalia, Dorothea Drummond: *John Edgar Wideman: Reclaiming the African Personality*, 57–58, 66
McAllister, Harold S.: "Incarnate Grace and the Paths of Salvation in *House Made of Dawn*," 143n. 16
McCarthy, Cormac, 6, 7, 129. See also *Child of God*; *Gardener's Son, The*; *Suttree*
McCarthyism, 31
McCullers, Carson, 84
McKay, Claude: "The White City," 77, 82
McNamara, Kevin R.: *Urban Verbs: Arts and Discourses of American Cities*, 8
Mead, George Herbert, 114
Melville, Herman, 86, 112; *Benito Cereno*, 20
Miraculous Day of Amalia Gomez, The (Rechy), 6, 73; analyzed, 113–28, 129, 135; Aztec mythology in, 117, 120; commodified violence in, 123–24; dialogism in, 114, 127; and family in Rechy's work, 114–15; gangs in, 117, 118, 120; homosexuality in, 121–22; magic realism in, 114, 116, 127; marginalization theme in, 116–17; Mexican Ameri-

can identity in, 118; as naturalistic protest novel, 115; popular culture in, 117, 123, 127; salvation theme in, 125–26
mock historical romance, 6
Momaday, N. Scott, 6, 129. *See also* House Made of Dawn; Names, The; Way to Rainy Mountain, The
Monroe, Earl, 67
Morrison, Toni: *The Bluest Eye,* 116, 119
Morrissey, James, 138n. 10

Names, The (Momaday), 103
naturalistic protest novel, 6
Neal, John Randolph, Jr., 141n. 16
Nelson, E. S.: "John Rechy, James Baldwin and the American Double Minority Literature," 145n. 6
Nelson, Robert N.: *Place and Vision: The Function of Landscape in Native American Fiction,* 101–2, 105, 109
Norris, Frank, 33, 93
Numbers (Rechy), 113, 115

O'Connor, Flannery, 18, 84
Oleson, Carole: "The Remembered Earth: Momaday's *House Made of Dawn,*" 142n. 5
Olivares, Julian: "Sandra Cisneros' *The House on Mango Street,* and the Poetics of Space," 72–73
Oprah (television series), 131
Orwell, George: *1984,* 133

Papajohn, George: "DCFS Files Show Boy Sought in Slaying Scarred by Abuse," 137n. 3
Papajohn, George, and Peter Kendall: "Law Opened the Door for Boy, 11, to Go Free," 137n. 4
Peattie, Elia W., 71
Pérez-Torres, Rafael: "The Ambiguous Outlaw: John Rechy and Complicitous Homotextuality," 121–22, 145n. 6
Philadelphia Fire (Wideman), 6, 15, 16; analyzed, 56–69, 129, 135; basketball theme in, 67; bombing of MOVE house (1985) in, 57, 64, 66–67; disease metaphor in, 16, 58–59; fathers and sons in, 68; postmodern aesthetic in, 56–57; Shakespeare's *The Tempest* in, 57–58, 61, 65, 67–68
Picano, Felice: *Like People in History,* 144n. 1
Poe, Edgar Allan, 18, 79, 84, 86, 89; "The Cask of Amontillado," 79; "The Fall of the House of Usher," 89; "The Masque of the Red Death," 16, 79
Poitier, Sidney, 45
Polk Street (San Francisco), 122
Price, Richard, 6, 129, 135. *See also* Wanderers, The
Proposition 187 (California), 122
Pynchon, Thomas, 4; *The Crying of Lot 49,* 124, 127

Queen for a Day (television series), 123
Quinn's Book (Kennedy), 6; analyzed, 8–25, 52, 129, 135; Albany cholera epidemic (1849) in, 12, 15–16; Five Points neighborhood in, 21; inadequacy of language as theme in, 8–9, 23–24, 25; New York City draft riots (1863) in, 19–20; Plum family history in, 14–15; Staats family history in, 10–14

Reagan, Ronald, 31
Rebel without a Cause (film), 45
Rechy, John, 6, 129; "All It Does Is Make You Hate," 144n. 2. *See also* Bodies and Souls; City of Night; Fourth Angel, The; Miraculous Day of Amalia Gomez, The; Numbers; Sexual Outlaw, The
Reed, Beverly, 132–33
Reilly, Edward C.: *The Big Book of Irish Culture,* 138n. 10; *William Kennedy,* 13–14
Rivera, Tomás: *. . . y no se lo trago la tierra,* 70, 74, 76, 119
Robinson, Edward Arlington: "Richard Cory," 62

Roosevelt, Theodore, 139n. 5
Rotella, Carlo: *October Cities: The Redevelopment of Urban Literature,* 45
Roth, Philip: "Writing American Fiction," 44
Rowell, Charles H.: "An Interview with John Edgar Wideman," 139n. 3
Rulfo, Juan, 114

Said, Edward W.: contrapuntal reading, concept of, 10, 100–101, 104, 106; *Culture and Imperialism,* 10
Saldívar, José David: *Border Matters: Remapping American Cultural Studies,* 145–46n. 9
Sand Creek massacre (1864), 139n. 5
Sandifer, Robert "Yummy," 1–3, 6–7, 44, 45, 46, 48, 55, 130, 132, 133
Satterfield, Ben: "John Rechy's Tormented World," 145n. 6
Saunders, James: "Exorcising the Demons: John Edgar Wideman's Literary Response," 59
Scarberry-Garcia, Susan: *Landmarks of Healing: A Study of* House Made of Dawn, 142n. 5
Schubnell, Matthias: *N. Scott Momaday: The Cultural and Literary Background,* 104
Scopes trial, 141n. 16
Selby, Hubert, 45, 46, 48, 50, 52; *Last Exit to Brooklyn,* 45
Sexual Outlaw, The (Rechy), 121–22
Shelton, Frank W.: "Family, Community, and Masculinity in the Urban Novels of Richard Price," 47, 52; "Suttree and Suicide," 141n. 10
Silko, Leslie Marmon, 100; *Ceremony,* 101, 102
Sommers, Joseph: "Interpreting Tomás Rivera," 144n. 3
Song of Bernadette, The (film), 123, 127
Steinbeck, John: *Cannery Row,* 96; *The Grapes of Wrath,* 146n. 13; *Tortilla Flat,* 96
Stevens, Wallace, 68
Suttree (McCarthy), 6, 77; analyzed, 84–99, 129–30, 135; Knoxville as setting of, 87; literary allusions in, 89; McAnnally Flats as setting of, 87–88, 92–93, 96–97; nature in, 86–87; racism in, 94–95; Steinbeck echoes in, 96; Tennessee River in, 89–90, 93, 95–96

"talking book": Henry Louis Gates's analysis of, in African American literature, 70
Tatum, Charles M.: "The Sexual Underworld of John Rechy," 145n. 6; "Stasis and Change along the Rio Grande," 146n. 14
Taylor, Charles: "The Politics of Recognition," 114
Toomer, Jean: *Cane,* 70, 74
Turner, Tramble T.: "*Quinn's Book:* Reconstructing Irish-American History," 138n. 11

Underground Railroad, 11, 21
Universal Studios (Los Angeles), 124
University of Pennsylvania, 61, 62

Valdez, Luis, and Stan Steiner: *Aztlan: An Anthology of Mexican American Literature,* 146–47n. 15
Vanderbilt, Cornelius, 31
Van Dover, J. K.: *Understanding William Kennedy,* 9
Velie, Alan R.: *Four American Indian Literary Masters: N. Scott Momaday, James Welch, Leslie Marmon Silko, and Gerald Vizenor,* 143n. 18; "N. Scott Momaday," 102
Vietnam war, 31, 61–62, 117
Vizenor, Gerald, 100
Voltaire: *Candide,* 24

Wanderers, The (Price), 6; analyzed, 44–45; popular culture in, 44–45, 46–47, 54; Selby's influence on, 45, 46, 53, 55; war films language in, 47
Watkins, Floyd C.: "Culture versus Anonymity in *House Made of Dawn,*" 105, 109

Way to Rainy Mountain, The (Momaday), 107
Welch, James, 100; *Death of Jim Loney, The*, 100, 101; *Winter in the Blood*, 100
welfare reform bill (California, 1996), 122
White, Edmund, 144n. 1
Whitman, Walt, 35
Wideman, John Edgar, 6, 129. *See also* Brothers and Keepers; Cattle Killing, The; Fatheralong; Fever; Lynchers, The; Philadelphia Fire
Wiesel, Elie, 133
Wiget, Andrew: *Native American Literature*, 100
Williams, Tennessee: *The Glass Menagerie*, 64
Williams, Raymond: *The Country and the City*, 26

Winchell, Mark Rydell: "Inner Dark: or, The Place of Cormac McCarthy," 141n. 9
Wolfe, Thomas, 91
Woolf, Virginia, 82
World War II, 31, 116, 134
Wounded Knee massacre, 139n. 6
Wright, Richard, 46, 63; *Native Son*, 27, 45, 54, 63
Wyatt, Edith Franklin, 71

Young, Thomas D., Jr.: "The Imprisonment of Sensibility: *Suttree*," 141n. 11

Zamora, Carlos: "Odysseus in John Rechy's *City of Night:* The Epistemological Journey," 145n. 6